BENEATH the Indigo Sky

Unexpected Love – Book One

Rayne Hawthorne

&

D.W. Michaels

Cover art by @lis_photoart
Editing by Steph White (Kat's Literary Services)
Proofreading by Paige Munnik (Kat's Literary Services)

Reader Advisory

Not all books are the right fit for all readers. I find this to be a wonderful thing as it allows each of us to steer clear of items we may not enjoy while finding works that truly resonate with us.

While this is a slow burn romance that offers some spicy open-door scenes, romantic gestures, and loving found-family support, (and of course a happy ever after), the characters also encounter various issues and situations which may trigger some readers.

This work's content warnings include:

- Intense on page-grief and depression due to the loss of a sibling (including passive SI) as well as the off-page death of another character's spouse (historical).
- Acts of violence (on page assault).
- Amnesia.
- Homophobia.

Please remember to practice self-care, and if you feel that any of these might make you uncomfortable, know that it is perfectly okay to pass on a book for that reason.

That said, I have fallen head over heals in love with Jayce and Namid, and I hope that you enjoy reading their love story as much as I enjoyed writing it.

This book is intended for an 18+ audience only. This book contains graphic language and adult situations.

Wolf
Who handed me his boys with a staggering level
of trust.
Look what we've made.

For everyone who has ever stared up at the stars

and wished for someone to love them...

exactly as they are.

TABLE OF CONTENTS

"All the art of living lies in a fine mingling of letting go and holding on."
— *Henry Havelock Ellis*

"You found parts of me I didn't know existed, and in you I found love I no longer believed was real."
— *J. Iron Wood*

Chapter 1

It's cold here. Remote. I like it that way.

I've heard it called freezing. Lonely. Desolate. The people who use those terms don't know it like I do. It's majestic and peaceful and teeming with life; a lot of that life simply isn't human. Here, there are caribou and eagles, pine trees and moss. The thick snow that blankets this world for most of the year brings a silent peace that can be found nowhere else, and when it melts for a few short months in the summer, all the life that's been quietly waiting to make its presence known emerges once more. The birds take flight, the bears wake up, and the salmon spawn. The air is always chilled and crisp in a way that burns your lungs and reminds you that it's a privilege to breathe. The night sky is an endless expanse of dark velvet, alive with flickering pinpricks of light and swirling with greens and purples and teals. There is a pureness here, a beauty only found in wild places.

The people here are wild too. They are strong and sensitive and resilient. They commute on ATVs and snowmobiles while bundled up in Carhart overalls, puffy coats, and beanies and mittens their grandmothers knit. They hunt - not to kill or to brag, but to eat and survive and provide for their families. They cook their own meals and do their own cleaning and work hard to ensure that their kids make it to school and their bills are paid. They play and love in the same way they survive - with everything they have. The small shops are their own tiny communities - gathering places where people congregate and gossip and acquire small conveniences that help to soften the harsh edges of their lives. You only need to ask for something specific once before the owners ensure they have it ordered for you regularly when their shipments are trucked up.

The small bar in the center of town is always full. People meet and drink and laugh and dance together to old familiar songs played on a new state-of-the-art jukebox. They keep their business to themselves for the most part, but if someone is ever in need, everyone comes together without hesitation. They're suspicious of outsiders, but fiercely protective of their own.

It's not quite the middle of nowhere, despite its isolation. We have high-speed internet, a small electronics store, a medical clinic - complete with a surgical theater and an MRI machine - and a Michelin-star restaurant that opens during the short summer months. It caters to tourists, of course, but like most other places here during tourist season, it offers a locals' discount.

I like it here.

I'm different than the people who were born and raised here though. Not like, "Oh, that guy has a few face piercings" different or "Yikes, he eats cereal with chocolate milk" different. For the record, I don't have any facial piercings, and I could never be the kind of monster that eats cereal with chocolate milk. I don't have an unusual accent. I don't dress in flashy, bold floral prints that stand out from the tan and green puffer coats and worn, black Henleys everyone else wears in this place. I don't have pink hair or three eyes or seven arms.

I'm different in other ways.

I'm different from everyone I've ever met, even though I don't really know who I am.

I don't mean that I don't know whether I'm bi or pansexual or that I'm questioning whether I'd prefer another job more than the one I currently have. I don't mean that I can't decide whether I prefer tacos or enchiladas, Pepsi or Coke, white or wheat bread.

No, I don't mean anything quite so straightforward or ordinary. What I mean is, I actually don't know who I am...or what I am.

Ten years ago, I was found alone on the side of the highway with no memory. I don't know where I come from or who I was before that day. I've never remembered a thing, and no one has ever shown up looking for me.

Even though I'm still a stranger to myself in many ways, I've done my best to build a life here, and I'm lucky in more ways than I can count. I know a handful of people in town, I have a nice place to live, and I enjoy my job. I get up every morning, go about my business, and curl up in a soft, warm bed every night. I do my laundry, cook my meals, pay my bills, and run my errands. When I stand in line to check out at the grocery store, I look like everyone else.

I don't feel like everyone else because I feel...everything. The young mom I pass in the bread aisle, she's exhausted - truly exhausted - and when I brush past her, for a moment, I'd give anything to take a nap because, in that moment, I'm exhausted. The cashier ringing up my apples, he's angry. I don't think he's "I'm planning a murder in my head right now" angry, but angry. When one of my apples escapes the conveyor belt and I place it in his outstretched hand after I catch it, I want to scream. I want to smash something with a baseball bat and drop to my knees and yell until my throat is scratched and my voice is hoarse because in the moment our fingers touch, that's what he's feeling. When I smile and take my canvas bag from the teenager who placed my groceries inside it, a rush of excitement bolts through me. It reminds me of the excitement I felt many years ago as I got ready for my first date, and I wonder what his plans are for the evening. Whatever they are, I hope they live up to the anticipation he feels in this moment.

The emotions of others get tangled with my own. Over the years, I've learned how to identify which are truly mine and which aren't, but even when I know whose belong to whom, the feelings I pick up from others make mine seem more intense. My emotions can overwhelm me if I'm not careful, and even simple interactions can affect me to the point that I get lost in my head for hours, simply observing every little shift and nuance my body experiences. The only time I don't risk being overwhelmed is when I'm alone in the woods, thinking about nothing but the beauty of the trees or studying the beautiful intensity of the grey storm clouds rolling over the horizon.

I feel things in a way others don't. I feel them with my heart and my soul. They set my nerves on fire and rearrange my cells and spread across my skin until they consume me.

I'm just different.

I am empty.

Hollow.

Lost.

There is nothing in this moment.

I'm thankful for that.

The last six days have nearly broken me. Today still might.

I know this moment of emptiness will pass. I know all too soon my eyes will burn and my throat will catch and the waves of grief will come crashing back to drown me.

I don't know how to explain what it's like to lose half of your soul. I don't think anyone can. That's what it feels like I've lost. Half of my soul.

I dream of him at night. Dreams that are gentle and sentimental. Dreams of a lighthearted young boy whose sun-bleached hair shines like gold when it catches the rays of light piercing through the trees as he runs through the forest on one of the few truly warm summer days that exist in this place. Dreams of a slightly too-tall teenager snorting as he tries to laugh quietly enough that our parents won't be able to hear us from their room down the hall as he regales me with a story about his night out with the football team and the way at least half of them caused trouble at the diner after practice yet again. Dreams of a man in his twenties who looks like me as he smiles and sprawls out on my couch to tell me about the new girl he's seeing and how he thinks it might be true love this time.

Then I wake up.

My heart is pounding, and my ragged breath sounds almost deafening in the oppressive darkness. I'm covered in sweat, and for one brief moment, I struggle to remember what could have brought me to this point. Then I lose him all fucking over again.

The people who say grief is just love with nowhere to go are full of shit. Grief is shit. Grief is an endless, heart-wrenching, soul-crushing struggle to remember to breathe. It's looking across the room for a smile you'll never see again or seeing a commercial on TV that has always been an inside joke that now makes you wish you didn't exist. It's skin you'll never touch again. A laugh you'll never hear. It's trips you'll never take, texts you'll never send, best man speeches you'll never write, nieces and nephews you'll never meet. It's growing old without your other half.

It's wishing you'd been the one to go instead.

But he was the one who left. So, I'm stuck here. I'm standing in this godforsaken joke of a room, with its burgundy drapes, soft music, and carpet thick enough to muffle footsteps and whispers as I wait for friends and family to arrive to say goodbye to my brother.

I want to leave this place. I want to run deep into the woods until my lungs burn with exhaustion and I fall to my knees and beg to take his place. I know that no one would be listening were I to ask, and I know that even if anyone were, they wouldn't let me. All I could do is join him. Maybe when this is all over, I will. But right now, I can't. Right now, I have to paint on a solemn, polite, almost smile and hug and shake hands and thank people for coming to apologize for my loss.

I've done this before, but before...I wasn't alone. Before...I had him.

We were only twenty-three when our parents died in a car crash, and we were left with nothing but each other. I never thought that nine years later, I'd be standing in the same room, offering the same bullshit thank yous for the same reason. Only this time, I'm doing it without Jordyn.

For nine years, we only had each other. For the twenty-three before that, we chose only each other. We loved our parents, and we dated, of course, but everyone knew that at the end of the day, our relationship mattered more than any other. That's just how twins are built. We're two peas in a pod, two halves of a whole, joined at the hip. We're inseparable. Or...we were.

I fight against the darkness that threatens to overtake me. It wants to drag me back to where I've been for most of the past six days, back to lying in bed, hoping that the next time I close my eyes, I won't wake up. To tears running in hot trails down my stubbled cheeks. To curling into a ball and crying out until my throat stings and my lungs are on fire. To praying to gods who don't answer me. I want the darkness to take me.

I close my eyes and listen to the sound of my breath, the beat of my heart. My eyes are still closed when I hear the doors open.

I force a pained attempt at a somber half smile on my face - it hurts the muscles I'm trying to use; they aren't built for smiling anymore. I tell myself that I'm okay. This is okay. *I'll be okay.* Maybe if I say it to myself enough times, I'll start to believe it. I won't, but I say it anyway.

I take the hands of the people who come up to me, cold or sweaty or sticky. I shake them as they speak condolences I barely hear. *"So sorry for your loss." "He was taken too soon." "Don't hesitate to reach out if you need help."* I nod and thank them for coming and agree that he was too young and tell them I'll certainly contact them if I need any assistance, and they walk away, filing into the next room where a simple cherrywood coffin sits on a dais. They can't even see him. I can't see him. The accident was too bad for that, they said. He didn't suffer, they said. It was painless, they said. Instant. That's what they said. That's what they have to say, isn't it?

The people continue after only a moment beside his box, shifting toward chairs that stand in long rows with an aisle down the center as if this could actually be a wedding. They find others they know. They form small groups, speaking in hushed tones at first, but their grief isn't like mine. They move on from my brother after a minute or two, and their muted tones transform into something just a bit lighter, just a bit harder to tolerate. Subdued laughter breaks through from time to time before they hug and shake hands and settle into the padded metal chairs.

I sit at the front, and I listen as our old priest speaks. I haven't seen him in years, neither had Jordyn, but he speaks anyway. I don't know if he believes we are worth speaking for even though we haven't seen him in years, even though we haven't spoken to his God in years, or if he simply speaks because it's his job, but he does it. Others speak. They tell stories about us in our youth, about how we became good men. They speak about us as if we're gone, even though I'm still here, because we were always *US*.

We sing a few songs that I don't remember picking, songs that have been sung by many who have found themselves sitting in this room. They've been sung by those who find themselves as lost as I do and those who simply sit on the metal chairs going through the motions because it's the socially acceptable thing to do.

We pray.

They pray.

I'm beyond prayer.

Mr. Johnson, the kind older man who owns this burgundy and gold room and spends his days discussing coffins and flowers and the logistics of cremations and funerals, tells us that the procession for the graveside service will begin shortly, and the people on the chairs stand and file out into the crisp spring air. The crisp spring air would be considered freezing anywhere else, but here, thirty-eight degrees is a nice balmy springtime temperature, despite the fact that every visible surface is still black and grey and white. It will be months still before the green arrives. Before we hear the songbirds. Before life returns.

I ride in the hearse with Mr. Johnson. The drive is short and quiet, and it's strange to think this is the last drive I'll take with my brother. Our last drive won't be speeding our motorcycles along Top of the World Highway or out to Prudhoe Bay on the few weekends every summer when temperatures finally reach the mid-sixties. It won't be the 2000-mile trek to Seattle that we embarked on each year just to get away from work and snow and small-town life. It won't be one of us driving the other home from Shelly's Hole-in-the-Wall bar on Main Street after one of the rare occasions the other has had too much to drink. It won't be on a double date where my bisexual companion ends up leaving with my brother's new girlfriend (that only happened once, but still). It's this. It's me sitting in the front of a long black car while he rides in a cherrywood box in the back before being lowered into the frozen ground.

There are more prayers at the cemetery, but not many. Even though it's spring here, it's still grey and snowy, and no one wants to stand outside for longer than is socially required. I've forgotten my coat. I had it this morning, I think. I must have left it in my truck when I arrived at the funeral home with the atrocious burgundy and gold room. I barely notice when my fingers and toes start to go numb. When they begin to tingle, I'm grateful for the distraction. It gives me something to focus on rather than sinking into the darkness that threatens to overwhelm me once again.

Mr. Johnson waits for me since I rode with him. He stands politely to the side with his hands deep in his pockets, his face a mask of practiced sympathy. Maybe it's real. He's done this for so long that I wonder if he can tell the difference. I know he lost his wife a few years before Jordyn and I lost our parents, and I wonder if he felt like he lost half of his soul when it happened. I wonder if that's changed over the course of the last decade, or if he's just learned to hide behind his caring voice and fluid movements and pretend that he's not broken anymore. I wonder if that's who I'll be in ten years. I don't believe I'll stick around long enough to find out. I'm not that strong.

He waits quietly while I stand and stand and stand as the workers wearing plaid flannel shirts and thick canvas coats and leather gloves and beanies with ear flaps wait for me to walk away so they can finish their work and go home. They're getting paid to cover my brother's cherrywood box with earth, but they have places they'd rather be - kids and wives and still-living brothers waiting for them to return home for dinner.

It's silent in the long black car as we drive back to the building with the burgundy room, and I wonder if Mr. Johnson is respecting my grief or if he's lost in memories of his own.

He walks with me through the parking lot with his hand gently resting on the back of my ribs. It feels like the gesture of a father. Did he walk this way with his son when Mrs. Johnson died? Does he feel her loss each time he makes this trek? He walks me to my truck and he tells me he's sorry, and his shoulders slump for the first time today as he leaves my side and makes his way toward the small brick building.

I sit in my truck without turning it on. I sit and stare at nothing. I stare at the way the road grime clings to the ice on the edges of my windshield and the patterns the wipers have tracked across the glass. I stare until my eyes burn and hot streaks of salt track down my cheeks once more. I suck in breath after lung-stinging breath of cold, stale air that has been trapped in my closed-up truck for too long. My throat cinches shut, and my heartbeat stutters; my eyes squeeze close, and I cry. I cry until there is nothing left, until I'm empty once more.

Ken thinks I'm an empath - a person who is highly attuned to the emotions of those around them. Someone who can tell what other people are feeling. He's not technically wrong, but I don't think he's technically right either. I don't tell him that anymore. We haven't talked about what I am...or what I'm not...for a long time.

Mr. Kenneth Johnson is a kind man. He's the one who found me on the side of the highway in the snow ten years ago, and when it became clear that I had no one who cared enough to come looking for me and nowhere to go, he let me stay with him until I could figure something else out. I never figured anything else out. I never needed to.

He was in his late fifties when he found me. His wife Katherine had passed away a little more than a year prior, and their only son had moved to Arizona, of all places. He isn't close with his son Ethan, and in all the years I've known Ken, I've only known them to speak a handful of times. Neither has ever visited the other. I know that hurts him. I don't know what happened between them, but I know Ken loves his son deeply.

Though I'm endlessly grateful for all Ken has offered me, there are moments in which I feel like I've inadvertently taken Ethan's place.

Ken owns the mortuary and funeral home where I work. I started helping him with small things when the days of not knowing who I was and having nothing to do became too soul numbing to tolerate. I lifted heavy boxes and drove with him into town to the mechanic's shop or the grocery store on cold winter days when the snow was bad enough that it was too risky for him to drive in the icy darkness alone. Eventually, I started helping him with his business as well.

Even though Ken usually sees people when they're at their worst and they're crying in his quiet rooms after losing someone close to them, they like him. Everyone likes him. He grew up in this small town. He's gentle and soft spoken and doesn't have a mean bone in his body. I'm lucky he's the one who found me. I don't think anyone else would have taken in a naked man they stumbled upon in the middle of the Alaskan wilderness who couldn't remember who he was or why he was there. Ten years later, a lot of folks are still a bit suspicious of me. They're polite, and they smile and make small talk when they're stuck behind me in line at the grocery store, but they aren't the same as they are with Ken.

That's okay though. I don't think I'd want them to be.

I like being alone. I don't mind being around one or two people on occasion, but most of the time, I prefer solitude. Ken knows this, and he's okay with it. He gives me plenty of space even when it's just the two of us, and he's always careful to avoid sending me on errands that will lead to prolonged contact with others. He understands that being around a lot of people is hard for me. While he believes that a lot of my aversion to being in public is because I feel everything so deeply, he also thinks I have social anxiety. I don't think I do; it's just overwhelming to experience multiple people's feelings all at once.

Ken and I never had a conversation about me staying with him forever. For the first three months after he found me, he let me live in the small backroom of the funeral home that houses a cot and a hotplate and a tiny shower stall. One day after work, he grunted in my direction to indicate that I should follow before leading me across the mortuary parking lot and down the narrow gravel path toward his house. He'd cleaned up the small one-room cabin that sits not far from his two-bedroom cottage, and he'd told me that I could live there as long as I wanted. Ten years later, it's still my home. I love it. It's made of logs - actual logs. The walls are scraped smooth, but they are still round, and the wood's grain is clearly visible. I've studied them for hours, running my fingers along their glossy surfaces, learning the whorls and patterns that formed when they were trees. I wonder what they saw as they grew large enough to be used for cabin logs. I wonder what they lived through. How many of their winters were harsh enough that they barely survived? How many summers were bright and wet, and they thrived and grew? How many animals had eaten their leaves or made homes in their branches?

There is a soft bed in one corner of my cabin. It's large enough for two people, but no one has ever joined me there. There is a coffee machine and a toaster oven sitting on the counter under my kitchen window. There is a fridge, and a stove, and a tiny pantry that holds more than enough for just me. There is a stacked washer and dryer next to my clothes rack inside the hallway closet, and the corner of the kitchen holds a small dining table and two chairs. I've never needed more than two chairs. There is a fireplace with a hearth where I set the beautiful rocks and pinecones and occasional raven's feathers that I find on my walks. Once in a while, on long, dark Alaskan nights, I pile my blankets on the floor and curl up close to the flames to listen to the wood crackle as it burns while storms rage outside.

Ken and I spend time together outside of work too. He's become my friend, and he's the closest thing I'll ever know to a parent. We eat dinner together most days, and sometimes we watch TV afterward. We talk while we eat and while we work. We talk about almost everything. I listen to him talk about his past and about his late wife, Katherine. He loved her with an all-encompassing completeness that I don't think many people get to experience in their lives. We talk about football, which I don't particularly care for, but he absolutely loves. I like listening to him talk about it even though I don't find the subject very interesting. I enjoy feeling the way he gets so excited about something so simple. Working where we do, I don't encounter a lot of happy emotions.

When it became clear that I wanted to stay, Ken began teaching me about his business. It's an odd thing, coordinating funerals, especially in a small, close-knit community like this. While I'm happy to help Ken in any way that I can, most of what I do doesn't involve interacting with people. I keep the inventory organized and do all the heavy lifting - things like moving coffins and chairs and extravagant floral arrangements. I've also taken over all the bookkeeping and accounting. I'm good with numbers, and Ken is decidedly...not. I also prepare people for their last moments with their families. I don't actually think they know what I'm doing for them. I don't think they're still around. I don't know where people go when they die, but as I get them ready - putting makeup on their faces and brushing their hair and dressing them in their Sunday best - I don't think they're with me. I treat the people I get ready like they're here anyway.

For me, people are who they are because of their emotions. People are always feeling something, usually more than one something. Sometimes, their emotions are so simple they don't even realize they're experiencing them. Sometimes, they sit on a bench in the sun and wonder at the marvel of bees and flowers and cool summer breezes. Sometimes, they find comfort in a box of fries or a bowl of ice cream. Sometimes, they're genuinely annoyed when they see their first mosquito of the year. These feelings pass by so quickly that they may not even notice, but if I'm near them, I do.

Sometimes, people's emotions are so big they engulf them completely as they fall into the depths of grief and depression, or laugh with delight at the birth of a child, or find a profound sense of achievement when they've finished their thesis or gotten a long-awaited promotion.

People never feel...nothing.

The people I get ready feel nothing. I think what I do is for those they've left behind.

It's not like Ken keeps me locked away in the basement far away from the living. He simply knows that I only like interacting with people one-on-one. Even that can become too overwhelming for me at times.

Sometimes, people come in and want to pre-plan their own funerals. I often take the lead on those occasions as I actually enjoy that work. I like the fact that when we begin the process, the people making plans feel overwhelmed or sad or depressed, but when we finish, they feel a sense of completion. Sometimes, they even experience peace over the fact they won't leave the burden of planning for their loved ones or that they know their wishes will be honored. I love that. I like the way their emotions slowly shift, like a gentle stream of hot water flowing into a cold tub until they blend in a way that leaves the water a comfortable, warm embrace. I wonder if their relief surprises them. I wonder who they truly are as we sit together and plan, and I wonder who they'll leave behind.

I wonder about the people who feel nothing as I get them ready for their last moments with their loved ones. I wonder who they were and what their lives were like and what emotions they got to experience. I wonder who they were close to and whether they knew what it was like to be loved. I don't get to see love in person very often. I read about it a lot. I watch it on TV and in movies.

When Ken thinks about Katherine, I feel the way he loved her. It's gentle and warm, and it washes over him in waves that seem to dampen the grief and sadness he still carries deep in his soul. Sometimes, I wonder what Ken's love for her must have felt like on its own. I only know it in combination with loss. That's usually how I encounter love - tinged with sadness. I've felt love coupled with relief a few times as well when those who come to the burgundy room have loved ones who were ill for a long time. Their love seems gentler when it's combined with the relief that the one they loved is no longer suffering.

There are so many kinds of love. I don't know if I had a family before I came here. If I did, I don't remember them. I don't know if they loved me or if I loved them. I love Ken now, and he loves me in return, but that is a soft love. It's kind and affectionate yet still somehow detached. It swirls peach and gentle and consistent, like the love I notice others feel for their children.

Just once, I'd like to feel the kind of deep, passionate, unbreakable love that I read about. I imagine it must be bright and vibrant and overwhelming and achingly beautiful.

I know that it's not something I'll ever find for myself, but I'd like to feel it through someone else one day just to know that it really exists.

I'm attracted to men, and this is a small, remote town. There is no one for me here, aside from the tourists who pass through a few times a year. They are where I've halfheartedly looked for love in the past and where my limited sexual experiences have been found.

The men I've dated, the men I've had sex with...I didn't love any of those men, and none of them loved me. What we felt for one another was grasping, almost desperate desire. It was nervousness when we first met, and hope that perhaps we'd like one another, that maybe we'd found someone who would like us. It was excitement and passion and pleasure and need and connection and aching. It was gasps and lips and tongues and heat and skin. Until it wasn't. Then it was resignation and acceptance and loss as we went our separate ways, having realized that what we'd found wasn't love and that it never would be.

I'm too different for the kind of love I read about. How would I explain who I am? What I am. I've been vigilant on the handful of occasions I've taken men to bed, always careful to act as normal as possible, to not react to every stray emotion that has swept through my partner's consciousness. I've been cautious to keep my shirt on the few times I've had sex as well, so the other ways I'm different haven't been an issue. My encounters have been quick and sweaty. They've been enjoyable yet ultimately unfulfilling liaisons in motel rooms or in the cool air outside behind the bar. Still, I wonder what it would be like to experience more. I wonder what it would feel like to be loved.

I wonder.

I wonder about the man I worked with today, the one who was in a car accident. It had been a bad accident, and he'd been badly injured. I was glad they'd told his family the casket should be closed. I wouldn't have wanted anyone who loved him to see him as he was.

I took care of him anyway. I'd seen him in town a handful of times, at the mechanic's shop, I think, but I don't know anything about him. Whoever he was, he deserved to be cared for. I cleaned him gently and dressed him in a deep-blue suit. I combed his light-brown hair and covered the cuts on his jaw as best as I could. He'd been handsome, with a strong jaw and high cheekbones. That sounds creepy, I know, but I don't mean it that way. It's just an objective observation. I like observing things. I like studying them. I like wondering.

When I'd finished, I closed the lid of the cherrywood box quietly. I was the last person to see him, and a rush of sadness washed through me as the lid clicked shut. It always does. I'd moved him into the gold and burgundy room where his friends and family would join him and rearranged some of the flowers. Ken doesn't have a good eye for that sort of thing.

I've never liked the burgundy room. It feels suffocating. I don't know if that's due to Katherine's heavy-handed decorating - which is something Ken will never change - or if it's the residual effect of so much emotion, so much sadness, being crammed into one place for so many years on end. I don't know if rooms can absorb emotions from the people who occupy them. I know some places feel like they have emotions of their own. Places like the forest that are filled with living creatures that have their own emotions, even though they aren't the same as those humans experience. The burgundy room feels like it carries emotion, but it's not like the forest. It's not someplace good.

Ken is in the other room with the man's family when I finish in the burgundy room, and when I hear their muted conversation heading in my direction, I discreetly exit down the back stairs. I don't really feel like absorbing others' grief today.

Chapter 2

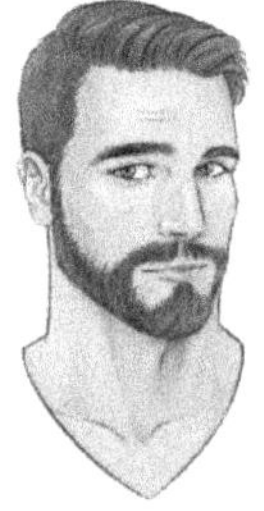

My jacket isn't in the truck. Of course it's not. Why would a task as basic as keeping track of a jacket be something I'm capable of anymore? I have other jackets, but this is the jacket I wear when I ride. This is the jacket I wore when *we* rode. This jacket matters. Maybe I took it inside this morning when I went to meet Mr. Johnson and started this whole fucked up mess of a day. I don't want to go back in there. I want to forget any of this ever happened. I want to drink and cry and curl up in the dark only to wake up and find it was all a nightmare.

I don't want to wake up at all.

I don't know the man who answers the door. It's certainly not Mr. Johnson. I've seen the man before, and I know who he is of course; everyone in town does. I've caught glimpses of his back in the supermarket a time or two and seen him smile at Jordyn and the shitty receptionist we employed for three months last year as he picked up Mr. Johnson's beat-up old Ford from the shop. I don't remember where else I may have encountered him. Though he's not completely unfamiliar, I've never seen him up close, and I've certainly never spoken with him.

Jordyn usually handled the clients at the shop, and it's been years since I've had to smile and make small talk about the weather while someone tries to convince me to take just a few more dollars off the cost of their brake job. I actually like people in most settings, and more often than not, I'm described as the "life of the party." I simply don't like spending my time haggling with folks over ten dollars when we're all better off if I'm busy getting actual work done. Jordyn and I have always been a good...*were* always a good team like that.

When Jordyn and I opened the shop at the tender age of twenty-four with our parents' life insurance money, not a lot of people thought we would succeed. After all, out here in the middle of nowhere, people are resourceful, and folks are primarily their own mechanics. At first, I think some people brought us small jobs like brake replacements that they'd usually complete on their own simply because they felt sorry for the boys who'd lost their family to a patch of ice on the highway. Eventually, they found it was worth the money to hire us so that they could free up their time for other things. A few other folks brought in old projects that had been sitting around waiting for them to get to "one of these days." Things like fixing up their old vintage Corvettes or figuring out why their tractor just "doesn't run like it used to." Work was slow, and money was tight for a year or so, but we managed to stay in business. Jordyn was good with finances and people, and I'm good with my hands. The business has more than stabilized over the past few years - it's flourished.

Now everything has changed.

Now, as I stand in the cold trying to figure out where I've seen this man outside of the shop, it suddenly hits me yet again that I'll have to find a way to do it all myself, and the suffocating darkness threatens to overtake me once more.

I force my mind back to jacket recovery.

I know the man who answers the door lives and works with Mr. Johnson, but I can't for the life of me remember his name. My life doesn't really matter to me right now, and I can't gather enough emotion outside of my grief to care that it might seem rude that I don't know it, even though I probably should. On more than one occasion, Mr. Johnson has said that this man feels like more of a son to him than his actual son. I know he's thankful to have been the one to find him all those years ago, and he's grateful that when it became clear the man would likely never recover his memory, he eventually decided to stay. I can only imagine how lonely Mr. Johnson's life would have been without him. I don't have to imagine because that's the life that now lies ahead of me.

It was an odd situation, the way he found an unknown young man, naked on the side of the highway in the middle of nowhere with no memory. I know that most people in town have reluctantly accepted him - though

they're hesitant to accept any outsiders - but a handful
still believe he's up to something nefarious. What evil
they think he's hoping to accomplish by living in a one-
room cabin, befriending a lonely older man, and helping
to run the funeral home that barely makes ends meet is
beyond me.

He's beautiful up close. Truly beautiful. His skin
is pale. Not in the way most people have pale skin in this
place that has far more darkness than sunlight, but in a
way that almost seems iridescent, though that feels like a
strange word to use to describe a person. He's shorter
than my six-foot-two - but only by a couple of inches -
slimmer too, and he's wearing a thin navy sweater that
clings to his strong shoulders and drapes across his
chest. He's not large or muscled or imposing. He's
athletic and lithe and perfect. His hair is jet black, and
when he opens the door and a ray of sunlight engulfs
him, it almost appears to contain hints of blue or purple.
It's cut tight on the sides - nearly shaved along his neck -
lengthening toward the crown of his head. The top
section is quite long and flows in soft, graceful waves.
Several strands dip across his temple and forehead as he
moves. His eyes are blue. Not the pale sky blue that
people write about in romance novels and gush to cast in
Hallmark movies, but a blue so dark it's barely still blue.
Navy or indigo. It's not a color I've ever realized eyes
could be.

I lose myself in that blue. I lose myself in such a
way that, for a moment, I forget about my jacket. I forget
about the aching darkness that threatens to pull me
under the tide. I forget how to think and breathe and

exist. There is nothing but the blue depths of the deepest sea staring at me in the form of this graceful man's eyes.

"Hi."

His greeting is so quiet that I'm not sure he really spoke, and he looks almost scared. I haven't said anything, haven't stepped toward him. I'm tall and muscled from lugging heavy car parts and working with my hands, and I know I can be intimidating when I want to be, but I haven't done anything other than stand here. Why does he look afraid of me? Maybe it's my certainly swollen red eyes. Maybe it's simply the grief and loss that must be rolling off of me in tangible waves in all directions.

I take a small step back. I don't want him to look at me that way anymore.

"Ya, umm. I'm sorry to bother you. I think I might have left my jacket. It's plain black leather."

He blinks a few times, confusion joining the fear on his face.

"I was here this morning."

I pause and force my throat to let the words pass through it.

"For my brother."

Relief floods his face. Relief, followed by sorrow, as he steps back into the building with a soft, professional smile.

"Of course. I'm so sorry. We haven't met, and you look..."

He trails off, clearly realizing that telling me I look just like Jordyn might not be the best choice.

"I know," is all I can manage to squeak out.

His smile softens further, and he gestures me into the reception area.

"Give me a few moments, and I'll look around for you."

His voice is deeper than I would have expected from a man of his size and build. It's gentle and smooth, but not in the way Mr. Johnson's is. Mr. Johnson has spent his life speaking with people during some of the hardest moments of their lives. He's trained his voice to sound comforting and supportive. This man's voice doesn't feel trained. It feels natural, like it's meant to be the smoothest thing in existence. It's like the voice of a lifelong monk whose throat knows only gentle songs of praise, or the sound of a waterfall cascading into a hidden spring, or the first sip of a twenty-year-old single malt whiskey. I want to listen to him talk forever.

All I'm capable of is a nod.

I watch him walk away as he leaves the room. He moves with an elegance and grace that I've rarely seen. He moves as if he is deeply and completely a part of the world rather than someone moving through it, like if he were to stroll through the forest, willows would part their branches, and birds would land on his shoulders just to be near him.

When he returns, it's with my jacket folded across his arm and a genuine smile on his face. It's still tempered by professionalism, of course; he knows why I was here this morning. Even so, he seems thrilled that he is able to help me with this, like this small offering in this moment might be able to lighten my burden somehow.

"Found it."

He unfolds it carefully and steps close to place it in my waiting hand.

"Thank you," I mumble, hopefully coherently.

"You're more than welcome."

His fingers brush mine as we transfer the cool, thick leather, and pain flickers across his face. So much pain. His expression is a reflection of the way I feel. It's almost like our brief, simple touch offers him a window into my soul.

"You'll be okay again one day."

His voice is soft and silken as it slides along my spine, our fingers still touching where we both hold my coat. Many people have said that to me today. People I've known most of my life. I didn't believe them. I barely even heard them, but for one brief, tentative moment, my heart wants to believe this beautiful man.

"Thank you."

I choke out the words like a prayer for salvation whispered in the depth of night.

Our skin separates, and he leads me back to the door, smiling kindly once again, his face holding no trace of the pain I thought I saw skitter across it.

I manage to nod and turn toward my truck, forgetting to shrug on the jacket I've retrieved as I cling to the memory of the sound of his voice.

Namid

He is beautiful, the man who comes back for his jacket. I suppose, in a lot of ways, he looks like many of the men I see in town. Tall and strapping are the terms I've most often heard used to describe them. His hair is a warm brown with hints of blond that must lighten in the summer sun, cut tight and short. It looks like it hasn't been trimmed in a while, though, and tussled ends poke out slightly over his ears. He wears a beard, as many here do. I don't know if facial hair genuinely helps keep a person warm - I've never grown a beard to find out - but I've heard that it might. I think that's probably just something people say, and everyone wears them simply because it's a popular thing to do in the cold wilderness.

The beautiful man's is short, more stubble than beard, and it's the slightest bit redder than the rest of his hair. His skin is darker than mine, though that's not hard to manage, and he's taller than me, over six feet, I imagine. His shoulders are broad, and his hands are strong and roughened from work. There are small black stains that likely never wash off ingrained in firm calluses on his palms. He's wearing black pants that hug muscled legs and settle low across his hips. His shirt, a button-down flannel in shades of green and black, has the top two buttons popped open, his thin black tie tugged loose. His biceps seem intent on testing the strength of the fabric that encompasses them. His stomach isn't large, but it's not flat either, and for some reason, I find myself wondering if the hair that must grow under his shirt is the pale chocolate of his hair or the slightly more auburn of his beard. He looks like warmth and strength and life, even though his heart tells me that he's falling apart.

For a brief moment, I'm absolutely terrified. I've never been terrified before, not even when I woke up with no memories and nothing and no one. Scared, yes, but not terrified.

I've never been convinced I've seen a ghost before.

The beautiful man standing at the door when I pull it open is the man I sealed into a cherrywood box early this morning before his family came to say their goodbyes. I don't believe in ghosts or zombies or the ability of a broken body to magically show up hours after it's been placed in the ground, healed of its injuries, and looking at me as if I might be able to offer it the meaning of life, but for one breath, one heartbeat, I can think of no other explanation.

"I was here this morning," he says in a voice that sounds like shards of broken glass are lodged in his throat.

"For my brother."

His brother. His twin. Clearly, they were twins. No wonder his soul feels so broken. I've never met twins before, but I've read about them. About the way they often feel more connected than other siblings. I've always wondered what it would feel like to be that close to another being. I've wondered if twins feel their sibling's emotions in the way I feel the emotions of others. I've wondered if their bond is the closest anyone might come to feeling things the way I do.

I know it's not likely. I'm not like other people. I know I'm alone.

I wonder if that's how the beautiful man feels now, as utterly and completely alone in this world as I am. His grief is so crushing that it's overwhelming anything else he's feeling.

I invite him in when he tells me he's forgotten his coat. His soul feels lost. It feels like he's drowning in darkness.

His coat isn't nearly as lost as his soul feels; he's simply left it sitting on a chair in the burgundy room, and I gather it up to return to him. Its scent wafts upward as I fold it gently over my forearm. Old leather and motor oil and cinnamon and sweat. It smells like laughter and comfort. Like the sharpness of an inhale on a winter's morning and the warmth of a blanket beside the fire. I've known all of these scents before, yet none of them have ever sent a rush of emotion surging through me like this. Maybe his jacket carries his emotions in the way the burgundy room seems to hold grief.

I offer him the kindest smile I can manage as I extend the coat in his direction. His gait is slow, his body and soul exhausted, as he shifts two steps toward me. Our fingers brush as he takes the scuffed leather from my grasp, and the world freezes. I've never been so overwhelmed by one person's emotions before. This is how it feels when I'm trapped in a crowd, everyone feeling something different, their emotions crashing together into a swirling, muddy mess that threatens to drown me. There is no crowd. It's just him. He's so hurt and so lost and so alone. His grief is so intense and burdensome that I wonder how he's able to stand and breathe in the face of it all.

Nearly hidden under all of the despair and heartache, there is love. A bright, swirling, all-encompassing love for the other half of his soul. It's love that now has nowhere to go. I'm overwhelmed by its radiance, still so visible and bright and teal and magenta and golden, even though it's buried in the black void that envelops him. It's the tiniest glimpse of the way I've always imagined love could feel, and I want more of it. I want him to know more of it, to remember what it feels like, and I hope with every fiber of my being that he's able to claw out of his darkness and find it again one day. Anyone who is able to feel love like that should get to experience it every day of their lives.

I know there isn't much I can do for him. I don't know him, and he doesn't know me, and while I've found that there are tools that can be useful when it comes to navigating anxiety and depression and fear, in the end, I can't take those emotions from him. He'll have to find his own way out.

"You'll be okay again one day."

The words slide through my lips before I even realize I've formed them. I hope he hears them. I hope that even the smallest part of his soul can believe me. I want him to hope.

He nods a mumbled thank you as I lead him back to the door.

He doesn't look back as he trudges to his truck, but I watch him. I watch as he slides behind the wheel and pulls away from the parking lot. I watch the space his truck used to occupy as the remnants of his emotions flow through me with an intensity I've rarely known, pulling mine to the surface to meld and dance with those he's given me. They move together through my heart and soul and across my skin in a way that they haven't before. I watch the way they shift inside me for long enough that the room becomes cold, and it's only when Ken startles me from my revelry that I close the door and return to work.

Chapter 3

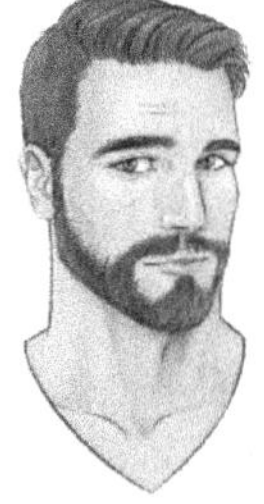

I can't do this.

How can I be expected to change spark plugs and replace alternators as if life is the same in this moment as it was three weeks ago, as if my heart and soul haven't been torn to shreds? How am I supposed to go to the front counter a dozen times a day and smile and take payments and return keys and say things like, "I'm hanging in there"? How am I supposed to magically know how to make numbers balance in the shop's checkbook when, a month ago, I wasn't even sure we had a checkbook?

I fight through every minute of every day at the shop. I cling to reality by my fingernails as I watch the clock, counting every minute and every breath and every heartbeat until I can leave my fake, painful smile in my toolbox with the rest of the heavy metal things I can barely remember how to use. I force the angst and the black and the despair into the pit of my stomach until I can get in my car and somehow make it home.

I don't know how I manage that either. I don't ever remember driving, only that there are trees and snow flying past the window and the sound of the tires on asphalt, and then I am in my driveway. I must be remembering to do laundry on occasion; I've only had to put on a shirt I've plucked from the floor a handful of times. I must be remembering to shower, as no one has told me that I smell or cringed and backed away when I've approached them at the counter. I must be remembering to eat; I'd probably have joined Jordyn by now if I weren't.

I don't want to do this. I don't want to live with only half of my soul. I don't want to try to fill in the gaps. I don't want to walk into rooms that are populated only by memories. I don't want to hear the voice of a ghost echoing in my head.

I do what I'm supposed to, what they tell me will help me move on. I go back to my routine, and I eat and I shower and I breathe...and I'm lost. I don't want to fall into the abyss, but I'm standing at the edge and I don't know how to find my way back. I don't know how to move on. I don't know if I deserve to.

Maybe I deserve this. Maybe I deserve to spend my nights with tears and pain and misery filling me until there is nothing else. It's my fault after all.

I've watched it all on repeat in my head for weeks now. I've listened to every word I screamed in anger, every word that was screamed back. I fight the memories and try to lock them away. I try to use logic and reason as I clutch tightly to the words offered to me in calming tones by the doctors, and the officer who had come to my door. *"Wrong place at the wrong time." "There was nothing he could have done to avoid it." "He wasn't speeding." "The semi blew a tire and rolled before he could swerve out of the way."* It doesn't help.

We were supposed to spend the afternoon together with beers and the game on my TV as I listened to him ramble about the demise of his most recent disaster of a relationship, just like I always did. I was mad at the world, not at him. I was mad at the storm that had raged for over a week, even though that's normal in March. I was mad that the shipment of parts I'd been waiting for had finally come in after a three-week delay, only to find that they'd sent the wrong things. I was mad at the fact the diner had gotten my lunch order wrong twice and that I'd ripped my favorite old T-shirt. I was mad at everything and nothing, but not him.

He was frustrated, but not with me. He was frustrated with himself and with his newest ex. He was discouraged that he wanted so desperately to fall in love and get married and start a family, and yet here he was, on my couch, crying again. He was frustrated with the world, but not with me.

It didn't matter. We took our anger out on one another. Isn't that what happens sometimes, even though it never should? We take things out on those we love the most.

We bickered over the television volume and what to have for dinner and whether to give Daniel a discount the next time he brought his plow in to be serviced. In the end, he'd left. He'd planned to spend the evening, but he'd left at 5:08. He'd left, and he'd never made it home. What if I hadn't yelled at him? What if he'd stayed? What if it wasn't just me now, desperately and hopelessly trying to keep myself together, if only to preserve our business - the only part of him I still have?

What if...

Namid

I wonder about the beautiful man as I curl up under a thick, fluffy blanket beside my fire with a book. Ken and I ate dinner together, as we do most nights, and I'd asked about the beautiful man. When I did, I felt Ken's soul begin to ache.

"He's a good man, that Jayce. His brother Jordyn was too. They lost their parents in a wreck, oh…eight or nine years back. I knew them well, the Stephens; they had dinner with me and Kat on more than a few occasions. Jayce shouldn't have to do this again, but the world ain't fair most of the time."

"Does he live in town?" I don't normally ask about clients, or anyone, really, and I wondered what Ken would make of my curiosity even though I'd made sure to give it a few weeks before asking so that I didn't seem too eager or curious.

Ken grinned at me like a cat who'd cornered a mouse in the pantry.

"Any particular reason you'd like to know?"

I'd shaken my head, careful to keep my gaze on the mug my hands were playing with.

"No reason. I was just curious."

His expression and voice and emotions all softened.

"He lives in town, owns the mechanic shop out on Westland. I'm sure you've seen him when you've taken in the truck or the hearse. Jordyn was always the front-end guy, not Jayce, but it could be hard to tell them apart."

His tone became contemplative as he continued. "I wonder what Jayce is going to do on his own now."

"Can he not run the shop on his own?"

Ken's brow furrowed. "Oh, I'm sure he can, but losing his brother has likely hit him harder than we realize, and I'm not sure he'll want to."

I stared at my fingers as they traced the swirled pattern on the ceramic mug.

"Maybe you should take the truck in soon, huh? Get a read on how he might be doing." Ken suggested hesitantly.

I cringed in his direction. "You always tell me that reading people with intent is an invasion of their privacy."

He had sighed as he reached over to take my hand, knowing that I'd be able to feel his worry for Jayce, knowing that I'd feel it too.

"I know, son, but sometimes I say that to protect you, not other people. The way you are, it's a gift, but I know it takes a toll on you to be around so much grief all the time. I know you can't help feeling what those around you feel, and I don't want you to have to go through life living with others' anger and pain and unhappiness. You deserve better than that. You deserve happiness, Namid."

It was one of the longest speeches I'd heard Ken string together in the decade I've known him. He's a caring soul, but he spends more time listening than talking. It was also probably the most he'd said about my abilities since our first year together. He's the only one who knows about me. While he's accepted me from the moment we met, it's still not something we ever really talk about outside of the few times he's made sure I know that he accepts me no matter what.

He was quiet as we cleaned up dinner, and if I couldn't feel the sadness radiating from him, I'd probably have thought he'd just used up all of his words for the day. I was quiet, too, as I thought about the way he'd spoken about me. The way he said that I deserve happiness. Does he think I'm not happy here with him?

I thought about the man I now know is named Jayce. About the way he felt one breath away from drowning when I'd seen him last and about him trying to run a business with only half of a partnership, only half of a soul. I thought about Jayce as I headed back to my small cabin. As I brushed my teeth and put on my flannel pajamas, I remembered the flood of helplessness and devastation that had rushed through me when his fingers brushed across mine beneath the folds of his worn leather jacket.

Shifting away from the warmth of the fireplace, I wrap myself tighter in my blanket. I grab another from the back of the couch as I make my way toward the door, wrapping it around me as well. It's a clear night, the first in more than a week. It's mid-April now, and the brilliant swirls of jade and magenta and azure and violet that fill the inky void during the winter months as charged electrons thrown from distant solar storms collide with oxygen and nitrogen in the atmosphere are starting to fade away. Soon, the thousands of blinking lights on their bed of velvet will be alone in the sky. I lie on my back on the small wooden porch and watch my breath rise in dense clouds that hover between my body and the silent wilderness that surrounds me. I watch the universe slowly spin past, and I remember what he felt like.

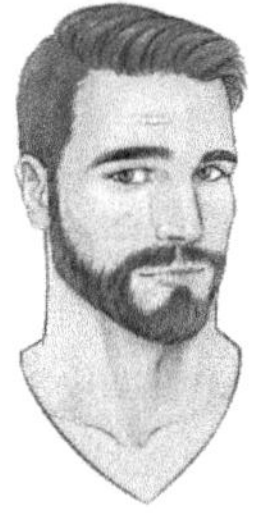

I'm staring at the cheese case as if it might hold the answer to the meaning of life, or at least like it might decide whether I want medium or sharp cheddar for me. I have no idea how long I've been staring at cheese. Definitely longer than a person should stare at cheese.

"Hi."

The gentle greeting disrupts my attempt to convince cheese to jump into my cart on its own, and I turn toward the voice. I'm slightly startled when I see him standing beside me with his indigo eyes and tentative half smile. I stare for long enough that he speaks again, apparently having decided I'm not going to return his greeting.

"You've been standing here since I came in. Can I help with something, maybe?"

A quick glance at his cart shows he's been here long enough to pick up at least a dozen things. It's not like it's the first time during the past month I've awoken from a god knows how long trance. It's just the first time anyone has bothered to say anything.

"No." I have to force out the word. "Thanks though," I hurry to add, not wanting to sound like a complete asshole.

His face seems to soften somehow as he steps closer and reaches past me, plucking up a small block wrapped in black plastic.

"This is my favorite. Now you can cross cheese off your list."

He offers me a kind smile as he places it almost gently in my cart.

"Thanks," I grunt quietly.

His head tilts like he's a confused puppy, and his pupils dilate as he studies my face. Sadness seems to overtake him for a moment - just as it did the first time we met - before his features return to the kind expression he's been offering me since he first spoke. Somehow, the look doesn't feel like pity. I can't handle any more pity. It's all people seem to offer me anymore. They no longer extend condolences and casseroles with empathetic sadness and shared grief. Their lives have moved on, and the looks they give me seem to say that they don't understand why mine hasn't as well.

"I'm going to ask you to do something for me. You don't have to say yes, of course, but I'd like you to consider it." His voice is calm and smooth, but I'm still startled by his request.

Nervousness grows in the pit of my belly. I don't really have anything to be nervous about; it's not like this small, beautiful man would be capable of harming me in any way, even if he wanted to. But I can't handle the idea of doing anything more than remembering to breathe - even that is touch and go, and I don't like feeling that I'm being set up to disappoint him.

I nod once, and a broad smile takes over his face. I've never seen a smile like his before. It's blinding. It's so much like staring directly into the sun that when it falls from his face slightly as he begins speaking again, I'm left with the residual memory of it branded into my retinas, like the pale-green spot you burn into your eyes when you look at an eclipse without glasses in the way everyone does even though you're not supposed to.

"Come with me."

He gestures with his head, and I follow without thought. Thankful that, for one moment, I don't have to think about what I'm doing or where I'm going.

He leads us to the front corner of the store. This is a small town in the middle of nowhere, but we aren't heathens - we do have a coffee shop. It just happens to be five small café tables and an espresso machine in the windowed front corner of the supermarket. He leads me to the back corner table, the one that's tucked away on its own close to the windows, and pulls out a chair, gesturing for me to slide in. I don't have it in me to resist. The seat he's chosen for me places my back to the shoppers and lets me stare into the black and white and shades of grey nothingness of a parking lot peppered with snow and stray metal carts and pickup trucks coated with road grime. I slump deeper into the chair, only to hear his footsteps fading away as he moves off without a word. I don't wonder why he's left me here. It doesn't really matter.

It's sunny today; it's the beginning of spring after all, and the sun was bound to poke its head out sometime. The light is blinding. After months of darkness and shadow and gloom, the rays that reflect off the barely melting snow and bounce through the windows and into my eyes are nearly painful. I stare anyway. Some part of me welcomes the pain. Pain is all I've known for a month now; it's become familiar.

The brightness dims as he slides into the chair opposite me and settles a delicate mug with a matching saucer onto the chipped and worn Formica table in front of my hands. He's backlit by the glow from the windows as I watch his long, graceful fingers toy with a small espresso cup, and it's hard to pull my attention away from the way they move in order to look at the drink he's placed in front of me.

The scent of cinnamon wafts up as I lift the fragile mug, and the first sip startles me, pulling me a fraction of an inch closer to reality. It's exactly what I would have ordered for myself if I were still capable of managing to complete human tasks like ordering a drink or remembering to drink at all. I feel my eyes widen in question as I look up.

He shifts awkwardly, and a blush spreads across his pale cheeks.

"Your coat smelled like cinnamon." He shrugs and mumbles as he lifts his cup and studies its contents after taking a small sip.

My coat smelled like cinnamon.

Is it creepy that when I returned to retrieve a forgotten jacket after my brother's funeral, this ethereal man noticed what other scents lingered on the worn leather as he carried it from the back room? I decide that it's not. No one has cared what I smell like for a very long time. I have to tell myself that the sip of chai is the only reason there is a pool of warmth spreading through my abdomen.

"Do you have a list?"

My eyebrow tries to escape my forehead in confusion. "A list?"

He takes another sip. "A grocery list."

Oh. "Oh. No, I don't."

He shifts to the side in his seat and pulls his phone from his back pocket. He presses on the bottom corner, and a small stylus pops out, which he uses to tap on the screen for a moment before sliding the phone across the table to rest beside my tea, stylus on top.

"Why don't you make one for me, and then I'll grab your shopping with mine while you sit here and enjoy your tea."

What?

Why in the world is he offering to shop for me? I don't know this man. The most effort anyone has extended to me has been to leave a roast or scalloped potatoes at the shop when they've dropped off their trucks.

I shake my head quickly. "No. That's not something you…"

He cuts me off.

"Please. Let me do this."

I search his face, all strong, sleek lines and soft skin.

"...Why?"

"Because I want to." He says it like it's the most natural thing in the world to want to grocery shop for someone he doesn't know. Like it would be the most natural thing in the world for me to agree.

He watches me struggle to say yes and seems to decide that perhaps an additional reason might sway the tide.

"Besides. I only allow myself one espresso a day, and if I do this, then you'll have to buy me a second as a thank you, and I'll have to drink it. It would be rude of me to decline."

A noise escapes me that feels like it's trying to be a laugh but manages to sound like nothing more than a choked sob.

His playful grin is wide and brilliant and all-encompassing, and I can't remember what it's like to look at anything other than his smile as his smooth voice winds its way across my skin and down my spine.

I can't say no when he looks at me like that, when his voice sounds like that.

I look away before his radiance blinds me, nod once, and quickly scratch out a list on his phone.

As he walks away, leaving me with my still steaming cup of tea, I realize that for the first time in more than a month, for one brief moment, I forgot to hurt.

I have no idea why I'm doing this. I'm shopping for his groceries. *Really, Namid, this is the choice you've made?*

I'd noticed him as soon as I entered the store. His emotions are so intense that it's hard for me to ignore them anytime he's near. I'd recognize the intensity of his despair anywhere. Not noticing him was never an option. My gaze had been drawn to him each time I left an aisle and walked the few steps along the main walkway before turning down the next. He didn't move. I made it through half of my shopping, and he'd still been staring at the cheese. He hadn't been wearing a coat even though it was thirty degrees outside, and his hair, which was longer than it had been when I last saw him nearly a month ago, looked like he'd just rolled out of bed. He'd looked so...alone. He felt so...alone. Somehow, that had been enough to convince me to prolong the agony that is the grocery store.

There are less than a half-dozen things on his list: milk and bread and cheese and lunch meat. I don't really think that eating nothing but pre-sliced deli sandwiches for weeks on end is going to do much to help his mental state, so I add a few more things: pastries and a rotisserie chicken, apples and broccoli. I don't know whether he'll bother eating them, but somehow, I feel a bit better knowing that he has the option.

I have his groceries loaded into paper bags since I didn't think to ask if he has canvas ones in his truck and there were none in his cart when I took it from him. Somehow, I doubt he brought them, or even if he knows whether he did or not. I settle his bags in the cart next to mine and head back to the coffee nook.

When I return, he hasn't moved, and I find myself studying him as I order a second round of drinks and park the cart to the side in a way that places it out of the way of other customers but also encourages them not to sit at the table nearest ours. Even with his shoulders hunched like he carries the weight of the world, his back is straight and broad, and I wonder what it must have been like to have known him laughing and loving and enjoying life.

He jumps slightly as I set a second cup down in front of him and slide back into the cold metal seat on the opposite side of the scuffed-up table.

I sip slowly as I wait for him to calm down and readjust to my presence.

"I was supposed to buy your second one."

I shrug. "You can buy me one some other time."

He nods almost imperceptibly and picks up his new tea, warming his hands on the cup and swirling it gently as he watches the pattern in the foam shift around.

"Thank you. For everything."

"My pleasure."

When he looks up and his eyes find mine, they're red and swollen; he's been crying again. They're jade green, and in the bright sunlight that streams through the windows and bathes him with its warmth, they're almost transparent. They're beautiful.

"I just realized I don't actually know your name."

I'm so lost in his eyes that his softly spoken words surprise me.

I offer a kind smile. "Namid."

"I've never heard that name before."

I have to suppress my laughter. That's the politest version of "What the hell kind of name is that?" I've ever heard - which is, of course, the first thing everyone I ever meet says when I introduce myself.

"I'm not surprised. It's Chippewa. It means star dancer."

His left eyebrow lifts in silent question, and I can't help but chuckle. He wants to know why. When I've had this conversation with others in the past, their expressions - and the confusion that radiates from them - always seem to come with wariness, as if my name alone somehow makes me seem even odder to them than I already do. I feel none of that from him. No judgment or confusion or fear. Under his pain, there is only a spark of curiosity.

"I know the Chippewa aren't from around here, but Ken - Mr. Johnson's - grandfather is Chippewa, and he speaks the language. When we realized that I likely wasn't going remember who I was, I needed a name."

Jayce's eyebrow has fallen back to its normal resting place, and he carefully sips his hot tea.

"I told him that I was fine sticking with John Doe, which is what the sheriff's office and hospital called me. Ken was...less than thrilled with that suggestion." I can't help but chuckle at the memory of how offended he felt on my behalf.

Jayce smiles. It's a rough, broken thing, but for one single instant, as his lips twitch upward, I feel something other than despair from him. Something that in another time and place might be akin to amusement.

"He found me in December, on a night when the sky was clear and the Aurora was so bright he was able to see me lying on the side of the road, even though it was nearly midnight. It's the only reason he was able to see me. When we got to the hospital, I was, astonishingly, unharmed. There's no way to know how long I was lying in the snow on a two-degree night, but I didn't have frostbite, and I didn't have hypothermia. I was cold but otherwise unharmed. Ken thinks it was a miracle. He says that I must have fallen from the stars, and they kept me safe until he found me."

Jayce's face is soft. It's the softest I've seen it; the small lines that have lived next to his eyes and across his forehead each time I've seen him are barely visible. The guilt and pain and desperation that have threatened to swallow me right along with him whenever I've been in his presence have faded as I've spoken. Behind the black and hurt and emptiness that I struggle to hold at arm's distance when I'm near him, I feel a hint of something else. It's subtle and soft and gentle and so quiet that I'm not even sure it's real, but it feels like hope. Like maybe he's realizing that if I was able to survive, he might too.

I keep talking, hoping to nurse the small spark somehow.

"When I told Ken I'd keep John, he told me he'd think about it and come up with something perfect, and then three days later, he lays this on me."

I laugh quietly. "He didn't do me any favors with a name like this in such a small town. John might have helped me seem slightly less like an outsider, but when he suggested it and explained his reasoning, I couldn't say no. He offered me his surname as well, so at least that half is easier for people to pronounce."

I shift in my seat, growing uncomfortable under Jayce's intense gaze and wishing I had more espresso to sip as a distraction, but it's long gone.

"I love it now. I'm...different. I know that. Fewer people expect me to fit in here with a name like this."

He smiles at me. It doesn't last long, but it's the first time I've seen an actual smile rather than a twitch of his lips as they try to shift into the ghost of an expression simply because he feels it's a social obligation to do so.

"It suits you."

Warmth rushes through me. Aside from Ken, I don't interact with many people outside of work, and I certainly don't sit through two cups of coffee with them, especially when their emotions are as strong as Jayce's are. It's hard for me to keep pushing them aside and telling myself that they're his, not mine.

The warmth that's slowing growing in my chest is my own. It's because of him, yes, but this feeling is mine.

"Ken says you own the mechanic shop?"

The smile is gone. "Me and Jordyn. It's always been the two of us."

The wave of guilt and loss threatens to engulf me once again. I don't know how he's managed to stay standing feeling like this. No wonder he'd been staring at cheese.

I sigh and hesitate for a moment. I don't want to impose, but he clearly has no one else.

"I can't pretend to know what it's like for you. I don't have any family that I remember."

His gaze shifts back down to the liquid that still fills his cup as I continue.

"But as strange as it might sound since I'm not very social, I'm pretty good at knowing how someone feels, and I just..." I trail off for a moment as I try to figure out how to continue. "I took over Ken's bookkeeping a few years ago. I enjoy it, and I'm good at it. Ken told me that was your brother's department at the shop, so if you ever feel like you need some help with it..."

He hasn't moved, so I trail off, afraid that I've overstepped some invisible line.

I watch him closely, wondering if he'll offer me thanks once more and then stand and walk away. He'll probably tell me to go, that he doesn't need my help, that he doesn't want it. I don't want to go, and I tell myself that it's simply because I'm trying to help someone in need, that it has nothing to do with strong arms and jade eyes and the bright magenta surge of love for his brother that I felt roll off him when we first met.

And then the world is blue. It's the vibrant blue of the sky and the sea where they come together on the horizon on mid-summer days as relief washes over him. His shoulders move with his breath, slow and smooth, and his fingers reach toward his cheeks. His head is bowed, his gaze averted, but I watch as relief settles into his bones. It's dimmed and covered by a shroud of hurt and emptiness, but it's there as I watch his knuckles brush away the tears that have found their way down his cheeks and gotten caught in the scruff on his jaw.

"Thank you," he whispers to the table. "I can't..."

His breath stutters.

"Thank you."

Chapter 4

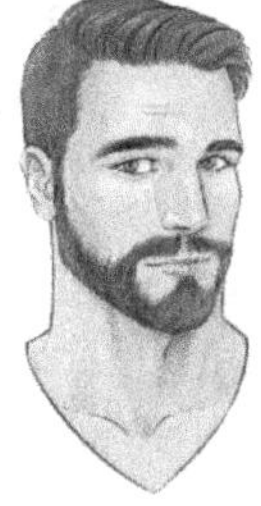

I never realized just how much I depended on Jordyn's presence to ground me, and I've been so lost, floating on my own without him. After our parents died, we were all the other had. We both wanted more one day, of course - a wife, a husband, kids. We wanted families of our own. I've always known that would be harder for me than for Jordyn; after all, how many single gay men are there in a backwoods town with a population under three thousand? Not many. As far as I know, it's just me. Still, I wanted that for each of us - to have someone to love other than each other. We'd always love one another. We'd always be a part of the other's soul; that's how twins are, but we both knew we needed more. Neither of us had found it, so we'd been one another's everything.

I knew the moment I lost him that his ghost would haunt me at the shop.

The vacant desk in the office is gathering dust because I can't bear to sit in his chair, and the absence of his bulky shoulders as he stood at the front counter plagues me every day, but it's the small things I've found somehow harder to bear. It's the thirty texts a day about football and food that never arrive. The online dogs that bark on my phone screen with no one for me to send them to or laugh at them with. The tea that no longer miraculously appears on my workbench at four every afternoon.

For the thousandth time in only a few short weeks, I'm sitting on the single high bar chair behind the reception desk holding my phone in my hand, willing it to beep or to vibrate or to ring until my knuckles whiten and the edges cut into my skin. What am I supposed to do now, alone with my thoughts and my hopes and my dreams? Alone in the shop and in my truck and at home. Alone with no one on the other end of the telephone line.

I crush my lower lip between my teeth hard enough that the metallic taste of blood floods my mouth as my thumb slides along the blackened screen. It's not the first time. Without the sound of my tools, the silence that seems to hang in the shop like thick fog is deafening, and my world is collapsing into a black hole of nothingness.

The sound of the door chime pulls my attention from the breath that sits trapped inside my lungs and the heat of the salt water that's found its way onto my face once again, and I manage to loosen my grip on my phone and set it on the counter in front of me.

Namid asked if he could come to the shop on a Saturday. He doesn't spend a lot of time around people, which makes sense, I suppose, as any time I hear people talking about him in town, it's always with a bit of uncertainty. They aren't sure what to make of him with his refined demeanor and almost otherworldly beauty. Objectively, I understand why they think he's out of place here. People here are kind enough, but they're hearty and boisterous and roughened by the cold and the dark. They are eagles and falcons - strong, sturdy hunters - fending for themselves in an obvious, almost predatory way. Namid doesn't feel out of place to me. He feels like a jay, bright and small and blue and beautiful. Happy to soar through the clear spring skies looking for seeds and berries. Yet there seems to be a quiet strength to him, like he's thriving by foraging in the crisp snow-covered woods. He fits here, just as the jay does. He simply doesn't conform in the way others expect him to.

He smiles at me as he walks in, and it's effortless and happy and brilliant. It's like he's offering me the gift of a single ray of light to cut through the darkness surrounding me, and I can't help but smile back, even though the movement is unfamiliar and awkward these days.

"Good morning." He crosses the room without hesitation and sets a paper cup on the counter in front of me.

"I thought I was supposed to buy the next round."

He looks almost playful. "You'll just have to get the next, next round, I suppose."

I'm not sure what to say to that, so I just mumble a, "Thank you," as I stand and take the cup.

"You want me to show you around?"

"I'd love that, thank you."

He keeps talking as he follows me through the glass door that leads into the work bay.

"I've been here before a few times, for Ken's shitty old trucks mostly. Ken says that he used to be his own mechanic before you opened this place, but as someone who's seen him try to fix the office's radiator, I'm grateful that I don't have to drive something that he's worked on."

We're standing in the shop next to the lift, surrounded by tools and the smell of oil. We're standing in a place where I stand a hundred times a day, but it feels different with him here rambling at me, filling the silence.

"I've never really learned to do much with cars. I'm good with math, and I read enough to enter some kind of reading triathlon if such a thing exists. I don't think it does though. I'm a pretty good cook, I think, and I'm handy enough when our plumbing has issues, but cars I've never really figured out."

He walks down under the lift into the pit.

"This is very cool. So, you don't have to slide under cars on those little scooters these days, huh?"

He glances briefly in my direction as he walks back out of the pit and resumes his exploration of the shop's diagnostic computers and the pneumatic tools

I've left on the floor since I usually don't have the energy to put them away at the end of the day anymore.

"I mean, I own one of those."

He spins around to face me with a grin.

"Can I play with it?!"

A laugh forces its way from my chest. *A laugh.* A short, tight, strangled sound that I don't quite understand anymore.

"Can you...play...with it?"

"Yes."

"No."

He shrugs and continues wandering around, trailing his graceful fingers along the edges of toolboxes and the curves of wrenches before coming to a stop in front of me.

"One day, you'll let me play with it."

He sounds so confident, so sure of himself, so...joyful. Like he intends to insert himself into my life and my shop for long enough that I'll agree to let him use one of my tools like a child's toy until he somehow smashes into the lift and brings an entire car crashing down on me...or himself.

I don't know how to respond other than to shake my head in disbelief and lead him back to the reception area.

His playfulness fades as we approach the office door. It's opened about a foot. That's how Jordyn left it the last time he walked out. I haven't been able to approach it since.

When I pause, unable to take the last two steps and push the door open, Namid lays his hand on my forearm.

His touch is warm through my thick flannel shirt, even though his fingertips rest so lightly on my arm that I can barely feel their pressure. The heat spreads across my skin, down through the muscle, until it feels like my arm is throbbing where we're connected. I don't understand this sensation. Even though there is no one in this town for me to build a life with, we get tourists in the summer, and I spend plenty of time letting them touch me and touching them in return. All the lips I've kissed, all the skin I've touched, it all blends together into something vaguely memorable but ultimately uninteresting and indistinguishable. Never has the brush of a hand through fabric sent my body reeling the way his does. I really have lost it.

"Do you want me to do this alone?" His tone is gentle, the type of tone one might use on a hurt or skittish animal.

"No. I'm okay."

I take a deep breath and force myself forward.

My fingers tingle as they fall from Jayce's arm when he finally steps toward the office door. There is so much complexity inside him, so much buried under the hurt. For a moment in the shop, he let me tease him. For a moment, he smiled and laughed and almost teased me back. He was so full of love and light and laughter; he just doesn't know where they are anymore. He doesn't know how to find them.

I take a deep breath and step into Jordyn's office, hoping that he's left everything in order. I want to be able to give Jayce good news, or at least not bad news.

"Do you want to grab a chair and join me? I don't know how long I'll be."

He shakes his head quickly. "No. I'll be...I'll work."

I smile as kindly as I can. "I'll let you know if I have any questions."

He hovers at my side for a moment before taking one shuddering breath and walking away without a word, and I settle in behind the desk. It faces out toward the reception area, and I leave the door open so that Jayce doesn't have to worry about what I might be doing in his brother's space. It doesn't take me long to learn just how organized Jordyn was. The software they use for scheduling appointments and ordering parts is connected and state of the art. The banking and accounting software is separate, but the two interface nicely. It doesn't look like any of the shop's bills have been paid since Jordyn died, but it's only been about five weeks, so I'm sure when Jayce reaches out to let people know what's happened and get his accounts up to date, there won't be any issues. It takes less than two hours for me to go through the entire system and pull together a detailed overview.

I find Jayce sitting at a small glass table in what can loosely be called the break room. It's little more than a large closet with a mini fridge, a table with two cheap plastic chairs, and a warehouse-sized box filled with individual bags of chips. I suppose with only the two of them, it was more than enough for them to grab a drink or eat lunch together, and my heart breaks at the fact he'll be in here alone with his pre-sliced deli meat sandwiches from now on. His arms are crossed on the table, his forehead resting on them as if he's trying to grab a cat nap. I don't think he's asleep. I think he might be crying.

"Hey." I startle him even though I deliberately keep my voice low and calm.

He jerks up quickly, twisting his head briefly and dragging his eyes along his sleeve. They're red again, and

I find myself hoping that one day, I get the chance to see them clear and bright.

"Something you need?"

I gesture to the other chair with the folder I hold in one hand. "May I?"

"Yeah. Yeah, of course."

The chair's metal legs squeak deafeningly across the tiled floor as I pull it out and settle into the small space with him. I take a moment to breathe, hoping that my pause doesn't worry him. He's in nearly as bad a shape as he was the day we first met, and even though I've been here for a couple of hours, being this close to him still leaves me needing a moment to focus in order to prevent his emotions from affecting mine.

He sighs deeply. "Should I be nervous?"

I can't help but chuckle. "You don't do much with the accounting, do you?"

His shoulders slump further. "No. That was all Jordyn."

"Well, you might be in for a bit of a surprise then."

He straightens in his chair and raises an eyebrow. "A bad one?"

"No." I laugh again kindly.

"It looks like you each took a yearly salary of forty thousand. Does that sound right?"

"Yeah. I mean, my house is old and small, and Jordyn lived in a condo, but you've been grocery shopping here; it's expensive."

Clearly, he thinks I'm going to tell him he's spending too much money.

"Well, Jordyn's records are immaculate."

He physically slumps back over, hunching his shoulders as relief floods through the small room and fills his soul. It's a welcome momentary change.

"From what I can see, the shop's accounts are in amazing shape. You do have one double booking next week, and you haven't paid March or April's bills yet, but other than that, you have a great business here. It looks like Jordyn kept a ten-thousand-dollar cushion in the checking account in case any emergent issues came up."

He cuts me off and sighs again as he sinks back into his chair. "Oh, thank God."

Considering what I found while going through his books, I can't stop the grin from spreading across my face at the fact that he thinks ten thousand dollars is a lot.

"You've been in business for what...seven years now?"

"Eight."

"Eight. Well. You've done well."

I open the folder and slide it across the table.

"There is a savings account as well."

He raises an eyebrow and shifts forward to examine the papers I've printed out.

"Every month, Jordyn would transfer anything that remained after your operating costs, salaries, and whatever it took to keep the cushion in the checking account. There is nearly a quarter of a million dollars there.”

A strangled choking noise escapes his throat as his eyes dart back and forth from me to the folder on the table.

“That...that can’t be right.”

I flip over a couple of pages to the highlighted account balance section. “It is. Your brother was good with money, and you’ve built a strong business. You have the money to do whatever you want for a while...if you need some time or something...”

His eyes shine as he tries to blink back tears.

“I can’t believe he...I just...”

I reach across to rest my hand on his arm. It’s thick and warm and strong, and there is so much sadness and disbelief, but underneath it all, something that feels almost like amusement.

“I can’t...I don’t want to...I need to work, you know?”

I nod and squeeze his arm tighter.

“But I...I can’t believe he never said. I mean, I can...but I can’t, you know.”

My thumb slides along the flannel of his shirt for a moment before I realize what I’m doing. As soon as I notice, I quickly pull my hand back to my lap.

“Well. I’m just happy I found good news instead of bad. Everything is incredibly organized. You’ll need to pay a bit more attention to scheduling in the future, and you’ll have to make sure you pay all of your utilities and vendors on time moving forward, but I'd be happy to show you where all those accounts are if you'd like."

His gaze is so intense that I want to look away as he searches my face. I'm not sure what he hopes to find.

"Could you, maybe? I mean, I know you have your own life, but I...I'd pay you of course. Would you have any interest in me hiring you to do things like that?"

God, he's endearing. How is it possible for such a giant, fragile man to be so...likable?

"I'd love to. I don't really think you need a lot of help, so maybe we could start with...I don't know...twice a month and see how that works?"

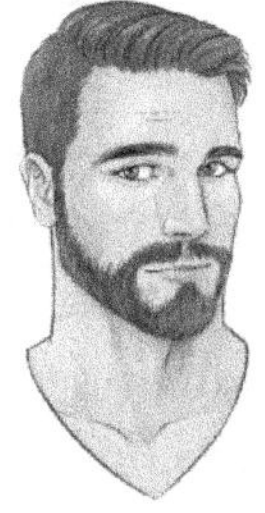

I quickly walk Namid out after he agrees to come back in two weeks to help me again. I don't want to risk my endless crying causing him to change his mind. While I say my goodbye, I do my best to keep my mind as blank as possible. I need to be on my own before I can even begin to process what he just told me.

I lock the door behind him and make my way back to the break room in a daze. Unless I take the time to close all of the blinds, it's the only room not visible from the parking lot aside from Jordyn's office, and I'm definitely not up to hiding in there while I have the breakdown I'm sure is on the way.

A quarter of a million dollars. A fucking quarter of a million dollars. The shop's savings account has a quarter of a million dollars in it. All this time. For eight years, Jordyn had been quietly putting money away for us to buy houses or for our retirement or for when one of us finally found someone to love and needed to pay for a big splashy wedding.

I drop my forehead to rest against my crossed arms on the shitty tempered-glass table and cry until I can barely pull enough oxygen into my lungs to stay conscious. Jordyn took care of me our entire lives. Everyone knew he was always the responsible one, while I was the screwup. It's not like I've ever done anything truly wild. I've never been arrested, never gotten anyone pregnant, never done drugs, but still. I was always the one to run out of money because I impulsively bought something stupid. I was the one who drove my motorcycle just a little too fast, the one who occasionally forgot to wear a helmet, the one who once insisted I knew how to paint my own truck when I was fifteen, only to have our parents come home to seventy-three empty cans of spray paint on the lawn and their son covered in a black, sticky film so thick it took more than a week to wear off. I was the one who flooded my apartment putting in a new dishwasher, accidentally bleached my darks, and spent three weeks' salary on a weekend trip to Vegas. Jordyn didn't do those things. Jordyn drove me home when I was drunk, helped me mop up the flood, and took pictures of me every day while the black paint wore off and then turned them in as a science project. Jordyn was the one who had apparently been saving for our futures. He'd been saving for a future he won't ever have. I should have been the one to go, not him.

What am I supposed to do with this kind of money? I can't buy a nicer house with it; I'll just wander around all my new empty rooms alone. I can't buy a shiny new motorcycle with it; I won't have anyone to ride down the coast and eat shitty roadside tacos with. I won't have anyone to laugh with when those tacos have us both pulling over and running for the bushes twenty minutes later. What am I supposed to do with this money?

What am I supposed to do without him?

It's dark before I manage to drag myself to my truck and head home. I've been at the shop since eight a.m., but I don't remember any time passing after Namid left. It disappeared into the abyss like so much of the past five weeks.

I don't eat when I get home. I pull off my jeans in my bedroom doorway and fall into bed without bothering to finish undressing. I curl up under the comforter, pulling it up over my head until the world disappears. Here, there is only my breath, loud and warm in the small, dark space. I'm left with only my thoughts. Only guilt and loss and emptiness. I shouldn't have yelled at him. I shouldn't have said okay when he grabbed his keys and walked out my door. I shouldn't still be here trying to survive without him.

I don't know how long I cry. I never do.

I dream again. I dream of a boy who convinces me we look enough alike that we should try to trick our teachers into thinking we're each other. I dream about sitting on cold metal stands as I watch a teenager play his first game of high school football. I dream about a man standing at an altar with a beautiful woman in a white dress at his side. I dream of their dog barking as I arrive for their summer barbecue, their two kids running through the gate and calling me Uncle Jayce. I dream of a life cut short, of a future that will never be.

Jayce is five minutes late. While I tend to be late for just about everything, I made sure to be ten minutes early today, and now it feels like I've been waiting for so long that I'm sure something must be wrong, and I'm starting to worry. It's been two weeks since I was last here at Jayce's shop, and he was in such bad shape when I left that I'm terrified of the possibility that he's somehow gotten worse. Worse for him might mean... No. Surely, he's just late.

I can't help but breathe a sigh of relief when his truck pulls up next to mine. Jayce hadn't hesitated when I'd asked if we could meet on a Saturday again since I'd be a bit uncomfortable if there were customers at the shop while I was working. He hadn't even snorted with laughter or asked me to explain or looked at me like something was wrong with me the way most people do, so, while I'm absolutely a night person, when he'd asked if nine was okay, I wasn't about to make any snarky comments about the fact that I consider nine a.m. to be nighttime.

I hop out and make my way over to him as he exits his truck and reaches back in for something.

"Sorry I'm late," he mumbles, with his head still buried inside the cab.

"No worries. I only just got here myself." It's just a little white lie. I don't want him to feel even worse if he happens to be one of those people who feel guilty about wasting five minutes of another person's time.

When he turns around, he's holding two paper cups, one that looks like it holds a human-sized beverage and one that looks like it's been miniaturized. The heady aroma of espresso and cinnamon curls up into the air and combines into something heavenly. He holds mine out without a word.

"Thank you." I moan in gratitude as I take the cup.

He gives me a single nod, and I can't help trying to make him smile.

"Four sugars, right?"

His eyes briefly attempt to pop out of his head until he registers the grin on my face.

He snorts and shakes his head as he shuts his truck door before leading the way to the shop. He doesn't smile, but he doesn't roll his eyes as if my attempt at humor has annoyed him either.

The wave of pain that washes over me the moment we step inside nearly knocks me down. How is it possible that he's able to get out of bed and pretend he's functioning while he feels like this?

"I'm going to…are you good if I work a bit since I'm here?" he mumbles.

"Of course." I smile as gently as I can. I'm terrified that something I do is somehow going to be the thing that breaks him. "I'll get your bills paid and reconcile things for the past two weeks, so you're all set for the next two again. I honestly doubt it'll take me more than an hour."

He simply nods once as he walks toward the bay door.

I settle in behind the desk and take a sip from the tiny cup in an attempt to wake up before starting on his finances. It feels like something I should be at least half awake for. Straight espresso. As out of it as he was at the grocery store, he'd still noticed and remembered what kind of coffee I drink.

The office is plain. The walls are pure white, and the desk is a basic grey laminate slab that holds two computer monitors, a tear-away calendar, and a single picture frame. Two teenage boys, identical save their haircuts and the color of their T-shirts, standing in front of a couple who are clearly their parents, smile back at me. That's all the room holds. There isn't a painting or a filing cabinet or a bobblehead or a baseball. The room holds the bare minimum Jordyn needed to do his job, and a picture of his family. That was all that had mattered to him.

It's silent. Disturbingly silent. God, no wonder Jayce felt so terrible when we walked through the door. There is nothing here. There is no music or conversation or television in the background. There is no life at all.

Somehow, I imagine it must be even worse in the shop, with the harsh metallic clang of tools echoing around the space with no radio or laughter to temper sounds. I've been to the shop a handful of times in the past, but those visits were fast. I'd just drop off or pick up whatever car needed repair, pay the bill, and that was it. Still, it felt different with the two of them here, with Jordyn greeting me as he stood behind the reception computer or yelling that he'd be right there from this very office as the sound of a ballgame quietly slipped out through the open door.

Shooting the rest of my espresso like a tequila shot, I get to work. Jayce is already here on a Saturday when he should be somewhere else, somewhere that isn't filled with the ghostly echo of a life that no longer exists. He doesn't need me dinking around and forcing him to be here longer than necessary.

He's done a good job with his scheduling these last two weeks. No one is double booked, and it looks like he's kept things just a bit lighter, which I think is probably a good thing for his clearly strained mental health. I pay his bills, shift the bit of leftover money into his savings account, and make a mental note to ask him if he'd rather give himself a bit of a raise than continue to shift it to the shop's account since it's all his now anyway. As I make my way through reception toward the mechanic's bay, I realize that I should probably give it a few more weeks before I deliberately point out that his brother isn't going to get to spend any of the money he so carefully put aside for their futures.

"Hello?"

I can hear some kind of...wrenching...but I can't see Jayce. The noise stops, and the car that is sitting floor level over the pit I'd climbed into a couple of weeks ago rises into the air.

"I'm finished." My voice echoes through the empty space.

The car has stopped its ascent and is floating in the air now, but Jayce doesn't respond.

"So...I'm going to take off. Would it be better if I came on a weekday next time? I don't want you to have to keep coming in on your weekends."

I'm a tad relieved when he hops out of the pit.

"It's okay. It's not like I have anything to do on the weekends anyway. Gets me out of the house, I guess."

He is heartbroken, and it is heartbreaking. I know there isn't anything I can do for him, but I wish there were.

"Okay." I offer the same soft smile I've been using nearly every time I speak to him. "I'll bring the drinks next time. Nine is still best for you?"

"Nine is good."

Shit. "Okay then. I'll see you in two weeks."

He looks like he wants to say something, so I wait quietly for a moment, but whatever words his lips have parted to release evaporate into the ether. His mouth closes once more, and he simply nods.

Chapter 5

Namid

Three plastic chairs with thin metal legs that look like they might easily collapse are arranged in the shop's lobby against the wall, opposite the office door. I can't imagine there's ever been a need for more than that. It's only ever been Jayce and Jordyn working here, so at most, they'd have two clients waiting on quick things like brake jobs. People picking up vehicles they'd previously dropped off likely just stand at the desk and wait for the few moments it takes to pay and collect their keys; that's what I've always done. Besides, I've seen Jayce's schedule, and the shop rarely has more than three ongoing projects at any given time.

A man I don't know sits in the center chair as I walk in holding two coffee cups. They're ceramic with silicone lids this time. If we're going to keep doing this regularly, I don't want to keep using disposable paper ones. The customer staring at the wall is an older, gruff-looking man, probably in his late fifties. He's wearing overalls splattered with paint and a worn Carhart jacket. His beard is unkempt, and wisps of greying hair peek out from under an old baseball hat covered in what appears to be grease stains. He looks like half the men in town.

The man glares at me as I walk in, and his jaw works as if he wants to say something to me, likely something not very nice. He certainly feels more than slightly annoyed that I'm here, but I smile and nod in his direction anyway as I head for the glass door that leads into the large work bay. I stack the cups on top of one another to free up a hand, and by the time I'm halfway through the door, the man is on his feet, taking a few steps toward me as if he's afraid I'm breaking in to steal heavy power tools while carrying two cups of coffee as a plausible cover. Even someone who can't feel his anger the way I can would be able to feel him glaring daggers at my back through the glass wall that partitions the spaces. There is no way he's going to sit back down until he ensures I haven't come to beat Jayce up, even though I'm clearly inferior in terms of upper body strength. Maybe he thinks I'm here to throw coffee on his face and kick him in the jewels just for sport.

Jayce is standing next to his tool bench with a couple of quarts of oil in his hands, and a shiny new pickup has its hood popped a few feet away. He glances in my direction as I walk toward him, and the heaviness that always seems to seep from his every cell lightens briefly as he greets me with a half smile and sets down the oil to take the mug from my outstretched hand.

Win.

"Thanks."

He studies the ceramic and raises an eyebrow in question.

"I don't like wasting the disposable ones."

Another half smile.

Double win.

I gesture with my head as subtly as possible toward the man I know is still standing at the glass behind me, watching to make sure I don't cause trouble.

"He's going to stare until he's sure I'm not a threat."

Jayce glances up with a frown, and for an instant, anger floods through him as he raises a hand and offers a wave and a pained smile to the man in the waiting room.

"Sorry. I know you don't like people. I just figured since I was going to be here for a bit, I might as well bust out an oil change."

"Don't be sorry. It's your business. And it's not that I don't like people. I mean, I can get overwhelmed when there's a few, but it's more that..."

I force on a smile and shake my head as I realize what I'd been going to say might sound like I feel sorry for myself.

"Never mind."

"No. What?"

"Well, it's more that most people around here don't like me than I don't like them. No one has ever forgotten how I ended up here. In truth, it's not going to do your business any favors to have people see me here with you regularly." I shrug and sip my espresso. "I can come alone if that's better for you so that you don't have to come in on Saturdays, and so people don't see me here. If you trust me with a key anyway, I mean, I know you don't really know me or anything."

Jayce stares at me silently, and I wonder if I've overstepped my bounds by suggesting that I'm trustworthy enough to be in his shop on my own.

He takes a step toward me, and I have to fight not to back away. I don't think he'd do anything to hurt me, but he feels upset, and it's just instinctive for someone who's spent their whole life basically alone.

He's close now, less than arm's distance.

"You're serious?"

I stare at the lid of my cup and pick at the rim.

"I'm sorry. You don't know me; of course you wouldn't trust me to be here on my..."

His hand falls heavily onto my shoulder, and I jump before I can stop myself.

"That's not what I mean."

His voice is the same deep rumble it always is, but there's a softness to it I've never heard before. Normally, it sounds like he can barely manage to choke out his words through a throat filled with glass. But these flow almost easily. Like they aren't a fight. Like he means them.

"You think I care if people know you're here? You're the only one in this entire town who has lifted a finger to do anything other than offer pitying looks since it happened."

I raise my eyes to search his face, overwhelmed by the rush of gratitude and concern that flows through his touch. I think he might actually be concerned *for* me, not *because of* me, and I'm not really sure how to process that.

He squeezes my shoulder.

"Come with me."

I follow him through the glass door, helpless to even consider declining. The moment he opens it, his demeanor shifts. His soul is still just as filled with anguish as it's been since the moment I met him, but on the outside, he appears to be brusque and confident and stubborn and in charge of the world.

"I can't thank you enough for everything you've done for me."

He starts talking the moment he opens the glass door and doesn't stop until he's escorted me the twenty steps through reception, and I'm settled in the office behind the desk.

"Truly, I don't know what I'd do without you, and bringing me tea is just above and beyond. I'm so thankful for your friendship, Namid. Just let me know if you need anything at all."

I'm so overwhelmed at the fact that his words feel genuine that all I manage is a stuttering, "Thank you," as he half closes the door on his way out and makes his way back to the shop.

"You'll only be another ten minutes, Bob." His tone is deep and harsh once more, almost threatening.

While I know that it's not the best professional decision on his part to welcome me so openly into his shop, I'm grateful. While folks in town are generally polite to me, aside from Ken, no one has ever actively made me feel wanted in this place during the decade I've lived here.

I try not to eavesdrop on their conversation as Bob pays and picks up his keys not long after I've settled in with the books. Instead, I focus on my work, although there isn't much to do aside from balancing the accounts. It's only been two weeks, and there aren't any bills to pay this time. It takes me less than an hour, and I reluctantly admit to myself that Jayce really only needs my help once a month.

When I make my way out of the office, I find Jayce sitting at the reception desk with his feet up on the counter, poking idly at his phone.

"I'm finished already. Honestly, you probably only need me to stop by once a month if you'd rather have one of your Saturdays back."

He drops his feet and quickly stands, slipping his phone into his back pocket.

"I don't want to be an inconvenience to you; you're doing me such a huge favor as it is, but if I'm being honest, I think I might get a bit anxious letting things sit for a whole month and just hoping it all works out okay when you come in. Is it too much for you to come every other week, even though there isn't a lot to do? I'm happy to pay you more."

Warmth rushes through me as I let myself pretend he's asking because he wants to see me more often than once a month.

"Every other week is no problem at all for me."

Relief floods through him.

"So..." He looks oddly nervous. "Would you like to maybe get a second coffee with me?"

I know the smart thing would be to say no and limit our interactions. His feelings are so overwhelming that sometimes it's hard to separate them from mine. Sometimes, it's hard to even tell which actually are mine because while I feel the depth of his loss and sorrow whenever he's around, I also feel sorrow of my own for everything that he's been through. They play off each other, combining and swirling into a whirlwind. Being around him is like getting caught in a tsunami. It's overwhelming and exhausting and emotionally decimating.

Still, I can't deny that a small part of me is thankful that he was so kind when I first reached out to him in the cheese aisle. I've always been happy with my quiet life, and I've rarely felt the need for more than my friendship with Ken. The occasional interactions I have at the store and the coffee shop have always been more than enough for me, and while I have no desire to suddenly walk into the bar and try to befriend half the town while dealing with the onslaught of their emotions, the warmth in my belly that accompanies Jayce's smile and his occasional kind words surprises me. Even though I know it's likely the wrong choice, I want to spend as much time with him as I can.

"I'd really like that."

I know I'm grinning like a moron. I really don't care.

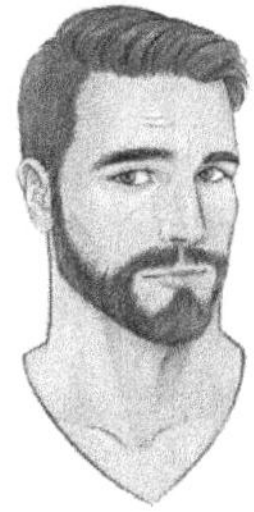

Why did I just do that? I don't want to go get coffee with Namid. It's not that I don't want to go with *him*. It's that I don't want another tea. I don't want to go to the coffee shop. I don't want to go anywhere other than home to strip and fall into bed until I have to drag myself out again on Monday morning, just like I have every weekend for the past two months. I want to hide in the darkness where the pain can't find me. Just like I have during every moment I haven't been obligated to do things I can't avoid - things like remembering to eat and shower. When I leave my bed, all I think about is the fact that when I'm asleep, I can't feel, I can't regret, I can't hurt. When I'm asleep, I don't have to try to convince myself that this lonely life is worth living, even though I'm not sure I believe that.

The invitation just fell out. I know that the way Namid keeps to himself rubs some folks the wrong way. I know the way he showed up with no history and no name and no anything still bothers them. I know people avoid him, and while they're polite to his face, he's not welcome enough to be actively included. He's still *other*. When he'd stood there with that sad half smile on his beautiful face, holding out a tea he'd gone out of his way to get in a new ceramic cup I hadn't had to ask for, telling me that the whole town hates him so much his very presence in my business is something he felt he should apologize for, my heart broke. I didn't even know the tiny pieces that were left could break any further.

I couldn't stop thinking about it the entire time he was working today, about the fact that I've never once seen him with anyone other than Mr. Johnson in the whole ten years he's lived here. Does he even have a friend? Losing my brother and finding myself alone has nearly broken me in eight weeks. Has he really been this alone for ten years?

"It's nice today. Do you want to walk?"

He shrugs on his thin coat. It's still cold outside, but it's nearly summer, and the sun has just started to peek out from behind the thin clouds, so it shouldn't be too bad. The idea of even a quick drive, squished into the cab of my truck, somehow sounds far more awkward than a walk.

"That'd be great."

His face lights up when he smiles at me.

The day continues to brighten as we walk the four blocks to the supermarket coffee shop, and once we have our beverages in hand, grateful for the decent weather, we decide to continue on for another two blocks to the small park in the center of town. It's the end of May, and still snowy, of course, but the short walking trail that circles the park and the few small benches that speckle the edge of the path have been cleared by the city. By that, I mean the mayor brings over his ATV with a plow bolted to the front and a broom for the benches. We find one that's in the sunlight and settle in side by side.

"You've been here for a long time now. Do you like living here?" I'm surprised when the words leave my mouth. I'm even more surprised when I realize that I mean them. I don't want to just talk about the weather; I want to know more about him.

"Well, it's not like I've ever been to the Bahamas or anything, so I can't say that this is my favorite place in the world. This is the only place I've ever been. I could do without the nine months of needing a snowplow, and it would probably be nice to actually feel warm when I'm outside for once in my life, but all that aside, I do really like it."

"Not quite convincing."

"It's peaceful here and beautiful. I spend a lot of time outside when it's nice enough, listening to the wind blowing through the trees and the sound of the birds and the squirrels and the deer just living their lives in the forest without humans bothering them. I love that. I love knowing that there are still wild, unspoiled places in the world. I feel very lucky to be able to observe that here."

At my noncommittal grunt, he just smiles and continues.

"The sky is my favorite thing about this place. We don't get to see the sky as often as I'd like since it storms so much, but when it's visible, it's spectacular. Even when it's five degrees outside, I bundle up and lie on my porch for hours, staring at the stars and the Aurora in the winter and wondering about the universe and my place in it."

I watch his face as he talks, and his expression is almost one of awe or reverence when he speaks about the sky and the universe. I can't remember ever having felt that way about something, at least not since I was a kid. Before I became jaded and worn down by the demands of daily life in adulthood. Before I lost my parents. Before I lost Jordyn. Before I lost everything.

"Jordyn and I have...had...motorcycles. Early every August, we'd drive them down the coast highways to Seattle - that's where our parents were from. On those trips, I'd notice things like that. I'd notice the way the trees move in the breeze and the rays of sunlight that broke through the packed canopies onto the pavement, but here..."

I sigh and look around in thought.

"I guess I've forgotten to do that for a long time."

There is a long pause before Namid speaks.

"You still can, you know. It's all around you still."

I can't trust myself with words anymore, so I only nod and turn my attention to my drink. This is the most I've spoken since I lost Jordyn.

It's quiet for a long time. I wonder if I've said too much, but the silence doesn't feel uncomfortable between us. Maybe it is, and I'm just too broken to recognize things like that anymore, but I don't think so. I shift down on the bench, my ass nearly sliding off so that I can lean my head against the backrest to stare up at the sky and listen to the breeze murmuring through the trees

that surround us. Large clouds float through a nearly
blue sky, but there is sunlight streaming out between
them, and for just a moment, I forget to be broken.

I find myself waiting anxiously each time I have to wait for the two weeks to pass before I get to see Jayce again. I want to be around him. I want to try to make him smile. I want to be there to catch the brief glimpses of the man I imagine he once was during the fleeting moments he forgets that he's shattered. I want to feel the rush of warmth that runs through my veins and makes my skin tingle when his expressive jade eyes look at me as if he's searching for the meaning of life. I've never felt anything like this before. This sense of contentment and wonder and joy. The lightness that settles over me when he's around is so strong that it almost erases the heaviness he carries. I wish I could share it with him. I wish I could wrap him in this feeling and help lift the sorrow from his chest.

I know he's not okay, and I know he doesn't feel the same way about me. I don't mean I know that in the way people always say, "Oh, he doesn't feel anything for me," because they don't believe it's possible that the person they have feelings for might like them back. I know he doesn't because I feel everything he feels. Once in a while, when we're talking or walking in the park, it feels like his pain lightens a bit, but there is nothing that joins it. There is no rush of attraction or sense of overwhelming delight when he sees me. He doesn't feel the way I'm starting to, and even though I know it means this will end in heartbreak for me, I don't really care. One day, I'm sure I'll look back and shake my head and tell myself I was stupid, but right now, I *want* to feel this way. I want to feel accepted. I want to nervously look forward to seeing him even though I just left his shop. I want to feel my heart rush when he steps into the room and my breath catch when his shoulder brushes mine as we stroll side by side. I want the knot that's slowly forming in my stomach. I'm not in love with him, but I think I could be one day, and I want to know what it's like to fall in love, even if that love isn't returned.

"You still okay working with Jayce, kid?"

Ken's voice snaps me back to reality with a jolt.

Ken and I are eating chicken parmesan, like we do every Thursday night, and I nearly choke when he asks about Jayce out of the blue. I talk about Jayce from time to time, of course. Ken and I talk about most things. I haven't told him about Jordyn's savings account; that's not my information to share, but I've told him that his accounts are all in order, and while there isn't much for me to do, Jayce asked me to come every other week to help him stay on top of things. I've told him that I've never encountered sorrow as intense as the waves that still threaten to pull Jayce under, but that even through that, he's kind to me. I've told him about the day Jayce stood up for me at his shop and asked me to get another coffee with him afterward so that people would see us together, and that it's something we've done the past two Saturdays I've gone in as well. I haven't told Ken I think I'm falling in love with him.

"Of course I am. Why?"

His kind brown eyes search my face before he speaks, and it somehow feels like my abilities must have transferred to him. Like he somehow knows what my soul is feeling.

"Just making sure. This life...it's not necessarily the one I'd choose for you, but you've always seemed happy enough here with me. I just want to make sure you still are."

I don't feel anything unusual from Ken. He feels as open and honest as he always does.

"Why wouldn't you choose this life for me?"

He sighs and grumbles something about me focusing on the wrong part of that sentence as he stabs his chicken with his fork, but that's just how he is, and I know he'll answer.

"You're alone here, Namid. I know that other people overwhelm you, and I know that you like being alone, but still, sometimes I wish you had...more."

"I'm not always alone. I have you."

"I know that, and you know I love you. But... well...we don't know how old you are, but you're not a teenager anymore; you weren't even when I found you. I'm an old man, and I just...I want you to be happy always, not just now. There aren't any other gay men here and..."

Fuck. Fuck. Fuck. He really can tell what I'm feeling!

I cut him off. "How did you asking if I'm happy working with Jayce turn into a conversation about my lack of dates?"

"By accident." Ken rubs the back of his neck, looking a bit surprised this is where we've ended up. Maybe he really just feels bad that I'm alone.

"You've just never worked for anyone other than me, and you don't have any friends to speak of, and I guess I just...I hope working for Jayce is good for you. I guess I hope maybe you've found a friend."

I have no words for that. I've never thought about how I must seem to the man who's become my father. How my differences must seem to set me apart in a way that hurts him. How many times has he wondered if I'm lonely the way young parents wonder if their kids will find someone to play with at recess on their first day of school?

I stand and pull him up into my arms, crushing him in a hug so tight that I worry that he might break.

He lets me hug him until I don't need to anymore and then grumbles about his chicken getting cold as he settles back in at the table.

"Jayce and I get along well, Ken. He might even be my friend."

"Was that so hard?" He snorts, and I can't help the laughter that bubbles out of me.

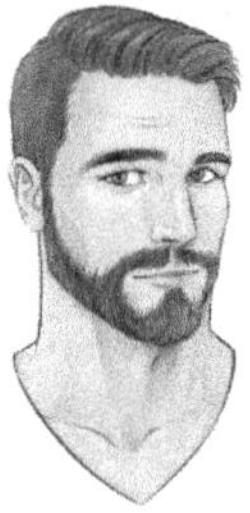

I still dream of a boy running through the trees on bright summer afternoons, and the teenager I snuck my first drink with, and the man who yelled at the football players on my TV every Sunday. I still wake up to find him gone. I still roll over and close my eyes for a moment and wish I could join him.

I force myself out of bed and into the shower before pulling on clothes that I somehow remembered to wash. I'm only half aware of the trees and melting snow and cars passing me by as I drive to the shop. I replace alternators and brakes and rebuild rear ends that were damaged in accidents. I don't like repairing those anymore. The shop is empty and cold and quiet. The world is grey and muted. It's been three months since I lost half of my soul, and I'm still here.

There are moments when I forget to hurt. Moments when I don't struggle to breathe. There are brief glimpses of a life less suffocatingly painful that are so short that I wonder if I'm imagining them. There are sips of tea that don't burn my throat, steps where the rub of my collar on my neck doesn't make me want to tear it off in a rage and crawl back into bed, sounds of life that don't grate on my soul.

These moments come on Saturday mornings. I didn't realize that at first. I'm too lost in the fog of survival to notice if it's Saturday morning or Wednesday afternoon, so it took a while for me to recognize that there is a pattern. The moments come when Namid is around.

He's here again this morning, working in the office like he has every other Saturday for the past two months, and I find myself wandering out to the reception desk and looking at the schedule when I know damn good and well what's booked without looking.

I try to watch him from the corner of my eye without it seeming like I'm hovering over his shoulder. I don't want him to feel uneasy here. I want him to stay. I want him to come back again. Having him here is comfortable somehow. He fits.

He finishes in just over thirty minutes, and I'm not ready for him to go. We've gotten coffee together after his last three days here, and I wonder if there is a way I can stay in his company for even longer as he shrugs on his light jacket and starts to tell me he'll see me in a couple of weeks.

"Do you want to get breakfast with me?"

He cringes. That's not exactly the reaction I want, and I start to shake my head.

"Nevermi..."

"No, it's not that I don't want to," he cuts me off, and then nervously glances at his shoes.

"I just don't handle busy places like Saturday morning brunch in public all that well."

He's right; it will be busy. It's the start of tourist season, and in addition to the town's fine dining restaurant that opens only during the three summer months, the local diner extends its normal lunch and dinner hours to offer brunch during the summer. Both places will be packed.

"You're right, I'm sorry. I didn't think about that."

His face lights up with a smile that seems almost conspiratorial, and I realize I can't wait to hear what he says next.

"Do you want to pick up some coffee and croissants and take them to the park?"

The muscles of my face split into a smile before I forget to stop them. I can't help it; he is so bright and joyful and full of life that when he smiles at me, all I want to do is smile back so that he never stops.

"I'd love that."

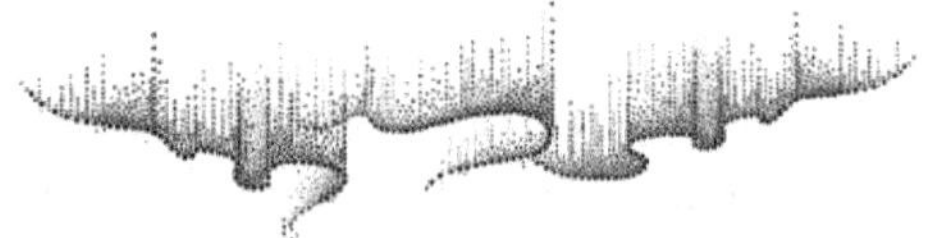

Out here in the middle of nowhere, you can get prepackaged, preservative-laden, pre-sliced bread in a bag anytime. Freshly baked goods, however, are harder to come by unless you make them yourself. On Saturdays, though, that changes. There are three bakers in town who bring the fruits of their labor to the market for a portion of the proceeds, and we can get everything from crusty sourdough loaves to chocolate croissants.

Namid and I are early enough that the case is still full, but there are a handful of other shoppers in the store, so that could change quickly. I grab the one-dozen-sized pastry box and snatch up two of my favorite onion and cheddar rolls before anyone can pop out of the dairy case and steal them all first.

"Well, that was decisive," Namid says with a laugh.

"Have you ever had these?"

"I have, and they are indeed the best, but I need another coffee, and people who drink coffee with savory foods are monsters."

I can't help the snort that escapes. "Agreed."

I slip a strawberry tart and an apple fritter into the box while Namid examines every single one as if his life might soon depend on how much knowledge he's absorbed about the store's pastry selection. Eventually, he lands on a cream cheese and raspberry Danish, a chocolate croissant, and a maple bar. As I struggle to put the lid on the box correctly, he picks up another box and loads it up with half a dozen donuts before glancing over and noticing the look on my face.

"For Ken."

"Uh-huuhh."

He flashes a smile and winks at me as he puts a lid on the box.

Pastries secured, we head to the coffee shop where he corrects the order I place.

"Americano instead of espresso on that, please."

The barista nods as if Namid hasn't just shaken my world to its core.

"What in the world is an Americano?"

He chuckles. "It's just my shot of espresso mixed with hot water so that it's more like a cup of coffee. I love espresso on its own, but it's not exactly a 'goes well with multiple pastries'-sized beverage."

"Ken likes donuts way too much, and an Americano is better than an espresso with multiple pastries. Educational day for me."

I'm joking with him. I'm not laughing or dancing or even smiling, but I'm joking with him, and it feels...okay. I'm not the person I used to be, and I'm not okay, but this, this is okay.

When we settle on our usual bench, I watch in amazement as he polishes off the raspberry Danish in a handful of bites and starts in on the chocolate croissant before I've made it halfway through one onion cheddar roll.

"That's...a lot of sugar."

He blushes and cringes as he looks down.

"I'm not exactly a morning person."

"It's almost eleven."

"Exactly."

He doesn't look back up at me as he nervously starts to pick the top flakes off of his croissant.

"You've been meeting me at the shop at nine."

"Mmmhmm."

His pale skin flushes even further.

"What time do you normally get up?"

He cringes and shoves half of the croissant into his mouth, delaying the inevitable for a moment. Clearly, he's not going to say eight a.m.

"I normally go to bed around three a.m. and get up around ten."

I can't help the note of disbelief bordering on panic that seeps into my voice. "Why in the world have you been meeting me at nine then?"

He shrugs. "You asked me to."

My heart aches at his almost innocent and effortless kindness. This is him shopping for my groceries all over again. I asked him to, and that was enough for him. He hadn't argued or debated or even asked if later would be alright. He'd volunteered to do me a favor when I was at my lowest, and when I made it inconvenient for him, he'd simply agreed. Time after time, two months later, he was still doing it.

"Namid...you should have said something. It's not like you'd have been interrupting my mid-afternoon Saturday squash game by asking me to meet later."

He simply shrugs again. "You need help, and if nine is best for you, then I can make it work."

How has a man this kind spent his life so alone?

"Well. How about we switch to noon next time?"

His smile is brighter than the sun. "My blood sugar would thank you."

We sit together for more than an hour. We talk about the fact that the weather is beautiful and about the way we're both happy summer is starting to arrive. We talk about the fact that dogs are infinitely better than cats. We talk about nothing, really; mostly, we just sit. We sit in the sun and enjoy the morning, and there is a peace that settles over me. There is something about him that comforts me, even when he's just sitting by my side. When he's there, the darkness that still threatens to drag me away is a shade lighter.

Chapter 6

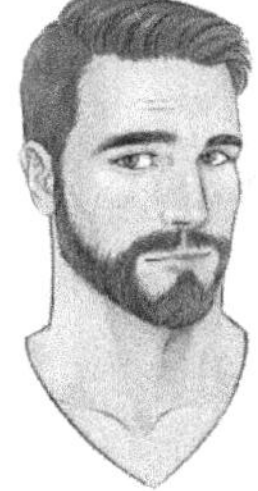

I have Namid's phone number; I've had it since the first day he came to help me in the shop. I haven't used it. I want to use it today. I've wanted to use it for a while now. I enjoy having him at the shop. My soul feels just a bit less empty when he's around. I enjoy the way we get coffee and sit quietly in the park together. I don't talk much, and it's still hard to find words when what I want to do most of the time is close my eyes and hide in some secret little corner of my mind where Jordyn is still here and everything is normal. Namid doesn't seem to mind my silence, and when we spend time together, I don't feel pressured to constantly speak.

I find myself noticing small things even though we don't say much, little details about his life and his personality. He's letting me see who he is, letting me learn about him in a way I don't think he's ever let anyone aside from Mr. Johnson. That's a responsibility and a gift. Even someone as heartbroken and miserable as me can recognize that. He's putting himself out on a limb, and I don't want to disappoint him. He's offering me more than help with my books a couple of hours a month. He's offering me friendship, and I don't want to mess that up. I can't mess that up. He's starting to feel important to me, and I can't lose this tiny little thread that's anchoring me in the darkness. I can't be the person who hurts a soul as pure as his when he's finally decided to let someone in.

The idea of my phone pinging with texts that don't come from Jordyn feels foreign and horrifying and heartbreaking, but I feel like I owe Namid something. I want to be able to offer him something...anything. He's already offered me so much.

I'm clutching my phone so hard that my hand has started to shake. I've been staring at it for almost an hour before my fingers twitch as I force them across the smooth glass, tapping a few letters.

Me: *Hey.*

I stare at the screen and will something to happen. Years pass. Probably only minutes. Then I realize...

Me: *This is Jayce, by the way...sorry.*

I put my phone down and force myself into the shower. I'm being stupid; he has a job and a life. He's not sitting around staring at his phone, hoping to get a text from some guy he only met a few months ago. Especially not one who can barely manage to pull himself together long enough to ramble a few semi-coherent sentences in his direction every other week.

I force myself to heat up some soup. I've been trying to eat actual meals again. I don't really see much point, but I'm still here and Jordyn still isn't and that's not going to change anytime soon, so I might as well learn how to pretend to be normal again.

The chime startles me badly enough that I drop my spoon, beads of tomato splattering across the table and the front of my old T-shirt.

Namid: *Hi Jayce. Nothing to be sorry about. I have your number, remember. What's up?*

My heart is racing, and I don't really understand why. It's just a text from someone I hope is becoming my friend. Hope. That's what's getting to me. The idea that some part of me is still capable of hope, still capable of believing that even just one thing that isn't darkness still exists, is foreign and uncomfortable. It's terrifying to recognize that if light still exists, then it's possible for me to lose even more somehow. Namid's friendship feels like hope.

Me: *I was wondering if you maybe wanted to get breakfast like we do this Saturday even though you won't be at the shop.*

Me: *No worries if you're busy or aren't into it or anything. Just thought I'd ask.*

I sound like a moron. I sound like a teenager asking his crush out on a date. This isn't a date, and I don't have a crush on Namid. He just makes me feel less alone. Like maybe my continued existence isn't a completely terrible thing.

Namid: *I'd love to.*

He'd love to. The breath rushes out of my lungs in relief. I don't know why I was so worried. Of course he'll meet me if I ask him. He's thoughtful that way, kind, always trying to help me.

How am I supposed to respond to that? *Thank you. You're saving my life somehow. I'm grateful for your friendship. Please keep saying yes.* Probably not.

Me: *I'll get breakfast and meet you at the park at noon?*

I'm on edge as I stare at the three little dots that appear.

Namid: *Sounds great.*

I stare at my phone, struggling to remember how to breathe properly. It's been so long since I've sent a text, so long since there's been someone on the other side to respond. It's the beginning of June now, and Jordyn has been gone for four months. It feels like a lifetime.

My soup has gotten cold, and I want to dump it out and crawl into bed. This has been overwhelming. It's so stupid. It's such a small thing. I sent a text to a friend. Still, the few minutes of feeling almost normal again have drained me. I get a rag and clean up the mess from my fallen spoon, reheat my soup, and force myself to eat before I crawl under the covers with the smallest spark of accomplishment settling in my chest.

Jayce isn't at the park when I arrive. It's finally summer, and the number of beautiful sunny days we get up here is finite. As a result, half the town seems to be wandering around the small pathway and lounging on the freshly cut grass. I don't really understand why they're all here; we live in a place surrounded by trees and meadows and wilderness. There is no shortage of places to enjoy the sunshine. Why would they all want to be in the same place? The only reason Jayce and I meet here is because our friendship is so new, and his ability to exist in the moment rather than sink into oblivion seems so tentative that I'm hesitant to suggest anything that might disrupt his fragile routine. If this is working for him, then I'm happy to continue.

I didn't expect him to text me out of the blue, and I certainly never expected him to ask to have breakfast on a day we weren't working. I know all too well that the way I'm starting to feel about him is one sided, I know that. I can feel it. Maybe he's at least beginning to think of me as a friend though. That's nice. I've never had a friend before, and it's...yeah...it's nice.

The benches are all taken, and while I hope that one opens up before Jayce gets here, it doesn't seem likely. Everyone appears settled in for the long haul with their snacks and dogs and blankets and Frisbees. I wander in a small circle near the edge of the parking lot, trying my best to stay away from the modest crowd. I've been more visible to folks over the past couple of months, but they are as standoffish as ever. I know that people have seen me with Jayce in his shop and the grocery store and coffee nook and here in the park, and while some tiny part of me hoped that being seen together might help people accept me a bit more easily, it's clear that it's having the opposite effect and they're wondering if I'm somehow taking advantage of Jayce after the loss of his brother.

I'm trying my best to keep to myself. The closest person is ten yards away, but I can still feel them. I can still feel the wariness and distrust and concern over my very presence. I don't let it bother me. It used to when I was young and new here, but it doesn't anymore. Not really. Not often, anyway.

I'm grateful when Jayce's truck pulls into the parking lot. I'm more than that, but I try to ignore the rush of excitement that races through me. That's normal, right? It's normal to be excited to see your friend.

Jayce walks toward me, carrying a large brown pastry box with two travel coffee mugs balanced on the top. They're ceramic. Between the two of us, we now have four ceramic mugs. He keeps two at the shop, and I keep two in my car; that way, we're always prepared when it's our turn to get drinks on the Saturdays we meet up. He's walking slowly, with his eyes on the cups as they shift ever so slightly with each of his steps. I speed walk toward him and snag the cups from the box before they have a chance to tumble to the ground. Once the mugs are safe from disaster, Jayce finally looks up, a smile spreading across his face. There is a dimple on his right cheek, one I've only seen a handful of times, and I want to trace my fingertip along it. Instead, I sip my coffee.

"So, the entire town seems to have had the same idea this morning," I mumble.

Jayce's mouth quirks up on one side.

"This afternoon."

"Oh. Oh, you have the jokes now. I see how it is."

He offers a gentle smile. He feels lighter than he used to. Not always, but in moments like this, his grief is soft. It's always there, but he's no longer constantly drowning. I'm thankful for that, and I hope that, in some small way, I've been able to help.

"Feeling adventurous?" I ask playfully as I lead him off the path and into the wooded area next to the park. I know there's a small meadow filled with long grass and wildflowers not too far into the tree line.

"Only if you promise not to murder me."

A snort escapes before I can stop it. "I suppose I can change my plans."

His lips twitch into a smile once more as he follows me without hesitation.

We don't have to go far before the dense trees and undergrowth thin, and a small sunlit clearing appears.

"Did you know this was here?" He sounds a bit awed as he pauses to look around, tilting his face to the sky to enjoy the sunlight.

I simply nod as I make my way over to a fallen log on the edge of the field and settle cross-legged with my back against the bark.

Jayce joins me, settling down onto the grass and popping open the lid of the pastry box before sipping his tea. We each make it through two bear claws in silence before he speaks. Our silences aren't awkward. They're peaceful. We're not quiet because we don't know what to say to one another; we're quiet because we know the other is there, and that's enough. We listen to the wind whispering through the branches, now covered in green leaves and filled with life, the birds that flit by on their way to their nests, and the rustling of squirrels in the undergrowth beside us.

"When Jordyn and I were kids, we'd play in the woods behind our house, like most kids do, I guess. We'd find places like this and spend entire days throwing rocks and building towers with sticks and searching for bugs."

He's never talked about Jordyn before, and I can feel the waves of grief and love rolling off of him. They surround me, threatening to pull me under, but it's not a bad thing this time. This time, the love tempers the darkness.

"In high school, he joined the football team. I was never really into sports, and I spent a lot of time alone when he was at practice. I'd wander through the places we'd frequented as kids and lie in the sun and listen to the sounds of life that humans don't usually take the time to notice. I haven't done that...haven't done *this* in a really long time."

I'm silent for a while. I don't want to break the spell that has woven itself around us, but eventually, I wonder if it might help if he continues to talk about Jordyn. I doubt he's spoken about him with anyone during the past few months.

"What was he like?"

My voice is soft and fragile and so quiet I'm not sure he'll be able to hear me.

Jayce sighs deeply. His smile is sad now, and the darkness is surging through him as he shifts to lie on his back in the long grass.

I want to reach out, to rest my hand on the swell of his chest and anchor him to this moment, to me. I never want to leave his side.

"He was...light." His voice is deep and hoarse, and he struggles to push out the words.

"I've always been a bit too serious. I was like this even as a kid."

He glances over at me for a moment before shifting his gaze back skyward.

"I've always been the less responsible one too, always in a bit of trouble."

His chest expands, and his fingers trail through the blades of grass at his side.

"He was my laughter and my support and my rock. Without him, I'm just...adrift."

I don't want him to feel lost anymore. I don't want him to feel alone. I reach out and let my hand fall to his shoulder, and after a moment, his fingers find their way over to rest over mine.

"When we were fourteen, we found an abandoned coyote pup. I wanted it so badly. I couldn't bear the thought of it dying alone in the woods. Jordyn knew that Mom and Dad wouldn't let us keep it if we said we'd found it, so he made it a collar out of some shoelaces and tried to convince them that a friend from school had a dog that had had puppies."

He laughs. Truly laughs. I haven't heard him laugh like this before. It's loud and brilliant, and it fills the small meadow with life and joy, and for a moment, it feels like we've carved out this small place in the universe just for us. It feels like nothing exists outside of his gentle, callused fingers sitting heavily on top of mine and the sound of his laughter and the warmth and love and amusement that radiate from his soul. I've never seen him like this before, and I know I should pull my hand away. I know I need to remember that he's becoming my friend and nothing more, but I can't. I want this. I want to sit with him and listen and laugh and learn who he is underneath all of his loss.

"Our parents knew, of course. Looking back, they knew from the moment we showed up with a mangy little coyote poorly disguised as a dog, but no one could say no to Jordyn, not even them. They wouldn't let us keep it as a pet, but they helped us find a sanctuary that told us how to care for it until we could get it to their facility in

Anchorage. We took a road trip the next weekend and dropped it off as a family."

Once Jayce starts talking about Jordyn, it's as if he can't bring himself to stop. He tells me story after story. Some bring laughter. Some leave his eyes shining with tears that threaten to trace along his temples on their way toward the earth as he lies in the sun. He talks of love and joy and companionship. He talks of sorrow and loss and darkness. For hours, he talks.

By the time we fall back to reality, his soul feels lighter. He's still hurting and grieving and lost, but the memories of love and contentment have softened his pain. It's quiet as we make our way back to the parking lot, even once we've stepped back through the thick trees and into the park. We've spent all day together, and the parking lot is empty and silent around us as we say our quick goodnights.

A light rain starts to fall as I follow his truck for a few miles before he turns off Main Street to head home, and as I watch his taillights fade into the dusk through my windshield, I want to follow. He's given me more today than I ever expected. I don't have stories about my past or family to offer him in return, and for the first time, that bothers me. I want to offer him something of myself.

I find myself thinking about the way the small lines beside his eyes seemed to deepen in the bright sunlight, and the way the rumbling timbre of his voice rolled along my spine and through my bones. About the shadows his eyelashes cast onto his cheeks and the strength of his fingers as they lay curled around mine all afternoon. Something warm and fluttery and aching settles in my belly, and I know that it's too late for me to rein myself in. I know this is one sided, and I know it's going to end badly. I want it anyway. I want to take every moment, every smile, every twist in my chest and wrap them up like the delicate and precious things they are and put them away somewhere hidden and safe so that one day, when I'm alone once again, I can take them out and remember the way it felt to fall in love.

Chapter 7

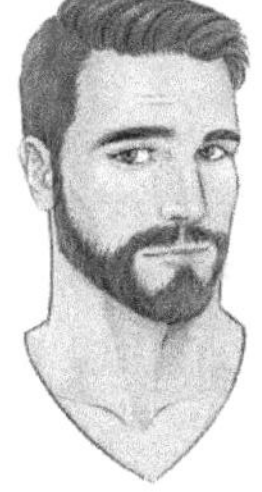

It's been three weeks since we sat together in the little hidden meadow and Namid listened as I spoke about Jordyn for hours, and even though he's only been at the shop twice during that time, we've had breakfast each Saturday.

The world feels different somehow. Lighter perhaps. The darkness that still clings to the edges of my existence seems slightly less oppressive, and there are times when it isn't a struggle to simply remember to breathe. I hadn't intended to talk to Namid like that. I never meant to tell him about Jordyn, never meant to make him listen to me ramble for hours. But he had, and as he smiled and laughed along with me, something changed. I hadn't realized just how much I've missed the easy comradery of friendship since I lost Jordyn. I know that I miss his presence and his light and his love every day, but I hadn't understood just how much I miss simply having someone to talk to.

How has Namid lived here for a decade without that? He seems to enjoy my company as much as I enjoy his. He feels like my friend. I want him to know that I care for him and that I support him. I want the town to know that too. He's so thoughtful and kind, and even though he's often quiet, he's clever and smart, and on the rare occasions he chooses to exercise his wit, I find myself shaking with laughter. It's something I never expected to experience again after losing Jordyn, and I can't imagine Namid having lived so long without it.

He's been an outcast for too long.

I know he doesn't like being around people, but the way I've noticed everyone treating him, who can blame him? I know I can't single-handedly change opinions that folks have held for a decade overnight, but I can try my best to help in small ways. The past two Saturdays he's been at the shop, I've deliberately scheduled small appointments so that my customers can see him there, so that word can spread that even though it's been months, he's still working with me. So that they can see me smile at him and welcome him openly into my life and my business.

He's not technically working today, but we've been meeting at the shop every week to have brunch whether he's working that week or not. I've been here since seven, and he's in the office waiting for me by the time I hand Mrs. Jackson back the keys to her beat-up old jeep whose spark plugs I just changed for the third time this year. The door to the office is open, and he's leaning back in the chair with his feet on the desk, poking at something on his phone. It's strange how comfortable it's become for me to see him sitting there. I still see Jordyn's absence as if it's a physical hole in my space on days Namid isn't here, but when he is, his company grounds me somehow, and the presence of ghosts in my life is just a bit fainter. He reminds me that maybe, just maybe, it's okay that I'm still here even if Jordyn isn't.

It takes him a moment to notice that I'm leaning in the doorway. Either that, or whatever he's staring at is so entertaining that he doesn't care.

An uncertain smile twitches across his lips when he glances up. He seems almost embarrassed to find me watching him.

"Must be something pretty good in there."

He chuckles and stands, slipping his phone into his back pocket.

"Wouldn't you like to know?" he teases as he rounds the desk, and we both make our way toward the coat rack by the door. He's been helping me for a few months now, and while we're heading into the peak of summer, this is Alaska, and some days are still chilly.

"Can I take you somewhere other than breakfast today?" I ask as I shrug on my leather jacket, the one that apparently smells like cinnamon. "There's something I'd like to show you."

A wickedly playful grin lights up his face, and small wrinkles I've only seen a handful of times crinkle into the skin beside his eyes.

"Only if you promise not to murder me."

Laughter I don't even try to hold back slips its way out of my lungs as he offers the same condition I used the first time we strayed from the beaten path and walked together in the woods near the park. I do my best to return the exact words he'd offered me.

"I guess I can change my plans."

As he flicks up the collar on his lightweight grey trench coat, his eyes sparkle in the sunlight that streams in through the shop's glass façade. I'll never stop wondering about his eyes. How they're somehow the dark blue of the deep sea or night sky, and how it feels like I can tell what he's thinking just by looking into them.

I bow slightly and gesture to the door.

"After you, sir."

He chuckles as he pulls open the door, and once I've locked up, he follows me to my truck without hesitation.

With jackets, it's not terribly cold, but I crank on the heater anyway. I don't want Namid to be uncomfortable, and I've noticed that he always dresses slightly warmer than I do, which makes sense as he's lithe and lean, whereas I'm bulky and a bit hairy.

"So, do I get to know where we're going?"

Namid's hands are tucked under his thighs, and I realize I'm smiling at the fact that I've come to know him well enough that I figured he might be cold even though I'm not.

I fish around the back seat with one arm as I reply.

"I want to show you something that not many people know about. It's a bit personal, and I don't have many close friends, but I thought maybe you..." I trail off, not quite sure how to finish the sentence.

He must be colder than I realize because when I glance over briefly, his cheeks are flushed and red. I keep searching the back seat awkwardly.

"If I didn't know any better, I'd think you were propositioning me."

His voice is light and filled with laughter, but I find myself sputtering as I panic to come up with a reply that somehow steers clear of the fact that I am indeed gay and that, yes, I think he's an attractive man, and that I suppose if I really stop to think about it, propositioning him might be something I could see myself doing at some point.

I manage to find what I've been searching for, and I thrust the small blanket toward him without shifting my eyes from the road.

"Bad joke, I'm sorry." He saves me from my spiraling panic as he continues, seemingly unfazed by the stroke I'm suffering through next to him.

"I'm honored that you consider me a close enough friend to show me whatever this is that's so personal for you. I shouldn't have made a joke instead of telling you that...and thank you for the blanket."

I risk a quick glance and find that he's looking at me the way he did so often when we first met, with something bordering genuine concern. He's clearly afraid that I've taken his joke the wrong way. He has no way of knowing that I'm not homophobic; it just hit a little too close to home.

"It was a good joke." I manage to find words and offer him a quick smile. "I just wasn't sure how you'd respond if I joked back in the same way."

His smile is blinding.

"If we're close enough for me to see your top-secret, friends-only...something, I'm going to say we're close enough for you to return a barely sort of kind of dirty joke."

"Deal."

It's the only response I can manage as everything else running through my head still feels like it would lead me down a road I don't want to follow. I don't want to risk losing this man who's become my friend. I don't want to lose him the same way I lost the only two people outside of my family I let myself be open with when I was too young to know any better.

He's quiet as I pull up to the large metal shop that stands on the edge of my property. I've never had him out to my house before, and somehow, I still don't feel ready for that, but this workshop is a couple of acres away from my small home, and I want him to see this. I don't really understand why, but I want him to know who I am.

"This looks like a good place to murder someone," he jokes as he hops out of the truck. The sound of the gravel under our feet seems loud in the crisp afternoon air that hangs heavy around us, threatening rain.

"Probably would be, but I promised I'd save that for another time." I grin and find myself standing perhaps just a little too close to him as I pull open the door and offer him an exaggerated, "After you," the same way I did when we left the shop.

It's not fancy inside. It's anything but. The place is nothing but a large sheet metal room, cold and echoey and impersonal. He stops only a few feet inside the door. He's staring at the machinery and steel that fills the space, sculptures that I've poured my heart into since I learned how to weld at fourteen. I watch silently as he takes a few more steps, his eyes darting around as he tries to take in everything at once. I'm staring at him, and I'm not moving, and the moment is growing, and my stomach feels twisted, and my chest is getting tight. I'm holding my breath and wondering if this was a mistake...if he's going to think I'm an idiot for spending my time thinking that I might somehow be able to offer glimpses into my soul simply by cutting and bending and putting fire to steel.

He's not looking at the sculptures anymore. He's looking at me.

"Jayce."

His eyes are bright, and he says my name in a whisper that feels laced with awe.

Joy and relief spread through my chest, and I'm able to breathe again as I step closer, my shoulder brushing his as he surveys the room once more.

"This is..."

I follow him as he steps closer to the nearest piece - a sharply angled, swirling work that towers over him at nearly fifteen feet.

"These are...yours?"

He turns to face me, his blue eyes searching my soul as he asks, and he's so close to me I can smell his grapefruit shampoo, and his body seems to radiate heat that sinks into my skin even through my jacket in the cold metal room.

"They're mine."

His fingertips reach out and trace along the steel's gentle curves and harsh edges.

"They're amazing."

I feel myself blush. I haven't blushed since I was a teenager.

My words catch in my throat, and I can barely manage to mumble a quiet, "Thanks."

I stay close to his side as he wanders through the sculptures, touching them, examining them from every possible angle.

"Do you sell them?"

I shove my hands into my front pockets, unsure what to do with them in my embarrassment.

"I've sold a few. I started dabbling a few years before my parents died. Dad was a painter, and he still had a couple of friends at his former gallery in Seattle. One of them, Max, came out for a visit once and expressed interest. I wasn't ready then, but a couple of years ago, I reached out to her, and she loved them even more than she had when I was younger. The couple of pieces I let her take sold fairly quickly, and once in a while, she pesters me for more."

The deep blue of Namid's eyes seems to shimmer like sunlight bouncing off deep water in the bright warehouse lights, and with no warning whatsoever, I suddenly realize that I want to get lost in them for the rest of my life.

"You don't want to sell them?"

There's no judgment in his tone; he's simply curious.

"They're like little pieces of my soul, I guess. I can't just sell them because the gallery is interested. I have to be ready to let them go."

I kick at a small piece of steel that has found its way onto the floor, despite the fact that I sweep regularly.

"Not sure that makes sense."

His hand falls onto my forearm. His touch is tender and warm, and it reminds me of the first time he touched me the day he first came to help me in the shop. The way the heat from his skin sinks into mine, even through my jacket, makes me wonder what it would be like to feel his skin against mine.

"It makes perfect sense." He smiles at me as if it's the most natural thing in the world.

Three hours have passed by the time I drop him back off beside his truck in the shop parking lot. He'd wandered my studio slowly, taking the time to study and touch each piece. He'd asked insightful questions and smiled gently at my answers. I've never seen anyone look at my work like that, not even Jordyn. It had felt like it wasn't my art he was examining. Like it wasn't sculptures he was touching. It was me.

We sit in silence for a long, weighted moment before he turns to face me instead of getting out of my truck.

"Thank you, Jayce...for everything."

His hand flicks out, and for the briefest of moments, it rests on my thigh just above my knee. His eyes search my face, and he seems to be looking for something. If I knew what it was, I'd offer it to him. I'd give him anything.

The silence drags on, heavy around us in a way it's never been before; then, with one quick pat, his hand is gone, and my skin is cold in its absence. By the time I realize what's happening, he's shut the truck door behind him, offering a quick wave through the window before hopping into his own truck.

Fuck.

It's not the first time I've started to develop feelings for a straight guy in town. Fortunately, I'm a quick learner and I know not to repeat past mistakes. I sit in my truck and watch through my rearview mirror as he drives away. For a single moment, I allow myself to remember what it's like to want someone before I sigh and remind myself that he's my friend, and that's all there is to it.

I shift into reverse and force myself to let go of the impossible dream that had begun to take shape at the edges of my universe. Back to reality it is.

Namid

Everything feels the same when I walk into the shop. I can hear the muffled sound of Jayce's tools, and coffee is waiting for me on the office desk. I can feel him, just like I always can, but today, that somehow feels wrong. It's not what I'd expected. There is grief, quiet and subtle and dim in the background of his soul. It feels the same as it has for weeks now. I feel a slight change when he hears the chime that announces I've opened the door. No one else is here today, and the door is locked, so he knows it's me. I'm the only other person with a key. He's happy I'm here, and the lightness that has slowly found its way into his soul expands ever so slightly at my arrival. It feels the same as it did the last time I was here. He feels the same as he has since the day we met for breakfast and he spoke for hours about Jordyn. He feels like my friend. I'm grateful for that, but I'd expected...more.

When we were together last Saturday, it felt like something had changed. As Jayce stood by my side, opening his soul and showing me something important and private, it didn't feel like friendship. It felt like more. He'd smiled at me in a way I'd never seen before, and it was all I could do to not reach out and wrap my arms around him. He'd lingered close to me, our arms and hips and shoulders brushing as we moved through the shop, examining piece after piece. His voice had been smooth and sure as he'd talked about what had gone into making each of them and what they meant to him.

A strange new tension had grown between us that had filled the room and sizzled across my skin. There were times I'd felt his eyes on me for a few heartbeats longer than they usually lingered. His laugh had felt deeper, his spirit had felt brighter, and there were touches of calm gold that floated from him in my direction. He'd felt different. He'd felt open and hopeful, and maybe, just maybe, it had felt like he'd been attracted to me.

We'd lingered inside his truck for a moment when we said goodbye, and I'd let myself wonder how he'd respond if I reached out and took his hand. His pale-green eyes had searched mine as if he were looking for something, as if he wanted more from me too. My world had been filled with the scent of oil and cinnamon and leather. I'd let my fingertips brush his leg through his beat-up jeans, and I'd wanted to kiss him so much that it hurt. His voice had been rough when he smiled and said goodbye. It had felt like...something.

Today, he's the same.

Today, there is no tension when he leans against the office door and talks about the weather and the car he's working on. His gaze doesn't linger on mine as he thanks me for being so kind about his art. He doesn't walk me to the door when I tell him I'm finished for the day. It's the first time since I began working for him that we haven't at least gotten coffee afterward. He'd texted me early this morning to tell me he'd have to skip our breakfast tradition today to finish a rush job, so I hadn't really expected it, but somehow, it still hurts.

Today, he feels the same.

I'm not the same.

I am in love with him.

I am stupidly, hopelessly, completely in love with him.

I sit in my truck in the empty parking lot in front of the shop and fight down the swell of emotion that clutches at my chest. My eyes burn, and the cool air in my truck stings my lungs as I try to suck in breath after breath. Nothing works like it should anymore; my throat is closing up and my heart is racing and I ache. I *ache* in a way I've never imagined was possible.

I want to watch him in his shop and walk with him in the park. I want to lace my fingers through his and rest my hand on his waist. I want to know what his skin feels like against mine, if his body trembles when our tongues tangle together, what it's like to lie with him in the dark.

I've known from the moment I met him that this is where I'd end up. That I'd fall so deeply in love with him that my soul would feel like it's on fire every time I look at him, and that's what's happened.

After our time in his studio, I thought maybe things wouldn't end up like this after all. For the past few days, I've let myself think...maybe. Just maybe there might be a chance he could feel the same way. But today he's the same. Today he's my friend.

I'll learn to be okay with that. I'll watch him and love him and find a way to be thankful that I've gotten to discover what it feels like to fall in love. It will fade, and I'll be forever grateful to have him in my life in any way I can. I'll be okay loving him from a distance.

Won't I?

Chapter 8

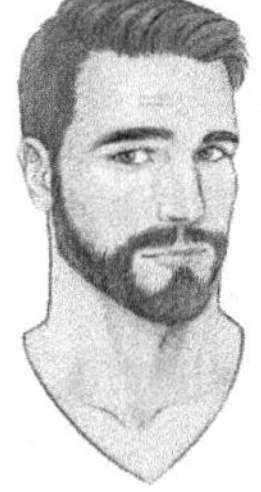

It's been a month, and everything is back to normal. Whatever it was I'd felt the day I took Namid to my studio was just a fluke. He's my friend, and I'm perfectly happy with that. I don't know what I'd been thinking that afternoon.

Namid has come to do my books every other week for months now, and ever since the Saturday I first told him about Jordyn, we've had brunch every weekend. As the short Alaskan summer has passed and it's gotten cold again, on the days he works on my books, we've shifted to having our coffee and pastries in my small break room before we head our separate ways to work for an hour or so. On the alternate weeks, we meet in the small café corner of the grocery store. Those are the boundaries of our friendship, and neither of us has pressed for more, so I was surprised when Namid texted me yesterday and asked if there was any way I could help him and Ken move some old metal cabinets out of the basement of the funeral home.

The basement of the funeral home is the last place I ever want to go. In fact, I'd be happy if I never even had to look at the funeral home again, but Namid has never asked me for anything before. After all he's done for me, I'm thrilled to return the favor in any way possible, even if this particular favor takes me into the realm of funeral home basement nightmares.

When I arrive, they have the door propped slightly open, and I can hear the slight screeching of metal sliding on concrete as soon I step into the building. I can't stop the chill that runs through me at being back here, but as the sound of Ken's voice and Namid's bright laughter floats up the stairs, I can't help but smile and head in their direction.

"Hi."

Ken jumps slightly at the sound of my voice.

Namid just laughs harder.

They're both filthy, covered with streaks of old dust and cobwebs, and there are half a dozen large metal cabinets that have been pried away from the wall sitting in the middle of the room. They've clearly been at this for a while already, and despite the dirt and hard work, they're obviously enjoying themselves. A fleeting wave of jealousy washes over me. They're family, something I no longer have.

Namid's eyes seem to darken, and his smile fades.

"Everything okay?"

Huh. Why would he ask that? I'm smiling, I'm sure of it. My expression must have changed for a moment, even though I didn't notice. I can't help but soften and smile once more at his concern as the momentary jealousy passes. It's hard for me to feel anything too negative when he's around.

"Just wondering if we shouldn't just burn the place down and move to the Caribbean with the insurance money instead of trying to get those upstairs," I joke in an attempt to bring back Namid's laughter.

Ken snorts out a laugh. "Not the first time I've had that thought."

"Sorry it's such a mess, but thank you for coming to help." Namid scrubs his hands through his hair in an attempt to push it off his forehead and out of his eyes. It falls back into place the instant it leaves his hands.

"Happy to." I grin as I roll up my sleeves. "Looks like they've been here a while now; what have these poor cabinets suddenly done to offend you?"

Ken chuckles as he grunts and shoves the last of the cabinets into the center of the room. "This room has been nothing but a pile of junk for twenty years now, and I'm at the point in my life where I don't want projects like this lying around anymore. I'm not exactly getting any younger here."

Namid rolls his eyes. "You're sixty-six, not ninety-one."

This is clearly a conversation they've had more than once.

"Which is why we're doing it now." Ken grins.

Namid rolls his eyes again and huffs out an annoyed breath. Somehow, it feels like Ken won this particular battle this time.

"Is there a game plan?" I ask no one in particular.

It's Namid who answers with a grin. "Umm. Get them upstairs."

I can't help but chuckle. "Good plan."

"Thanks, I thought so." His smile lights up even this depressing, dirty basement.

We've congregated around the cabinet closest to the stairs as we've talked, and they both join me as I bend down to lift one corner. It takes a bit of time and a dozen tries to get it situated, but between the three of us, we're able to slowly lug it up the stairs and out into the yard.

Namid falls into the few inches of fresh snow that coat the driveway. "Good job, team. I'm going to tap out; you get the rest."

Without giving it much thought, I slip my hands under his arms and lift him back to standing. He groans in protest, but the smile on his face shines even through the grey mist that hangs heavy in the air.

Three dirty, exhausting hours later, there are only two cabinets left, and we all look like we've run some kind of mud obstacle course marathon. The dust and grime of forty years in a basement covers our snow and sweat-slicked faces and exposed forearms.

There is nothing different about the weight of the second-to-last cabinet, nothing different about the way we lift it or the route we take, but four stairs up, Ken's foot slips. Namid and I scramble to redistribute the weight of the cabinet as Ken falls back toward the cement floor, but it's awkward, and there is nothing we can do other than watch in slow motion as the unrelenting steel clangs into the wall, slips from our hands, rolls down the stairs, and lands squarely on Ken's bicep, pinning him to the floor.

Ken's cry is loud in the sudden silence.

Namid's is louder.

"Ken!"

"Jesus. Ken. Are you okay? Oh my god. Okay. Let's just. Can we..."

We're both at his side in an instant, and it takes only seconds more for us to lift the cabinet from his arm and chuck it, uncaring, toward the center of the room. Even through the flannel of his shirt, it's clear his arm is broken; arms aren't meant to bend that way.

"God. *God.* Ken. It's okay. Jayce, call 911. It's going to be okay, I promise."

I already have my phone in my hand as Namid rambles, drops to his knees, and grasps Ken's torn shirt sleeve. He rips it open, and there is blood and bone where there should only be skin.

Ken is pale and quiet as he tries to grasp at the damage until Namid covers his searching hand in both of his, clutching it until his knuckles whiten.

"Hey. Ken. Hey."

Namid's voice is shaking, but his tone is calm and steady.

"Hey, look at me, okay? There ya go. Hey, it's just your arm, okay? You're going to be okay. We'll get you taken care of."

"Ambulance is on its way," I offer. My voice sounds more scared than supportive. *How is Namid doing this? How is he staying so calm?*

"I mean, if you didn't want to help anymore, you could have just told us, old man." Namid's voice breaks only once as he tries to engage Ken in any way he can.

Ken's body shakes in a pained laugh. "Why didn't I think of that?"

"Drama queen." Namid's voice is gentle and caring as he curls his body over Ken's, gripping his hand and distracting him as best as he can.

I'm in awe as I stand frozen in place at the bottom of the stairs, watching the way he cares for Ken. While it takes less than fifteen minutes for the ambulance to reach us and for the EMTs to get Ken strapped onto a board and carry him upstairs to a wheeled gurney, it feels like a lifetime.

"I'm fine."

Ken hisses as his shoulder jostles when the gurney hits another dip in the gravel driveway.

"I'm fine. It's an arm, not a neck."

I squeeze his hand tighter as a laugh that's barely more than a sob shakes itself from my throat. I can feel how much he hurts. He's being brave, but I can feel that he's scared. If he's ever been hurt this badly, it hasn't been during the decade I've known him.

We're at the ambulance, and they're trying to load him, but I won't let go of his hand. I can't let go of his hand. I need to help him; I need to do something. Anything.

I'm no good to anyone in situations like this.

"You need to let us get him into the ambulance. He's going to be okay, but we need to get him to the hospital." The EMT's voice sounds like it's echoing through a long tunnel, and they're trying to pry his hand away from mine.

"It's okay. Just let us get him loaded and you can ride with us."

Panic.

Pure, ice-cold, blood-curdling panic.

I shake my head, and my hand is trembling and gripping his so tightly.

"No. He'll be staying here." Ken's voice seems so far away.

I try to fight the burn in my lungs and the sting in my eyes.

"It's okay. I know you need to stay here. I'll make sure the doctors know to call you as soon as they can." He's the one who's hurt, but he's trying to take care of me. He knows I can't go with him.

The medic finally wins. He pries my hand away, and I can only stare, frozen in place by panic. Ken needs me, and I can't go with him. I can't and he knows I can't, and he says it's okay, but it's not. It's not okay that I can't.

"Hey."

Ken nearly yells to get my attention, and his gaze is soft and loving when my eyes snap to his.

"It's okay, kiddo."

I fall to my knees as they close the doors, and Jayce's hand that has been on my shoulder blade this whole time shifts down my arm as he sinks to a squat in front of me.

"Hey, it's okay. It's okay."

His arms are around me, and I'm shaking so hard I might break. He's so strong and warm, and all I want to do is disappear into his embrace.

"Let's get in the truck, and we'll head to the hospital and..."

"I can't." My sob cuts him off.

Pain. Pain and fear and desperation and anguish.

So much of it.

I can't be at the hospital.

"I can't." All I can do is repeat myself as I curl against his chest on my knees in the long gravel driveway.

"It's okay. I'll be with you; we can just..."

"I can't!"

I'm yelling and my hands are fisted in the front of his shirt so tightly my knuckles have turned white, and Jayce pulls me tighter into his arms as I sob. His hand is running along my spine, and his breath travels along my temple.

"Okay."

"That's okay."

"It's going to all be alright."

Jayce is telling me that it's okay, and it feels like he means it. He's confused, but it doesn't feel like he's upset with me. He doesn't know. He doesn't know who I am...what I am.

I love Ken like a father, and I can't help him. I can't hold his hand and reassure him that he's going to be alright. I can't be there like he's been there for me because I'm so different and so broken and so wrong.

Jayce holds me while I cry. He holds me until I'm wrung out and there are no tears left to fall.

He's confused. Worried.

"Come on," I say with a sigh that nearly breaks me.

"I need to explain."

Jayce is silent as I settle him at my dining table and move to make coffee. He's never been in my cabin before, and under any other circumstances, I'm sure I'd be a nervous wreck having him here, but in this moment, focusing on the task at hand is all that's holding me together. He doesn't interrupt me as I grind the beans, and boil the kettle, and place mismatched mugs on the counter in my small kitchen. He knows I need a moment, even though he doesn't really understand why. He's scared now. Scared and confused. Scared of what I might need to say. He doesn't understand why we're not on the way to the hospital with Ken.

I settle in across from him and stare into my cup. I can't look at him while I explain. I'll feel what he feels either way, but I can't bring myself to watch if he decides to leave. If he decides to hate me. I can't watch our friendship fade away in an instant.

"I'm going to tell you some things. Things I maybe should have already told you, but I haven't known how, and I need you to know that if you have nothing to say, if you want to just stand up and walk away, I'll understand.

I'll let you go, and I won't follow you or reach out or text or call you again."

When Jayce reaches across the table for my hand, I pull it back. If I scare him, I'll feel it. Of course, I'll feel it. But I don't want it to be as intense as it will be if he's touching me. He is so much more to me than I've ever imagined anyone could be, even though most of what I feel is one sided. Not touching him when he decides to leave is the only thing I can do to protect myself, even though it's far too little, far too late.

"You don't know who I am...I mean, you don't...I don't..."

I shake my head, trying to clear my thoughts.

How do you tell someone you're secretly in love with that you're a freak?

"I'm different."

"I know that. I love that about you." His fingers reach for my arm once more, and once more, I pull away.

I shake my head.

"No. Not like quirky or endearing or *bless his heart* different. I mean really different."

I sigh as my shoulders slump even further. My table is so small, and we're so close together that I can almost feel his breath.

"I can feel things. Not *can* I guess...that implies a choice. I feel things. Emotions. I feel what others do. Not in like an 'Oh, that guy is sensitive or empathic' kind of way. I feel things in a way I've never even read about. I feel all of them. It's why I keep to myself. It's why I don't touch anyone. I feel other people's emotions as if they're my own."

He doesn't feel scared. He feels confused but not scared as I force myself to lift my eyes.

"How? Is it from whatever accident you were in before Mr. Johnson found you?"

I can't help the sigh that slips from my lungs.

"I don't know. When I first told the doctors, they didn't really understand what I meant. I didn't know how to deal with it at first when I was in the hospital. All I knew was I felt fear and pain, and all they knew was they couldn't find anything wrong with me."

I watch my fingers play with the handle of my mug so that I don't have to watch his beautiful eyes study me like I belong in a lab somewhere.

"With no medical explanation, they brought in a psychologist who did two full days of testing, thinking I might be schizophrenic or something, but eventually, Ken could see they were making it worse. He told them it was enough and took me home."

I risk another brief glance up, and while he still doesn't feel afraid of me, his brow is furrowed in concern.

"Those first couple of years, we did a lot of research, talked to a lot of experts. We flew to Portland once to talk to someone who said they specialize in things like this, but in the end, they hadn't met anyone like me. We've never found any real answers. I don't know if something is broken because I sustained a head injury that didn't show up in the tests or if I was born this way…I don't even know if I'm human, I guess. Sometimes I don't feel like it."

Jayce's fingers reach for mine across the table, and I don't pull away this time. He hasn't run yet, and I want to feel his skin against mine in case it's my last chance. I know he doesn't feel the same way I do; I'd be able to tell if he did, but I can't help wanting his touch anyway.

His thumb slides along my skin in the silence.

When he finally speaks, his voice is gentle and strong.

"I don't know what I believe in, Namid. I don't know if I believe in a god or aliens or faeries or science, but I know that I'm not so closed minded as to question what someone tells me is their truth. There are so many things in this universe that we don't understand, and not understanding something doesn't make it scary or wrong."

My eyes burn as I force my gaze up to search his face, my arm twisting so that I can clutch at his hand with mine.

"I'm not going to stop being your friend because you're unique." His smile is gentle and accepting and it feels like the mid-summer sun shining against my skin.

"If you say this is how you are, then this is how you are."

I can't stop the shuddering sob that lodges in my throat, making my voice deep and harsh.

"Thank you."

His hand squeezes mine, and his smile broadens.

"How close do you need to be to feel someone?"

I shrug. "It's not exact. It depends on how strong their feelings are. Pretty close. A room or two away when I'm inside."

"Could you wait in the hospital parking lot?"

Panic.

I shake my head and tighten my grip. "No. People heading in...visiting or to get care...I can feel them as they walk past. I know the hospital here is small, but it's still just...it's too much."

He nods thoughtfully. "Okay. My house is a couple of miles away from the hospital. Why don't I drive you there, and then I'll head over and wait for Ken. I can call you as soon as I know anything."

Warmth rushes through me. Comfort and desire and gratitude, and I'm overwhelmed by his kindness.

"You'd do that?"

"Of course."

He stands and pulls me tightly into his arms before I can move away, and my body melts against his completely.

"Thank you. I can't thank you enough."

I lock Namid's fingers tightly between mine as I lead him to my truck and open the passenger door. I don't know what to do with what he's just told me. I've never heard anyone say anything even remotely like that, but he obviously believes it. Mr. Johnson clearly believes it too. He's the one who told the medics that Namid wouldn't be joining him on the way to the hospital.

Namid was so afraid to tell me. My god, he actually told me that if I just stood up and walked away, he wouldn't follow or call or text ever again. After all the months we've spent together, after everything he's done for me while I've been at my lowest. He's the only one in the entire town who's helped me since I lost Jordyn, and he thinks I'd simply walk away.

Has that happened to him before? Has he tried to open up and ask for acceptance and been left because he's different? I meant what I told him. I accept him no matter who he is, even though I don't really understand exactly what he means. It honestly sounded a little crazy, and I hope I have the chance to discuss it a bit more with him in the future, but right now, his best friend - his father - is hurt, and he can't do anything other than sit in another building and wait.

He's silent as we drive the few miles into the center of town. His forehead is resting on the glass, and he's staring at nothing through the window. He startles as I place my hand on his knee. I'm not sure why I do it, other than he seems so sad and so alone, and I know all too well what that feels like. I don't want that for him. I don't want that for anyone, of course, but there is something about Namid that makes me want to protect him, care for him.

He's silent as I lead him up the front steps. He's never been to my house before. I haven't had anyone in my house for months, not since the night Jordyn stormed out and I lost him. He follows me inside but doesn't move once he's through the door.

"Hey."

His eyes snap to mine, and I offer the most comforting smile I can manage.

"It's going to be okay. Okay?"

He only nods. The small muscles in the side of his jaw are twitching, and it's blatantly obvious how upset he is. I reach out carefully. I want to help, but as tightly wound as he is in this moment, I'm afraid that any quick movement might spook him.

"Let's get you settled in, okay?"

I try to mimic the way he'd spoken to Ken as we waited for the ambulance, offering soft, repetitive reassurances as I unzip and remove his coat and guide him to my sofa with my fingertips on his elbow.

"You have your phone?"

He pulls it out of his pocket, clutching it tightly in both hands as he sinks into the cushions.

"Good. Okay. I'm going to go, but I'll call you as soon as I know anything."

His cheeks are wet as he glances up at me, and it's all I can do to nod and walk out the door instead of sinking down next to him and wrapping him up in my arms as if I can protect him from the world.

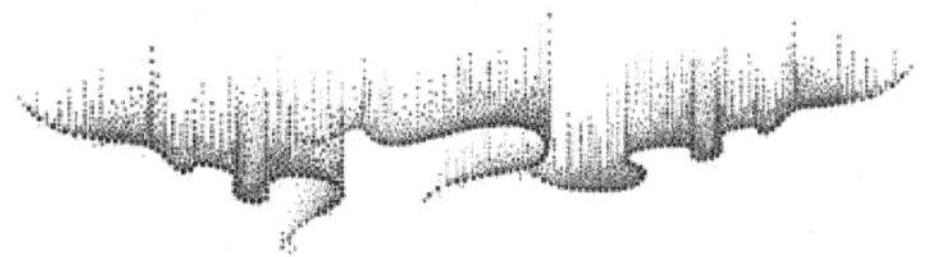

I rush into the medical center's small emergency department and sigh internally as I speed walk up to the young blonde woman who sits, half hidden behind computer screens, at the small reception desk. While the hospital has a dozen or so nurses, the woman at the desk is Cindy Buchannon, a woman whose heart Jordyn broke sometime in our early twenties. That's her take anyway. When Jordyn talked about their four whole dates, it sounded like they simply weren't a good match. I've run into her in town a few times since I lost Jordyn, and while she has never been my biggest fan, she's at least been civil in the past. Apparently, however, with Jordyn gone, the resentment she still holds has been redirected...to me.

"Cindy, come on. You know me. It's not like I'm some stranger trying to break in to steal narcotics," I beg for what feels like the tenth time. This is getting me nowhere.

"You're not his emergency contact, Jayce. How many times do I have to say it?"

"It's not like I'm trying to get back there so that I can trick Mr. Johnson into changing his will and leaving me the funeral home. Come on, Cindy."

Her smile is fake and icy as she continues. "Look, Jayce, these are federal privacy regulations. I can't just ignore them because I know who you are. Only emergency contacts are allowed in the emergency room."

"As I'm sure it says in Mr. Johnson's chart, Namid is his emergency contact, and he can't be here right now."

I'm sure her derisive snort is loud enough to be heard in the parking lot as she rolls her eyes.

"Of course he can't be. Why Ken would ever put that..."

I cut her off. I don't even want to guess how she plans to finish her sentence.

"Don't, Cindy. He's my friend too."

God. How has Namid survived in this town? I've always known that he's not overly welcome, but before getting to know him, I'd thought everyone to be politely indifferent, maybe even slightly curious or wary. I had no idea they were this rudely passive-aggressive. I still can't get over the way Bob watched him with suspicion while he waited for me to finish his truck the first time he'd seen Namid in Jordyn's office or the side-eyed looks we get just walking down the street or sipping our drinks together in the park. How has he managed to stay the generous, almost innocent man I've come to know?

What if the things he told me about himself are true and he really can feel what others feel? He's just been walking around town his entire life feeling the way others resent and dislike him?

"CINDY!"

Mr. Johnson's voice breaks me out of my momentary introspective trance. His yell is loud and angry enough that he could be Thor or Apollo or the goddess of death herself. I suppose the one saving grace of a small-town emergency room is that Ken knew we'd be able to hear him out at the reception desk.

"You let that boy back here right now, Cindy, or so help me!"

I offer Cindy a sticky sweet smile and take off at a jog through the doorway to the exam room.

It took nearly an hour for Namid to tell me about himself and for me to get him settled at my house, and Mr. Johnson is already hooked up to an IV with his arm strapped into place when I pull back the thin curtain and step next to his bed.

"Namid?" Even with whatever cocktail of drugs is flowing through his veins, Ken sounds concerned.

He's the one lying here with part of his skeleton sticking out through his skin, but his first concern is Namid's well-being, and somehow, I understand that.

There is something about Namid that makes me want to shield him from the world.

"He's shaken but okay. I dropped him at my place; it's only about ten minutes away, and I promised him I'd stay here with you."

Mr. Johnson's face softens slightly, but he's cut off before he can reply as the town's surgeon pulls back the curtain and joins us. Normally, a town this size wouldn't have a surgeon. They'd be lucky to have a family practice doctor and a semi-stocked urgent care, but we're fortunate. Dr. Susan Robinson had a glamorous and successful surgical career in LA before she decided she'd had enough of city life at fifty-five and moved here in semiretirement. She doesn't work rounds or even take regular patients. If someone needs to schedule a surgical procedure, they typically need to travel to Anchorage. She is, however, an outstanding surgeon who loves being able to keep one foot in the game on her own terms, and on the few occasions a year we need some type of emergency surgical intervention that doesn't require an entire intensive care team or larger facility, she's happy to step in.

She's carrying several films, so she must have been close enough to the hospital when Mr. Johnson arrived that she was already able to take imaging scans before I got here. She glances my way and offers a brief nod in greeting before addressing Mr. Johnson.

"Well, you did quite a number on yourself. A man your age, I've no idea how you managed to shatter your humerus before one of your joints blew out, but that's what you've done. It's a clean three-piece break, though, and it will be easy enough to set with a few plates and pins. Lucky for you, it's something I can do in town, and I don't have afternoon plans, so what do you say we head back, take care of it now, and you'll be on the mend by dinnertime?"

It's not really a question. She's the kind of person who sets the game plan, not the kind who follows someone else's.

"Sure, Doc, whatever you say." Mr. Johnson nods.

"Great. I'll go get prepped, and they'll come get you in about fifteen." She turns back the way she came with a quick nod.

"Hey, Doc?" Mr. Johnson's voice stops her, but she only turns her head and raises an eyebrow in question.

"Jayce here isn't my emergency contact, but he's going to be the one waiting for me today. Can you keep him informed? Namid isn't...well, he's not available, but he's worried sick, and Jayce will call him for me."

She nods briefly and continues out of the room.

"Thanks, Doc." Mr. Johnson's voice follows her as she closes the curtain on her way out.

We don't have the fifteen minutes that Dr. Robinson says we do, and things move quickly from the moment she leaves the room. I've barely taken two steps closer to Mr. Johnson's bedside to continue our conversation when the two nurses on call join us to wheel him back to the surgical suite. They distractedly state that the repairs will most likely take three to four hours and direct me back out through reception and down the left wing of the small hospital to the surgical center's waiting room before letting me know that someone will be out with an update for me in two or three hours.

Namid

I am so useless.

Ken has always said that the way I feel is a gift, but it's not a gift. It's not a gift when it means that the only person in the world who has ever felt like my family is in the hospital hurting, and I'm not able to be with him because I'd be overwhelmed and useless.

I've never felt panic like that before. The moment Ken fell down the steps, the world started to move in slow motion, and as I watched the cabinet fall onto his arm, there was nothing I could do to stop it. There was nothing I could do to fix it as he lay there in pain. Nothing I can do now.

Somehow, even worse than feeling useless is the way I feel like a burden. Ken is the one who was hurt, but the whole time he'd been worried about me. I'd sat there holding his hand, trying to ignore the waves of pain that rushed through us both, and he'd tried to laugh, tried to minimize what he was feeling even though he knew I could feel the truth. When they'd loaded him into the ambulance, he wasn't worried about whether his arm would heal or how much he hurt, or even whether he'd survive. Instead, he was telling me that it was okay that I couldn't come with him. He couldn't even focus on himself because he felt like he had to take care of me.

I'm thankful that Jayce was with us. I'm thankful that he called 911 and brought me to his house and agreed to go to the hospital to be with Ken. He took care of me just like Ken did, and he didn't even bat an eye. I'm grateful that Jayce accepted me into his life so easily and that he's become my friend. Even though I'm overwhelmed and scared and worried beyond reason, logically, I know today could have been so much worse. This could have been the day I lost both my father and my only friend. When I'd sat Jayce down and told him about myself, I fully expected him to mock me and leave. He didn't. I don't know if he believed me or even really understood what I was telling him. It's not like I'd picked the most opportune time to try to explain, but he hadn't left. He'd been confused, but he'd reached out and taken my hand without fear and told me that it was okay. That I was okay. He'd told me that he accepted me whether or not he understood. He'd settled his fingers on my arm, and they'd burned my skin even through my shirt. I'd wanted to pull him into my arms and feel his body crushed against mine. I'd wanted the scent of oil and leather and cinnamon to overwhelm me.

He'd asked questions, genuine and insightful questions, about how close to the hospital I thought I could get. He asked as if he believed me. He'd let me take his hand, and he'd offered to be with Ken in my stead, and he'd hugged me tightly. He'd brought me here, to his house, and he'd gone to the hospital with the promise he'd call as soon as he knew anything. He'd been everything.

It's been nearly forty-five minutes, and he hasn't called. I could call him, I suppose, but I don't want to bother him if he's with Ken or a doctor. What if it's bad news, and he is trying to work up the nerve to call me? I don't really want to find out even a few minutes earlier than I need to if that's the case. Ken's arm looked bad. There was bone sticking out of his skin. Still, it was only an arm, right? It's not like the cabinet landed on his chest. He'll be okay. He has to be okay. As long as he's okay, we can find a way to deal with anything else. If his arm never works the same way, then I'll just help him out even more than I already do. He's the only family I know, and I'll do anything for him. He just has to be okay.

I've been pacing around Jayce's front room for half an hour, clutching my phone like it's a lifeline, willing it to ring, but with my adrenaline finally starting to dip as I wait, I take in my surroundings for the first time. I've never been inside Jayce's house before.

I'm not sure what I expected. The shop is almost sterile with its pure white walls and cheap utilitarian chairs. The single family portrait that still sits on Jordyn's desk is the only personal item in the whole building. I guess I've always thought that was a deliberate choice, but now, wandering around Jayce's home, I wonder if it's because he's so private rather than because he harbors an all-consuming love for minimalist decor.

His house is...cozy. There are shelves that hold pictures of Jayce and Jordyn and their parents. There are a few baseballs, a couple of vases, rows of stacked books, and one random stick that I'm sure has an interesting story behind it. Vines hang from macramé suspended pots in front of the large east-facing window, and a tall palm tree takes up an entire corner. There are paintings on the walls, landscapes. Two large oceanscapes that almost appear photographic with their attention to detail, and one of sunlight streamlining through a dense copse of pines onto the forest floor. A pair of leather boots and a set of sneakers are lined up neatly on a small rug next to the front door. There are a handful of dishes in the sink, old Christmas cards on the fridge, and a laundry basket full of clean towels waiting to be folded on the kitchen table. It feels lived in. It feels like a home, and I find myself wondering what it would be like to spend time here with Jayce, to curl up on the couch with a book and his arm draped over my shoulder or his head resting in my lap while my fingers play with his hair.

Almost without thought, I find my fingers trailing along the edges of picture frames and the old dry leather of the baseballs, tenderly touching his things in the way I know I'll never get to touch him. Some of the leaves on the palm tree are dusty, and I wet a paper towel in the sink and carefully wipe them down. I'm useless at the things that matter most to me in this moment; I can't sit in the hospital at Ken's side, and I can't take care of him, but Jayce has become my friend, my best friend, and he's there for Ken in my place. Cleaning up a bit is the least I can do for him in return.

I fold the towels in the laundry basket and clean the dishes that have been left in the sink, and I wait for my phone to ring.

Chapter 9

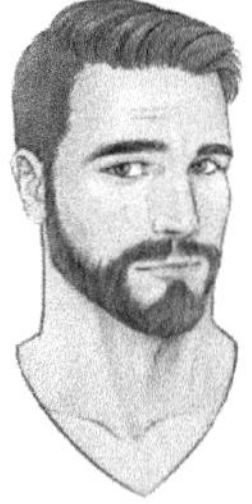

Namid answers my video call on the first ring. The way he sinks into my sofa, his blue eyes glistening as tears trace their way down his pale skin, makes me long to be there with him. I know he told me that he can feel other people's emotions, and I find myself wondering how overwhelming that must be because, in this moment, the intensity of what he's experiencing is palpable even through the phone. I can't help but smile as he thanks me again and again for being there for Ken. It's clear that he's never had anyone else he can turn to, and I'm grateful that he's allowing me the opportunity to show him that I can support him in the same way he's supported me. I let him know what Dr. Robinson said, that it should be a relatively easy break to repair, and show him that I'm already in the waiting room. He sinks back into the pillows on my couch, and I can't help thinking that even though I'm not at home, it's nice having him there.

He keeps me on the phone for more than an hour, but eventually, his voice begins to slur, and he slowly drops off to sleep. I watch him for a moment before hanging up and leaning my head back against the wall to close my eyes as well.

Mr. Johnson is already awake in the recovery room when Dr. Robinson comes out to get me. As she leads me through the sterile halls, she tells me that everything has gone well. He'll need to stay in the hospital for a couple of days, and then he'll have a couple of months of recovery and physical therapy ahead of him, but he should be out of the sling and can even attempt things like driving in six to eight weeks. He's lucked out that it's his left arm he's broken, and Dr. Robinson lets me know that as soon as the pain stops in a week or so, he'll be able to adapt to doing most regular things on his own with one hand quite quickly.

"How's Namid?" Ken's voice is scratchy, and he sounds groggy, but once again, his first concern isn't for himself.

I settle into a chair next to his bed as I take in his IV pumps and the huge pile of straps and bolsters that support his arm.

"He's okay. We talked for about an hour, and he fell asleep on the phone while you were in surgery."

He nods once. "Good."

Mr. Johnson studies my face for a long time. I don't know him well, but it's clear that he's become Namid's father, and he cares about him deeply.

"You and I should talk for a bit before we call and wake him up." His gaze and tone are serious, and I wonder if he's worried that I treat Namid like the rest of the town seems to. I don't want him thinking that. I want him to know that I'm Namid's friend.

"Look, Mr. Johns..."

He cuts me off.

"I think it's time you started calling me Ken, don't you?"

He raises an eyebrow in a way that seems to imply something, but I'm not entirely sure what.

I just nod as he continues.

"Namid is a good man. I'm glad he has you now. He's never really had a friend aside from me, and I hate that for him."

"I hate that for him too."

Ken's face relaxes almost instantly at my words of support.

"He's so kind and caring and funny. I don't understand why he doesn't have friends here or why everyone seems to be so on edge around him. He's done nothing to harm anyone."

Ken's smile is soft, almost hurt. "He's different, you see. People don't like those who are different."

"I know he's different, Ken. I mean, it's obvious he's a little more refined than most people here, and I know he's not very social or anything."

"It's more than that, son." His voice is quiet, and his gaze is intense enough I feel like I might melt under its force. "He's different in a lot of ways, and people can sense that somehow. He's very selective about who he interacts with for a lot of reasons, and that seems to rub people the wrong way too."

I nod. "Because he's...sensitive."

Ken's eyes narrow almost threateningly as I continue.

"He told me..."

I shake my head. It's not really my place to say what Namid does or does not trust me with. "Never mind...but I know he's different."

Shock crosses Ken's face briefly before he schools his features back into a glare. He scrutinizes me as he speaks.

"He told you what?"

How in the world am I supposed to say this? If Namid is somehow crazy and making it up, then I'll be the one who sounds crazy.

"Is it...he said you believe him."

Ken's face softens into something nearing a smile. "Yes, I believe him. We tried to find answers for a while. Doctors and shamans and spiritual healers. I know who he is, but there aren't any answers to be found in books or hospitals. He's just different, and if he told you about himself, then you're only the second person in his entire life he's ever trusted enough to share himself with."

Ken reaches his good arm over the side of the bed toward me, and I slide closer to take his hand in both of mine.

His voice breaks as he continues. "Don't you hurt him."

Ken loves him. He loves him like a father, and it's clear he'd protect him with his life. There is something inside of me that needs Ken to know that I understand.

"He's my friend, Ken. I'll protect him."

The ring from a video call startles me awake. I can't believe that I fell asleep on the phone with Jayce while Ken was in surgery; what kind of useless asshole does that? I fumble my phone as I try to answer, barely managing to stab at the green button before the ringing stops. Ken's face pops up, and I burst into tears before I can stop myself.

"Hey. I'm okay, kiddo. Everything is just fine."

I can only nod while I fight to pull myself together, and Ken's face quickly disappears, only to be replaced by Jayce's.

"Hey there."

I can't help the thankful half laugh, half sob that tears its way out of my throat.

"Thank you, Jayce. Thank you so much for everything. I can't begin to thank you enough."

He shakes his head on the tiny screen. "It's nothing. I promise it's been a pleasure getting to know Ken a bit."

It's the first time he hasn't called him Mr. Johnson.

"I'm going to hand you over and step out to get some coffee so you guys can chat, okay?"

I nod in thanks, and the image on the other end shuffles. I stare at the hospital ceiling for a few moments before Ken appears once more.

"You promise you're really okay?"

Ken laughs. "I'm fine. It's just a broken arm. I'll be home in a couple of days, and then aside from having to learn how to button a shirt one handed for a few weeks, I'll be good as new before we know it."

"I'm sorry I couldn't be there with you. You know that I wanted to, but I just…"

"I know, son. I know, and it's fine."

All I can manage is a nod. I'm barely holding my useless self together.

"Speaking of…" Ken trails off in an odd tone of voice, and I raise an eyebrow in question.

"Jayce tells me you've told him about your feelings stuff. That's a big step. Anything else I should know about?" He wiggles his eyebrows suggestively.

I flush with embarrassment as I try to convince Ken that I don't have feelings for Jayce.

"Ken! God! No. Jayce is my friend. It's just…it's nice to have a friend, ya know. I think I can trust him."

Ken's smile is soft and kind and loving. "I think you can too. He seems like a good man, and I'm so glad you boys have each other to lean on now."

Ken and I talk for a few more minutes before Jayce reappears at his side, and Ken transfers the phone back with a yawn.

"You should go home Jayce." Ken's voice is distant with the phone now in Jayce's hand. "You both need to get some rest. You boys have had a long day too, and it's getting late. I'm sure they'll be in here shortly to drug me into a coma for the night."

I hadn't realized how much time has passed since Jayce first showed up to help us this morning, but it's nearly midnight.

"Ya, of course. I'll see you soon?" I know my voice sounds unsure.

"Couple of days, kiddo, then you'll have more of helping me around the house than you can handle. Love ya."

"Love you too, Ken."

I can't feel emotions over the phone, but when Jayce pops back onto the screen to hang up, the emotion on his face looks like...longing.

Jayce's house is only ten minutes from the hospital, and I find myself pacing again as I wait for him to get home. He's been so kind to sacrifice his time and sit at the hospital all day, and it was so generous of him to let me wait here so that I could be close to Ken if there were an emergency serious enough that I had to pull myself together enough to brave the hospital, but he's never invited me over before. We don't have that kind of friendship. Now that he's had time to think through it, what if he doesn't like that I'm here?

Jayce had said that he was going to get a cup of coffee even though he rarely drinks coffee, and it was ten thirty at night when he'd stepped out of Ken's room. I wonder if he really got coffee or if that was just an excuse to give us privacy. *Shit.* I wonder if he even ate today. I don't know if he'll like me snooping through his kitchen, but making sure he eats tonight seems like the least I can do before he takes me home. By the time the door squeaks open, I have some sauce heating, some pasta boiling on the stove, and some vegetables cut up and ready to cook.

I step out of the kitchen and into the front room like I've been caught going through his underwear drawer.

"Hey." He looks startled by my sudden appearance, and I nervously run my hand through my hair.

"Hey. You okay?" He doesn't feel upset with me, just concerned.

"Yeah. Yeah, I'm okay. You?"

Relief spreads through the room.

Oh. He's not concerned that I'm here; he's concerned that I might not be okay. After everything that's happened today, after everything I told him, he's concerned *for* me. God. Could he be any more perfect?

His gentle smile abruptly disappears, only to be replaced by confusion. "Are you cooking something?"

I shuffle my feet nervously. "Yeah. I didn't know if you ate at the hospital, and it's late. I didn't want you to go to bed hungry. It's just pasta. If you give me five more minutes, I can drain it for you and then it will be ready when you get back."

"Back?"

"From taking me home."

His head tilts slightly. "Did you eat tonight?"

"Not yet, but I have food at home. I don't want to intrude or anything."

Small lines appear beside his beautiful green eyes as he smiles and steps closer. "Namid. I'm not kicking you out. Jesus." He laughs softly. "Have dinner with me. If you want me to take you home right after, I'd be happy to, but I have a guest room. You're welcome to spend the night here so that you can be closer to Ken if you'd like."

"Seriously?" My voice is small and cracked, my throat sore from stress and worry and tears, and my own emotions threaten to overwhelm me.

"Of course." His voice is strength and laughter and peace as he closes the distance between us and wraps me in his arms.

I melt against his body, burying my face in his shoulder and taking what feels like my first deep breath since the cabinet slipped from our grip this afternoon. He holds me tightly, enveloping me in his warmth for a long moment before I find the strength to force myself to step back and clear my throat. If I allow myself even one more moment in his arms, I'll do something stupid enough to ruin our friendship. I never want to let him go.

I run my fingers through my hair as I step back.

"I wasn't really sure what you liked or anything. I mean, I know you like bear claws, but I didn't have the time to burn your kitchen down trying to make those at midnight."

Jayce's soul lightens a bit more, and his deep chuckle runs along my spine, leaving me trembling as goosebumps rise across my skin. I turn on my heel and quickly make my way back to the kitchen in the hope he doesn't notice.

A mumbled, "It's just pasta with some vegetables," is all I can come up with as I dump the noodles into the strainer I have waiting in the sink, put an inch of water back in the pot, and slide the veggies off the cutting board into the water to steam.

"It's perfect, thank you."

He moves through the kitchen behind me as I face the stove, idly stirring the vegetables around even though they don't need any attention. I can't bring myself to face him; it's too intimate, being here in his small kitchen, and I'm too emotionally on edge to trust myself not to do something I'll regret - like blurt out that I'm in love with him. Jayce pulls out bowls and fills glasses with water from the sink. I hear him pop the caps off two beer bottles, and I jump a bit as he reaches over my shoulder to dangle one of them in front of me.

"Thanks." I hope he can't hear the way my voice seems to quiver over the fact that he's standing so close behind me that I can feel the warmth of his body along my back.

By the time he's loaded the bowls with noodles and sauce, the veggies are done, and I spoon them into the bowls he holds out for me before we settle silently at the table together.

I want this. I want this always. I want this so much.

We're quiet as we eat, both exhausted and lost in our own thoughts. It's not like silence is new for us; we spend plenty of time together without feeling the need to fill the space between us with unnecessary words. The silence isn't awkward - it's comfortable and companionable, and I'm grateful to be with Jayce instead of alone in my cabin tonight. He's tired and concerned, but he's not scared or worried, and it makes me feel like everything just might be okay.

"I'll get you some pajamas, and then you're welcome to shower first." His voice is steady as we stand together at the sink cleaning the few dishes we've dirtied.

Shower. Here. I'm going to shower in Jayce's house? I glance over, a bit startled at the suggestion, somehow only now taking notice of the streaks of grime and dust that cling to his skin from hours in the dirty basement. I always notice everything about him, and it's a testament to my frazzled emotional state that his disheveled appearance has escaped me until now.

I can't help laughing and pushing my hair back self-consciously.

"Right. No basement dirt in your bed."

Panic.

"Not your bed. Your guest bed. I mean, you'll probably shower too so that there isn't any in your bed either, but..." I groan and close my eyes.

His laugh warms my soul, and I want to step close and curl up in his arms again.

"Come on. I'll show you the bedroom and bathroom."

I quietly follow him down the short hall. Clearly, I can't be trusted to speak without making a fool out of myself, so silence it is before I say something even more incriminating.

He opens the first door we encounter and steps inside, squatting down to rummage under the counter.

"Bathroom. Nothing fancy, but everything works. Here." He holds out a wrapped toothbrush as he stands.

"Thank you."

I want to make a joke about the fact that he has extra guest toothbrushes lying in wait for overnight guests, but that would definitely be a bad idea, and in truth, I don't really want to think about anyone else that would need a new toothbrush spending the night here.

He pauses for a moment at the next door, and I'm almost knocked to my knees by the weight of the grief that rushes through him. He hasn't felt sorrow this intense for months.

"You okay?" I let my hand reach out to rest on his arm.

He shakes his head abruptly, almost as if he's pulling himself out of a trance, and he turns to face me.

"Yeah. I'm sorry. It's just..."

He cocks his head to the side, and his eyes move to my hand, still resting on his forearm. I pull it away quickly.

"Could you...I mean...did you feel that from me?" His eyes narrow.

I blush and shift my gaze to the floor. I can't help it. Ken is the only person who's ever been aware of the way I can pick up their emotions before, and I'm not sure how to respond.

"Yeah. You were upset. You felt like you did when we first met. It wasn't quite as intense, but it was the same heartache."

He stands unmoving at my side until I force myself to raise my eyes and meet his gaze.

"That's amazing, Namid."

His voice is gentle and soft, and he searches my face as if he really does believe me. He believes me, and he's not scared of me. I force an embarrassed half smile as he continues.

"Jordyn was the last one to use this room, that's all. I don't usually have guests."

Fuck. I probably shouldn't take Jordyn's room.

"I can take the couch; it wouldn't be a bother."

"No. It's okay. It's just...it's hard, ya know? But he'd want you to use it. I want you to use it."

I don't know what to say. I can only nod as he continues.

"I'll go get you some pajamas, and then I'll change the sheets while you shower."

"I really would be fine on the co..."

When his brow furrows, warning me that he's not going to lose this argument no matter how many times I offer to take the couch, all I can do is smile at the rush of affection that flows through me.

"Thank you, Jayce."

A smile that seems almost tender flits across his lips before he turns and heads further down the hall.

Standing under the hot water, I'm too exhausted to fixate on the fact that I'm naked in Jayce's home, but when I step out and find pajamas on the counter and realize that he'd popped in to set them there while I showered, it takes a few deep breaths before I can pull myself together enough to get dressed and towel off my hair.

As I curl up in freshly laundered sheets, wearing a soft old T-shirt that smells like Jayce, I can feel him from the next room. He's exhausted and concerned, but there is relief there too. I feel the same way. I feel more than he does though. As I lie in the dark, separated from Jayce by only two thin wooden doors and a short walk down a quiet hallway, I'm filled with longing. I'd give just about anything to be able to slip into his arms and fall asleep against his chest.

Chapter 10

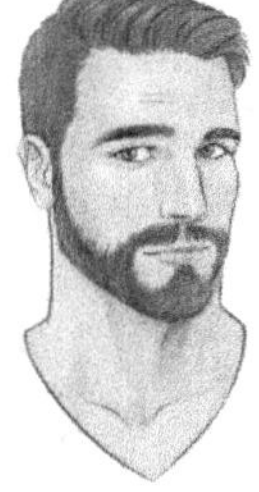

Aside from the time I've spent in my truck driving to the hospital and back home, I've been in the same room as either Ken or Namid for almost seventy-two hours, and it's been...nice. I hadn't realized just how much I've adapted to spending so much time on my own since I lost Jordyn. Aside from my weekly brunches with Namid and the few hours a month he spends at my shop, I've been alone.

Oh sure, there are a handful of people in town who would probably call me their friend, but they're acquaintances at best, and after Jordyn died, they all sort of vanished. We were always *US*, so my friends were his friends, and I know that his loss has been hard on them, too. Still, I guess some part of me expected more from them somehow, and I've been better off on my own than trying to reach out and force something I wouldn't have enjoyed anyway. I was barely capable of keeping myself alive at first, and even though my grief has faded over the past few months, being alone has just become my default.

I woke hours earlier than Namid the day after the accident. No surprise there, as he's mentioned before that he typically sleeps from three a.m. to ten a.m., and I'm more of a ten p.m. to six a.m. kind of guy. I drove down to the shop, put a sign on the door saying I'd be away for a couple of days, and had breakfast ready before he woke. It's not like closing the shop on short notice inconvenienced anyone. There are only two big project trucks at the shop - neither of them rush jobs - and everyone in town has my cell number anyway. The shop doesn't have its own phone line. It's not like I dropped off the face of the earth in case there's a true emergency, but in a town like this, a true mechanical emergency that can't wait a couple of days doesn't really exist.

Namid had stumbled out of the guest room around nine, hair tousled, wearing my plaid flannel pajama pants and one of my T-shirts that was somehow hilariously large on him, even though he's only a couple of inches shorter than me. His lean, athletic torso couldn't fill the fabric that had stretched from its original shape to fit my broad shoulders and the bit of cushion my stomach carries these days. He'd looked close to tears as he sipped his coffee and thanked me over and over when I told him I'd taken a couple of days off to be his and Ken's liaison.

I've spent a couple of hours the past two mornings and a couple more the past two afternoons in the hospital. I haven't interacted much with Ken over the years, maybe because he's so much older. Maybe because he runs the funeral home, and that doesn't exactly scream, "I'm the pleasant type who's looking for piles of friends." It might be because he lost his wife not long before I lost my parents, and we were both too lost, drowning in our own grief to spend our time trying to make any other relationships work. Whatever the reason, I hope that will change once he's home. It turns out I really like the guy.

Namid has spent his time trying to repay me for my support no matter how many times I tell him it's my pleasure to help and that he should just take advantage of the days Ken is in the hospital and rest. Every time I come home, he has lunch or dinner ready, the house has been vacuumed, my laundry has been folded, or some other trivial task has been completed. I don't want him to feel indebted simply because I'm being kind, but I know that it's killing him to just sit around and wait for Ken to be released so they can go home, so I've thanked him and tried to get him to simply sit with me and talk whenever possible.

The hospital told us that Ken would be released this morning, so we'd arrived around nine, ready to take him home. But by the time the paperwork was complete, we had him all packed up, and we'd navigated driving through the pouring rain from the hospital to his house, it was close to three this afternoon. I'd settled a thankful and relieved Namid and an exhausted Ken at home and told them I had some work to catch up on at the shop. I don't. The shop can wait. Over the past few days, I've found something with Ken and Namid that I thought I'd lost forever. A family.

Family.

I can't seem to remove the small smile that won't leave my face as I stand in the checkout line at the grocery store. I never thought family was something you could find a second time, but maybe if I'm lucky, really, really lucky, they might think of me as family one day, too.

After I've finished grabbing a few days' worth of groceries, I'll stop by the diner to pick up the order I managed to sneak in before Ed decided to close early because of the storm. We're so used to bad weather, even during the summer, that businesses rarely close because of heavy storms, but even though it's still tourist season, with this much rain thundering down, the diner won't see much more business this evening, and it makes sense for them to get home to their families.

Ken was only at the hospital for three days, so it's not like he and Namid were away for long enough for all of their food to go bad. I'm sure they both have plenty of groceries at home, but I remember all too well just how much it meant to me when Namid made sure I had fresh food at home when I wasn't capable of such a feat on my own after I lost Jordyn. Ensuring they're taken care of for the next few days as they settle in and getting them a good hot meal tonight is the least I can do.

The storm is raging as I pull into Ken's driveway, and I do my best to curl my body around the cloth bags in an attempt to protect them from being soaked through as I unload them from my truck and settle them on the porch before knocking.

"Hi." Namid is clearly surprised to see me so soon.

"Hey." I grin as he looks around, noticing the bags piled at my feet on the porch.

"What is all this?"

"You were so good to me when I lost Jordyn, and I know that the two of you have a lot of work ahead of you over the next few days, so I wanted to make sure that you didn't have to worry about food."

I hoist the soaking-wet plastic bag from the diner with a triumphant grin.

"I also brought you dinner for tonight, since I don't imagine either of you is up to cooking."

"Jayce..." His blue eyes sparkle as he shakes his head with a smile. "You've done so much for us already. This is absolutely above and beyond."

I don't need to have Namid's gift to realize just how much such a small gesture means to him. After all, aside from Ken, it's not like there's ever been anyone else looking out for him. I hate that. I know I can't change the past, but I can certainly make sure that he knows he's not alone now.

"Come on. Let me help you get all of this inside, and then I'll leave you guys to rest."

Namid cocks his head and frowns. "You're not staying to have dinner with us?"

"I only got dinner for you guys. I figure you've had enough of me by now."

His frown deepens. "What was it you told me the first night I stayed with you? I'm not kicking your ass out? Come on, let's get this into the kitchen, and then you're staying for dinner. I'm sure there is plenty for the three of us."

Ken is settled on his old, overstuffed, navy couch, surrounded by blankets, and piles of pillows are propping up his arm in its complicated sling. Even though I saw him a few hours ago, he seems genuinely happy to see me again, and he quickly seconds Namid's demanding request that I join them for supper.

By the time we've put the groceries away, dished up three plates, and joined Ken in the front room to eat, the storm outside is starting to calm. Namid and I settle cross-legged on the floor to share the coffee table while Ken struggles not to spill everywhere with his plate resting on a pillow on his lap. The fire has warmed the small living room, and it's comfortable here with them. I don't feel out of place or like I'm intruding. It feels like I belong as we eat and laugh and ramble together. I never expected to feel like I belonged anywhere again.

Ken is exhausted by the time Jayce and I get dinner cleaned up, and the two of us help him to his bedroom and tuck him into bed, almost as if he's our child. I make sure that his pills, a glass of water, and his phone are all within easy reach on his nightstand before Jayce and I tell him goodnight and head back down the hall. It feels comfortable having Jayce here with me, and I ache at the fact that this isn't real. He's only here helping me for the night. He's not actually mine. I know that I'm in love with him, and I've been trying to find peace living with unrequited love burning through my soul. But now I'm learning what it would be like to actually spend my life with Jayce, and it's more perfect than I ever imagined. This is the life I yearn for when I lie alone at night, and I don't want to let go of this dream. Even though I know I'm going to end up heartbroken, I find myself holding these moments close and cataloging each of them so that I have something to look back on when they're gone.

"It looks like the storm has cleared for now. I'd like to show you something if you're not in a hurry to get home." I don't want to press Jayce into staying, but I don't want him to leave. I don't want my time with him to end.

He shakes his head quickly. "No hurry at all."

He means it. He's happy and content here with us. He's always happy and content when we're together these days, but here in Ken's home, it's more intense than it's ever been before.

The afternoon storm was windy and brutal, and in its wake, mud and large puddles cover the gravel drive. We don't bother trying to find boots before making our way across the yard to my small cabin, instead opting to simply try, relatively unsuccessfully, to dodge the worst of the new murky driveway water features. We quickly discard our wet shoes by the door, and I light the fire as Jayce wanders my small living room, taking in the collection of rocks and pinecones that graces my mantle and the pile of books on a nearby shelf.

"It's nice here...cozy. I can see why you decided to stay with Ken." His voice is low and warm. It fills the small space, and I can almost feel it vibrate across my skin.

I sink back on my heels and grin up at him.

"I'm happy here, and Ken is a good family."

A hint of longing flickers through Jayce, but it's not enough to overpower the contentment he feels here with me in this moment.

"Wait here for a minute?" I ask as I stand.

He nods with a gentle smile, and I head into the bedroom to gather blankets.

Jayce raises an eyebrow as I reappear. "I've had a good time with you tonight, Namid, but snuggling in front of the fire seems like a bit much, doesn't it?"

His tone is light and teasing, and he chuckles as he finishes talking. He has no way of knowing just how much I want that, and I force myself to laugh with him as if the idea of us curling up together is nothing more than a joke between friends. As if it's not something I want with every atom of my soul. I force on a smile instead of breaking down and confessing everything, risking our friendship in the process.

"They aren't for snuggling."

I hold out two of the four blankets I've grabbed and sling the other two over my shoulders to wrap myself up tightly. Even in August, stormy nights can dip into the thirties.

"Come with me."

My porch is set at an odd angle, and even though its half covered, most of the western sky is visible. The wind typically blows across the grey, worn boards in a way that doesn't allow much rain or snow to accumulate, but when it does, I always make it a point to keep it clear so that it doesn't freeze or ice over. Tonight, we've lucked out, and even though the storm raged for most of the day, only a few inches near the edge are wet.

Jayce pauses in the doorway, shivering and pulling his blankets tighter, but he follows me outside. When I lie down on the rough wood on my back and squirm around to make sure I'm completely covered by the blankets, crossing my legs and tucking my feet under my thighs, he watches me as if he's starting to doubt my sanity.

"Come on then." My blanket-covered hand pats the ground next to me.

Jayce raises an eyebrow.

"Come on. I lie out here like this all the time. If I'm warm enough, I'm willing to bet you'll survive for a little while."

"Fine, but if I die of frostbite, it's on you." He awkwardly drops to the floor and struggles to get himself both comfortable and covered.

Eventually, he stills.

Through the chilled, calm air that surrounds us, even with several inches and four blankets between us, I can feel his body heat. The way I feel him these days is different from the way I feel everyone else. I can't always tell which emotions are his and which are mine, and even when he's not with me, there are moments when I swear that I know what he's feeling anyway. After a few moments, peace settles around us. The peace I feel when I'm by his side is the same peace that I feel when I lie here alone and watch the stars for hours on end, and as the world seems to slow as we silently lie side by side, his emotions slowly shift to match mine.

"This is one of my favorite things in the world." My voice sounds small and quiet, as if the open wilderness surrounding us absorbs the vibrations and scatters them through the air.

"Every time I lie here, it's different. The weather, the placement of the stars, the time of night - they all change, but somehow, the peace I find is the same. Some nights, the clouds nearly cover the sky with rolling blacks and greys. Some nights, the Aurora swirls with teals and pinks so bright that the colors seem to drip down and cover the world. The vibrant lights reflect off the snowbanks, and it feels like I'm bathed in something ethereal and endless. Like I'm a part of the universe, and each of us is somehow deeply important. On other nights, like tonight, the cold air is crisp and thin, and thousands of stars sparkle overhead; their light seems to hold back the darkness, and if you really look, the sky is a deep blue instead of black. So many stars and so many worlds so far away, and I remember just how small we all really are."

Jayce doesn't speak when I finally stop rambling. Instead, he shifts until our sides are nearly pressed together.

Hours pass as we lie together, each bundled up in our own blanket cocoon, yet somehow, it feels like the most intimate moment I've ever spent with another person.

Chapter 11

I don't know how to not want Jayce. It's been a month since we spent the evening together on my porch, and every day, it gets harder to keep my hands to myself when we're together. I want to slip my fingers between his when we walk down Main Street with our coffees. I want to lay my head on his shoulder in the park, pull him into my arms in the shop, and brush my lips across his every time he smiles at me.

When we spent the night lying side by side, watching the stars, I wanted to slide over and curl up against him with my head on his chest. I wanted to kiss him and ask him to stay. I wanted to take him to bed and show him that I could be enough if he'd let me, that I'd give him everything I am, and that I'd be everything he could ever want.

I can't be what he wants though. I can't kiss him or touch him or tell him he's everything I've ever wanted.

He's straight and he's my friend, and in all the time we've spent together, he's never felt anything remotely romantic for me. For one brief moment when he showed me his studio, I thought...maybe, but then it was gone. He cares for me and he enjoys being with me, but there is nothing more. There is no rush of joy or excitement when he sees me. There is no longing, no want, no *need*. He doesn't feel the way I feel. I wish I could at least pretend that he does.

All I feel anymore is Jayce. All I feel is desire and frustration and love, and there is nowhere for any of it to go.

I need to get him out of my system. I need to fuck into someone hard and fast and watch their fingers curl into the sheets as they scream my name. I need to lick the taste of salt from the back of a stranger's neck and dig my fingers into sharp hip bones until bruises are left behind. I need to dull my need for him with something more than my own hand and memories of his smile haunting me. I need to lose myself in another body until I stop wondering what his looks like undressed. I need something. I need someone. Anyone.

Tourists usually stay out of the old part of town. They rent small cabins along the river and rooms in the tiny condo complex that was built specifically to bring summer tourism money into our small town. Once in a while, they stray far enough during the day to eat at the diner instead of the summer restaurant or pick up cereal and milk and apples at the grocery store, but that's about it. They normally book locals as wilderness guides to take them hiking in the woods and fishing on the river.

They sit in the sun and enjoy the trees and remember what it's like not to have six a.m. meetings and eight p.m. kids' basketball games every day.

The tourists who come to this town are mostly families, parents with their 2.5 children who have saved up enough money to go somewhere other than Disneyland for their one-week-a-year summer vacation. There are also men's groups - packs of two, four, or six men in their fifties or sixties who have talked about fishing in Alaska together since they met in college and are finally making their dreams come true. There are fathers trying to build memories with their teenage sons and young couples on their honeymoons. They have evening glasses of whiskey on their small balconies and split bottles of wine while they barbecue in the fire pits at their rented condos or guzzle martinis in the restaurant bar. They don't venture to the Hole-in-the-Wall bar on Main Street.

Occasionally, there are other tourists. There are groups of men in their twenties and thirties who come for bachelor's weekends before one of their members gets married and abandons them forever. Rarely these groups do find their way to the bar. Once in a great while, one of their ranks is gay or bi or curious-only-while-on-vacation-in-the-middle-of-nowhere.

I've spent the past three weeks at the bar on Friday and Saturday nights. It's grating on me, the onslaught of unchecked drunken emotion that I can barely manage to keep at arm's length. The whiskey helps. I sit at the bar night after night, trying to find someone, anyone, to help me carve out the longing in my chest for a fraction of a moment. Shelly slides me over a third drink. We're not friends. Before Jayce, I never really knew what it was like to have a friend, but she's kind to me, and she's one of the few people in town who doesn't feel uncomfortable simply because I'm around. Aside from Ken, she's the only person in town who knows I'm gay, and it doesn't seem to bother her. I don't make a habit of trying to pick up men in her bar - I've only attempted it a handful of times in the decade I've lived here, and I've only been successful twice. The last time was four years back. That was the last time I had sex.

I'm sitting in the corner, watching the throng of bodies laughing and dancing while I nurse a bourbon and a headache, when a hand brushes across my lower back. The lust that rolls off the stranger is unmistakable, and it's strong enough that I'm almost sure everyone else is somehow able to feel it, even without my abilities. As the man leans over the bar and orders another tequila shot, his hand lingers on my T-shirt, one fingertip slipping lower to brush the thin strip of exposed skin between my shirt and belt. He leaves a twenty for Shelly, downs his shot, and heads for the front door without a backward glance.

I follow.

He's leaning against the bar's red brick façade, lighting a cigarette when I walk out, and when I walk the nine steps to the edge of the building and turn down the alley, he follows.

I pluck the cigarette from his hand and flick it into the street before hooking my fingers through his belt loops and pulling his body close. His mouth crushes mine, the taste of tequila and tobacco and ash filling my senses as he grinds against me. He's desperate as his hands work the buttons of my jeans. Good. I'm desperate too. I need this. I need the scent of bar and smoke and liquor, so different from leather and cinnamon and motor oil, to fill my senses. I need to yank and groan and feel teeth on my skin, so different from the gentleness that fills my soul when I'm around Jayce.

I shove the stranger's pants over his hips. He does the same to mine, and then I'm in his hand. He has our cocks crushed together, and he's stroking fast, dry skin on dry skin, and it's so rough it nearly hurts. It's too cold to be doing this outside, but that's good too. It's different and distracting and perfect, and I let my head fall back against the cold brick and try not to think about work-roughened hands and auburn scruff and pale jade eyes hovering over me.

It's not working. My soul feels him all the time now, and it's almost like he's with me, like he's close. He's felt close all night. I didn't see him in the bar as I glanced through the writhing, sweaty bodies and tried to sort through the emotional onslaught that accompanied them. I felt him, but I didn't see him. I always feel him now. He's always with me, even when he's not.

I squeeze my eyes tighter and groan as a mouth sucks along the underside of my jaw and a rough beard scratches the skin of my neck. It's not Jayce's beard. I lean down, catching the mouth with mine, demanding the taste of smoke and the tongue that thrusts itself just a bit too hard down my throat. I need this stranger to make me forget.

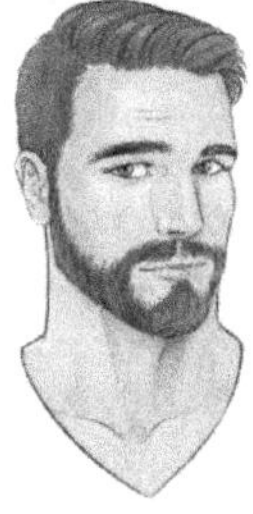

The pale skin of his throat almost glows in the silver moonlight; it's slender and strong, the tendons rippling as his body tenses in pleasure. His head is tipped back, his raven-black hair resting against the crumbling red brick wall. His eyes are closed, and he's lost in the sensation of the man's hands moving across his body, across his skin.

They don't know that I can see them. Even though they're technically in public, the space behind the bar is largely hidden. It's only visible for a few feet and only if you're walking along the sidewalk close to the bar, which few do this time of night. The nights here are cold, and there aren't many people stupid enough to linger outside for long. Tourists rarely make it to this part of town, and none of the regulars inside are likely to clear out of the bar before closing time. I didn't see Namid inside. If I had, I'd have asked to join him, and maybe the night would have ended differently. Maybe I wouldn't be standing here, frozen in place, watching a stranger touch him.

They know they're on stolen time. The stranger's hand is rushing, wrapped around both of their hard cocks over the top of open jeans that have only been shoved down far enough for him to gain access. The man leans in, his lips brushing along Namid's jaw until he leans forward to meet the man's lips in a kiss. The way their mouths move is raw and desperate and aggressive. So is the way the man's hand is moving between them.

Namid is so beautiful like this, undone and lost to the world - his chest pulsing as his breaths rush from him, his long fingers curling against the brick beside his hip as they search for something to grasp.

I nearly fall to my knees with the weight of the realization that I want to be the one touching him. I want to trail my fingertips along the curve of his throat. I want to be the one to lean in and taste his collarbone, sucking blood to the skin in prickly tingles until he gasps and whimpers. I want him naked and writhing against me as I take him apart inch by inch until he's keening and begging incoherently, until he's not even sure what he's begging for. I want him to slide down my throat. I want his fingers to clutch at my hair as he thrusts into me, taking pleasure that only I can offer him. I want him to shatter in my arms over and over until he's spent and sated and sleeping against my chest.

Their kiss breaks, and Namid's head rolls to the side against the brick, his eyelids fluttering as he squints into the darkness, almost as if he's looking for something. His eyes snap open as his gaze finds mine through the dark, and the world stills. I no longer see the man possessively touching him. Namid no longer seems to feel him. It's just the two of us. This is what it would feel like to stare into his eyes as I touch him.

Then it's gone.

His eyes rip from mine, and he's shaking his head no and pushing the man away and talking quickly. I've already ruined this for him, already been caught watching when I should have passed by. He knows I saw, and he's not going to understand why I was standing there staring at them. I can't explain why I was doing it, can't tell him that I'd sat in the darkest corner of the bar with half a beer and a plate of half-eaten fries for hours because I hadn't known what else to do with myself when he'd told me he had other plans tonight when I'd asked if he wanted to have dinner. I don't know why I glanced down the small opening into the ally instead of walking with my head down like I always do. I can't explain the life-altering epiphany that was the view of his throat in the moonlight. I can't explain that I want to be that stranger. I can't tell him that in a single instant, my world has turned itself upside down. I can't tell him that I've realized I love him.

I turn and nearly run to my truck. I have the door open and one foot inside before I hear Namid's voice behind me. I don't look back. I hop into the seat and shut the door behind me as I twist the key.

He's here now, just outside my window. His lips are swollen, and there is a red patch on his throat where it's been rubbed raw by a beard. Not my beard. The top button of his pants is still undone. He's talking to me, but I don't hear his words. I shake my head and back the truck into the empty street. I can't tear my eyes away from the sight of him as I pull away. He's shaking his head, and his arm is stretched in my direction. The corners of his eyes are glistening, and his lips move in the same motion again and again.

"Please."

I drive away.

I fall into bed without undressing, hiding under the covers in a way I haven't in months, not since Namid first came into my life. How did I not see this? My grief has been so deep and so overwhelming that I haven't even noticed myself falling in love with him. He's my friend, and I've been so sure that he's straight. Everyone here is straight; that's why I've picked up tourists in the past when I've needed to fuck. I've had a few momentary crushes on men from town, sure, but I tell myself they're straight and that I'm being ridiculous, and after a few weeks, those feelings fade, and things go back to normal.

I did that with Namid months ago. I thought that once I'd convinced myself he was my straight friend, the feelings that started to appear the day I showed him my studio had disappeared, just like they always do. I truly didn't realize that I'd simply shoved them into a locked box in a deep closet and that the moment I saw him with another man, the lock would fly open and my world would collapse into a flaming pile of lust and need and despair.

There are six missed calls and eighteen text messages when I wake up.

Namid: *Hey.*

I'm sorry.

I'm so sorry.

Can we please talk?

Please.

I am so sorry that you saw that.

Jayce?

Please don't do this.

I don't want to lose your friendship.

I know I should have told you that I'm gay, but I didn't want you to hate me.

Please, can you just talk to me about this?

Jayce...

Please don't do this...

I'll keep it to myself like I have been. I promise I won't tell you anything. You can pretend you don't know. You can pretend this never happened; you never saw that. It's been years anyway. It's not like I do that a lot and you're going to stumble onto it again. You can keep thinking that I'm straight. Really. I'm ok with that. I like our friendship; I promise I'd never hit on you or anything...I promise.

Jayce?

...it's ok.

I'm sorry. I can leave the shop key in the mail drop so you won't have to see me again.

I understand.

They started at 12:46 a.m., a few minutes after I left the bar. The last arrived at 8:32, twenty-three minutes ago.

I am an asshole.

I was so worried that what…that I realized I've fallen in love…and with someone I might actually have the tiniest chance at a shot with because he's miraculously gay too, that I ignored him all night and let him sit alone, panicking and thinking that I'm some homophobic douchebag who has dropped my best friend without a word because I found out he's attracted to men. There are no words that accurately describe this level of asshole-ness.

Six curse-filled minutes later, I finally find my keys under the coffee table and tear out of my driveway fast enough to leave divots in the gravel. I didn't know it was possible to get to his house in thirteen minutes. When I was driving there daily to help with Ken, it took twenty-one.

He doesn't answer his door…or his phone. I bang louder, pounding the wood with my fist and calling his name.

He's in the same clothes he was wearing last night when he finally answers. The pants the stranger had opened, the T-shirt that clung to his collarbones as he strained and tensed at the man's touch.

He says nothing as he opens the door. His eyes are red, his hair is disheveled, and his arms are curled around his body like he's hoping to hide or disappear. I can't seem to find any words, so I just stand, staring at him as he curls further into himself, his gaze on my chest. I step toward him, and he flinches back.

This is what heartbreak feels like.

"Look, I don't know why you're here. I told you, okay? I'm really, really sorry, and I'll leave you alone. We didn't see each other during the first decade I've lived here; it won't be hard for us to avoid each other for the next fifty years." His voice is deep and harsh and filled with gravel. I've never heard him sound like this. I know his throat is sore. I know crying all night will do that. God knows I know that, but this time, it's not my voice that sounds that way, it's his. It's his beautiful, smooth, silken voice that has been shredded, and it's my fault.

One arm is bent across his stomach, his long, beautiful fingers clutching at the opposite forearm, nails digging into his pale skin. I can see the marks they've left when he shifts slightly. What the fuck is wrong with me that I still haven't said anything to him?

"I'll get your key now so I don't have to come by the shop."

He turns to walk away, and my hand is on his arm before I can stop it. I'm pulling him into my arms and crushing him to my chest. He's stiff and tense and scared that I'm going to hurt him, but I'm not. I just want to erase the hurt I've already caused.

He's only a couple of inches shorter than me, and it feels so natural to bury my face into the bend of his neck, to press my cheek and lips against his skin until he relaxes in my arms.

"I'm sorry."

"I didn't..."

"I never..."

"I don't..."

I can't find actual words, so I just squeeze him tighter and hope he's able to feel what I need to say. I hope he can feel that I didn't mean to hurt him, that I'll never hurt him. That I'll protect him from anyone, always. That I was stupid and scared and confused. That I love him, and I never want to let him go.

Chapter 12

Namid

Jayce feels like anger and confusion and frustration even through the door, and when I open it, he just stands there staring at me. I always knew this would end badly, but that doesn't mean I'm ready. I'm not ready, but there isn't anything I can do standing here in the aftermath. Maybe it's better that I have to let him go now before I fall even deeper. At least I got to know what it feels like to fall in love.

He doesn't reply when I say that I'm sorry yet again or when I tell him I'll get his key; he just stands there radiating fear and confusion, and I don't know what to do. I don't know how to save our friendship.

When I turn away, his hand grips my wrist, and I brace myself. I don't know why he's grabbing me or what he plans to do, but it can't be good. He doesn't feel anything good right now.

He pulls my wrist.

He pulls me close, and he's holding me, and in a single instant, everything has changed. The whole world has transformed. He's confused and afraid, but there is love. There is so much love, and it's joy and passion and magenta and gold, and it's so much more intense and all-encompassing than I'd ever imagined it could be. It's so much deeper and more powerful than even the pain and sorrow I felt from him when he lost Jordyn. It's so much stronger. It's more than I ever imagined it could be. It's everything.

He's rambling, and he can't find words and...

"It's okay." I let my hands move to his back the way they've wanted to so many times before.

"It's okay. I feel you now."

He sobs into my neck, and there is no more fear and no more confusion. There is only love burning across my skin and sinking into my bones and swirling around us until the air is full and heavy and nothing else exists.

His feelings mirror my own, and they combine inside my chest and sweep me away until there is only warmth and cinnamon and leather and strength. I tighten my arms around him, and a trembling exhale shakes itself from his throat to settle against the skin of my neck. I melt into him, crushing our bodies together until there is no space, no air. There is nothing but him.

My fingers trace along his spine as he crushes me against his chest. He's broad and thick and strong as he curls his body around mine.

He is everything.

"It's okay. Everything is okay now. Come on. Let's talk...yeah?"

He nods against my shoulder and sniffs quietly before he pulls away. His sudden retreat feels like diving into ice water. He's standing close and his fingers lace their way into mine, but I still have to remember to breathe as I adjust to the absence of the warm crush of his body.

I lead him to my small couch and settle next to him, one leg curled up tightly under my hips. His hand hovers briefly before he lets himself rest it gently on my knee, and I swear I hear him sigh into the touch.

"Jayce."

My voice is quiet, almost a whisper, almost a prayer, as I watch him cautiously. I don't understand what's happening here. How has he been hiding this?

"I don't understand. You've never felt like this before. People can hide what they feel from everyone else. They can change their behaviors and smile and pretend, but not with me. I *feel* Jayce. I feel everything. How? How am I feeling this from you right now?"

He flinches as I speak, but his hand stays on my knee.

"You're my friend. You're my friend, and I thought you were straight."

His voice is broken and harsh, and he stops like that's enough, but it's not. It's not nearly enough. He's my friend, and I've always thought he was straight as well. Hell, a part of me still thinks he is, but I fell in love with him anyway. I've always known I was in love with him.

For the first time in my life, I'm not sure I can trust what I'm feeling.

"Jayce. It doesn't work like that. That's not...that's not an explanation. What I'm feeling from you doesn't just appear in an instant. Am I wrong? Is what I'm feeling wrong?"

He shakes his head, eyes bright with tears that threaten to fall.

"I don't think you're wrong about anything. I think you know what I'm feeling. I hope you do anyway, and I don't think feelings like this just appear out of nowhere either. I think I've had them for a long time, I just honestly didn't realize it. I hid them away, even from myself. I didn't know I still had them until I saw you last night."

"Still?" My voice is a whisper. *Still.*

"I mean, there was a moment a few months ago when I let myself think...maybe, just maybe. But then, like I said, you're my friend, and I thought you were straight, so I just forced myself to shut it down. I spent plenty of years in my youth living in a fog of unrequited love. It wasn't exactly enjoyable. So, I just sort of learned to turn that part of myself off whenever I'm starting to feel anything even remotely...romantic. It hasn't happened a lot, thank God, but there have been a couple of times over the years. I guess that with you, I managed to hide what I felt from even myself instead of erasing it completely. I mean, it happened so slowly that until I saw you last night, I just told myself it was friendship. I believed myself when I said it was only friendship."

I'm stunned into silence. Even though the pressure in my chest and the ache in my stomach over the past few weeks have been nearly unbearable as I've fought to ignore what it would be like to build a life with Jayce, and okay, yeah, even though last night was maybe the worst moment of my life, I can't imagine giving it all up. I can't imagine having the strength to kill the tiny ember of happiness and hope that had sparked inside me when I'd opened the office door and found Jayce looking for his jacket. I don't think I could have smothered it into non-existence. I'd never have gotten to experience all the beauty that has come with the pain. I don't know how he's had the strength to do that each time he's felt some small spark of hope appear.

Jayce is staring at me in the silence. His hand has left my knee, and his fingers are twisting on themselves anxiously.

"The day you showed me your studio." My whisper seems to fill the small room.

His eyes blow wide, and his fingers freeze.

"You noticed that? You really do feel...everything."

I can only nod. What if I hadn't been so scared that day? What if I'd let myself lean into him? Touch him. Kiss him.

"You really remember that?" He sounds almost awed.

The rush of warmth that travels through me at the memory is my own.

"Of course I remember. It's hard to forget the moment when you think there might just be a chance that you'll get what you've been hoping for."

Color rises across his cheeks.

"You wanted...you want me too?"

I can see his heartbeat racing in the side of his neck, and he's leaning ever so slightly toward me. I've never felt like this before and worry that my heart might explode as my voice comes out in a deep, harsh whisper.

"Please."

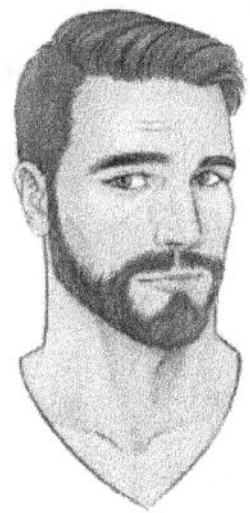

Please. He said please. Did I really hear him say that? Namid wants me too?

His face is so open, and his eyes are so blue, so deep and dark and indigo. There is red there too. That's my fault. I'm the reason he spent last night thinking he'd lost a friend. No. Not just a friend. Someone he wants. Someone he...loves? His lips are slightly parted, and he's leaning ever so slightly toward me, and he might just let me.

My fingertips hover in the bright ray of light that streams in through the window. They're so close. He's so close. I bite my lower lip as I let them slide to trace along the stubble of his jaw. I've never seen him unshaven before. It's dark, as black as his hair, and rough on the pads of my fingers. His eyelids flutter when our skin meets, and I swear his head leans into my hand.

My fingertips trail down the side of his neck, and his heart is racing so quickly under my touch. His eyelashes are so long and black, and his lips look so soft.

Is he closer now? He's closer now, and his hand is on my thigh. *Jesus, his hand is on my thigh.* I've never wanted anyone like this, never known it was possible to want someone this much. The ache that has lived in the pit of my stomach my entire life, the fear that I'd always be alone, that I'd never get to know what it feels like to fall in love, is suddenly gone, and there are butterflies in its place, and they are so fluttery and bright, and he's so very close.

When my lips brush his, the world no longer exists. There is nothing other than the smoothness of his skin and the warmth of his breath as he exhales sharply. I inhale, taking his breath into my lungs as if he's the only thing keeping me alive.

His hand is resting over mine against his throat, long fingers curling tightly, clutching at me like he's afraid to let go. His grip is strong, stronger than I'd expected, and I want him to overpower me. I want him to consume me. I want to be his. Only his.

His mouth parts, and his tongue traces my bottom lip, tender and slow, and I let his body into mine without hesitation. The sensation of our tongues and breath and skin together drags a moan from deep in my chest, and then he's moving. He surges forward and swallows my moan with his kiss. He pushes me back against the couch, his lips and his body desperate and hungry as he moves to straddle me, knees tucked in against my sides as he lowers himself to my lap, the fingers of his free hand gripping the back of my neck. I clutch at his hip, tugging him against me tighter and tighter, erasing the space between our bodies.

"Can you read minds?" I exhale the words against his lips.

He pulls back slightly and cocks an eyebrow. He's flushed and panting, and I never want to look at anything else again. Only him. Only like this.

"This is exactly what I want. You. Like this. Just like this."

His lips curl into a smile as his body surges back against mine, pushing me into the sofa cushions, and I let go, letting him cover me, letting him move me. He can have me. He can have anything.

I want him to kiss me for the rest of my life.

A loud chime breaks through the muted, desperate sounds of breath and skin and fabric, and suddenly, Namid's lips are no longer pressed to mine. His head drops to my shoulder as he exhales a pained, groaning laugh.

"That's my alarm. We have a service at work today." His words and breath roll across my skin, and I dig my fingers tighter into his hip.

"Of course you do." I can't suppress the laughter that's forming in my chest. I've never felt this light. I'm almost weightless, and Namid's lithe body is the only thing stopping me from floating away.

He lifts his head from my shoulder, and his indigo eyes hold my gaze as my fingertips wander along his throat, just above his T-shirt. I don't think I've ever felt anything as intense as the wave of love and lust that rushes through me when his body trembles under my touch.

"What time do you think you'll be finished?" Is that really my voice? It's at least an octave lower than normal.

He tightens his grip, his fingers curling through my hair until my scalp tingles.

"Maybe three? I just help get things ready and then clean up once people leave. I don't actually interact with anyone or go to the graveside services or anything. Things like that are too overwhelming for me."

I can't stop myself from touching him. My hand has slid down over his collarbones, and my palm is pressed to his chest, his heartbeat pulsing against my skin.

"Can I see you after?"

His smile is brilliant enough that it could guide ships into a stormy harbor.

"Yes."

I lean in and trail my cheek along his jaw, and his heart races as if it's trying to escape his chest.

"I want to take you on a date."

"Jayce..."

He doesn't look happy anymore. *Why doesn't he look happy anymore?*

"You know I'm not very good in public most of the time as it is, and it'll be too cold for us to wander the park with the storm coming today. I'm not sure it's a great idea for us to be seen dating anyway. I don't know any queer people here, do you?"

He doesn't wait for me to answer.

"I don't really know how that would go over even if you were seeing someone who people liked, but for it to be me on top of us suddenly being visibly queer..."

"Hey..." I cut off his rambling with a gentle smile. "Trust me enough not to do something stupid?"

The least attractive sound of skepticism I've ever heard snorts its way out of his mouth. I adore it. I lean up to brush my lips across his once more. I don't know how I'm going to convince myself to let him leave my lap and walk out the door, even if it's just for a few hours. My whole life I had no idea it was possible to feel like this, and I'm terrified that if I let him out of my arms, it will disappear.

He's kissing me again, and it only takes an instant before his lips part and his tongue asks for entry once more. I grant it gladly and with a whimper. It would be so easy to tighten my hand on his hip and roll to the side, sweeping his body underneath mine and pressing him into the cushions. But right now, in this moment, as much as I want that, I want this more. I want the slow, tender, delicate taste of him. I want the contrast of his petal-soft lips and his strong fingers digging into the back of my neck. I want to get lost in the way his heart rushes and how the air from his lungs escapes into mine and the weight of his body against me.

When he finally pulls away, I'm trembling against him.

"Pick me up at five?"

Jesus, if his voice sounds this wrecked right now, how is it going to sound when I touch him like the stranger in the alley did? *Oh my god.* He's going to let me touch him like that. He's going to touch me.

When he slips from my lap to stand in front of me, the line of his cock, long and hard and straining against last night's jeans, falls right into my line of sight, and I can't help the strangled groan I utter as I tilt my head back and catch his amused, lust-filled gaze.

"Later."

This time, my groan is long and deliberate, and I'm pretty sure that I might not survive the next seven hours.

Chapter 13

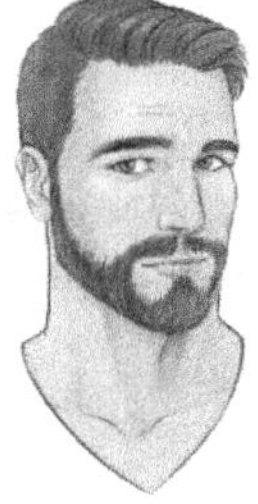

I'm nervous, standing in front of Namid's door. I've never done this before. Sure, I've trolled tourists for hookups, but even that has only ever been once a year at the most. I'm dressed in the same thing I wore to Jordyn's funeral - my black dress pants and a green and black flannel shirt. It's not fancy, but it's the nicest thing I own. I run a mechanic's shop in a small Alaskan town; it's not like I need a wardrobe full of expensive couture pieces. I've never been on a date, not really, and I'm not sure what I'm wearing is okay. I hope Namid will like what I've pulled together for us this evening. I think he will, but what happens if he doesn't? What if the first real date I ever have ends up being a fiery crater of awfulness?

He opens the door the moment I knock. Did he move to stand at the door when he heard me pull into the gravel driveway? Was he standing there waiting for me? Tonight's storm is blowing in a cold front. The strong winds will bring snow within the hour, and it's possible he didn't even hear me pull up. Could he feel me arrive when I got close to his cabin? Can he tell how nervous I am? Is he nervous too?

My breath rushes out in a startled exhale as I take him in. He's beautiful. He's always been beautiful, but I've never seen him like this before. He's wearing all black - a soft, fluffy sweater and skintight black jeans, the ends of which are tucked into tall, black leather boots that hug his lower calves. There is some kind of product in his hair, not much, but enough that the stray long strands that normally threaten to cover his eyes are held in place just over his forehead.

"Jesus, Namid."

He grins as he grabs his jacket and shrugs it on over the sweater.

"Acceptable then?"

"We could stay here, and I can see if I can make you come without even undressing you instead."

We've never even suggestively joked with one another before, but if I've startled him with my directness, he doesn't show it. If anything, he looks like he's thinking about taking me up on the offer, and it makes me wonder just what goes on in his head when he doesn't have to hold his comments back for fear of misunderstanding or disapproval.

He wiggles an eyebrow as he finishes pulling on his jacket.

"Maybe later, and only if I can return the favor, but right now, I was promised a date."

He interlaces his fingers through mine as he steps close and pulls the door shut behind him, and the shiver that runs through me has nothing to do with the crisp fall evening and everything to do with the warmth and strength of his touch.

When I walk with him to the passenger side of the truck and open the door for him, he pauses for a moment, indigo eyes smiling up at me.

"Thank you."

There is something almost unsettling about the slight tremor in his voice. I don't think anyone's ever done anything as simple as opening a door for him before, and he doesn't seem to know how to process it. It breaks my heart a little, and I want to open every door for him for the rest of my life.

He seems a bit confused when I follow him into the door's opening as he hops into the cab. When I parked, I'd turned the dashboard defrost on high and piled a small throw blanket on the vents so that it would be heated by the time we got into the truck. I reach in, leaning over him slightly, to grab it and lay it across his lap.

His hand catches my wrist as I step back to shut the door.

"Jayce." My name falls from his lips in an almost pained whisper.

I raise our hands and bush my lips across the back of his knuckles before lowering them back to his lap and slipping my hand away.

"Get used to it." I offer a grin as I step back and make my way to the driver's side.

I take a few deep breaths of air so cold it burns my lungs to steady myself on the short walk around the truck. He'd looked like he was going to cry for a second there over something as simple as a the offer of a warm blanket.

The moment I have my seat belt fastened, his hand comes to rest on my thigh and I curl my fingers around his. While the drive into town is quiet, it feels right. Neither of us feels the need to fill the time with unnecessary small talk. We're already comfortable enough with each other that we can sit and process our emotions while we watch the flurries starting to swirl in the beams of pale yellow that the headlights carve out through the darkness.

When I park in front of my shop and finally turn my head to look at Namid, he's grinning over at me with one aggressively raised, questioning black eyebrow.

"Shall we?" I ask as formally as possible.

"I've definitely got to hand it to you. No one is going to give it a second thought that your truck is parked in front of your own shop."

"Told you that you can trust me."

His smile softens slightly. "I know I can. Now come on, I'm excited to change some spark plugs."

He laughs as we run to the door through what can now be called a small blizzard, and the sound of it seems to ride through the air on the twirling wind, wrapping me in a kind of joy that I thought had abandoned me forever.

It's pleasure and breathless excitement and hope. He's carefree and alive…alive in a way I'd forgotten could exist.

I've drawn the blinds on all the windows between the waiting area and the shop's work bay. It's something I do on occasion when I'm working late and I want privacy from the rest of the world. If anyone happens to be out in the storm and passes by, they won't think anything of it. I lead Namid straight to the bay door; I don't want both of our coats hanging in the waiting room tonight, and I doubt he does either. When I hold the door open and he steps through in front of me, I follow close behind, only to nearly crash into his back. He's stopped just inside the door.

I settle my hand lightly on his hip and step us forward so that the door can close behind us. He hasn't moved, and I'm starting to panic. Is it too much? Is it stupid? As I look over his shoulder into the bay, everything is, of course, right where I left it. We're the only two with keys, after all. I've spread several thick blankets on the floor and sprinkled LED candles around them. In the center is a large charcuterie board loaded with grapes and figs and meats and cheeses - including the one he'd called his favorite as he put it into my basket on the day he'd helped me shop. A bottle of champagne sits chilling with two glasses just off to the side. Is it too high school? Too cliché? This may possibly be the worst decision I've ever made.

"Is it okay?"

"Is it okay?" His voice breaks.

Before I even realize what's happening, he spins in my arms, and his hands are on my jaw, his forehead pressed to mine. His cheeks are wet, but his eyes are sparkling and smiling only inches from mine.

"Is it okay…" He laughs.

His thumbs drag across my cheekbones on the smooth skin just at the top of my beard, and his lips pepper across mine over and over as he whispers.

"It's the most…amazing thing…I've ever seen. It's perfect."

My hands grip his ribs, and I grin so wide that I'm afraid my cheeks might split open.

"Not quite yet, it's not. There's one more thing."

Even though I don't ever want his lips or eyes or hands or body further away from me than they are in this moment, I haven't shown him the best part. The romantic picnic is something anyone taking him on a date might offer; the rest of my surprise can only come from me.

Still clinging together, I walk us back a few steps and then pull away, throwing my arms to the side and extending aggressive jazz hands in the direction of the floor.

"Ta-da!"

He laughs. He laughs so loud and brilliantly that it echoes around the bay as he throws his arms around me and squeezes me within an inch of my life before stepping away and lowering himself onto one of the two under-car creeper rollers I have sitting side by side, straddling it and sinking down onto his ass the same way he'd climbed onto my lap this morning.

"I told you that one day you'd let me play with it!"

I can't feel him the way he can feel me. I don't need to. I've never seen anyone look so innocent and carefree and ecstatic in my life. It's contagious. Everything about him is beautiful and light and perfect, and all I want to do is make him smile and laugh...and kick his ass in a race. I drop myself down onto the vacant roller at his side and offer the most serious and threatening look I can manage while my heart is joyfully exploding.

"You ready to race?"

"Ohhhh, it's on. Five. Four." We both shift to sit cross-legged with our hands on the floor. "Three. One!"

Wait. *One?!* He's laughing as he takes off, his long fingers pressing against the cold concrete floor as he zips away from me with his stolen head start.

I don't normally believe in cheating, but Jayce is a couple of inches taller than me, so his arms are probably longer than mine and definitely more muscular. Plus, it really just sounded like fun to tease him.

I can hear him behind me; he's gaining ground already as we speed across the shop. I've never heard him laugh quite like this, never felt him this jubilant. I've never felt this way myself either. Light and weightless and elated, as if every moment is somehow more enjoyable than the last.

There is movement out of the corner of my eye, and then he's beside me, grinning over at me with a smile so wide and bright and happy it seems to light up the room. My first instinct is to push harder, propel myself forward faster. It turns out I'm far more competitive than I thought I was, and I fully intend to win this race. Then his eyes change; their bubbly sparkle is replaced by something that looks almost mischievous, a slight wrinkle appears on his forehead, and his lips curl up into a smirk. I don't have time to process the shift before he launches himself in my direction, wrapping his arms around me with a growl as he tackles me. He curls his body around mine, nearly crushing me in his arms, flipping us around as we fall so that we skid across the cold concrete using his back as a sled. When we stop a few feet away from the rollers, we're both breathless with laughter. Unflattering gasps and snorts escape us both as we cling to each other.

"Cheater." I nip at the thin line of exposed neck skin between his beard and the collar of his flannel.

"If you're unhappy with the results, you can always request a rematch."

"So you can tackle me again when you realize you're going to lose?" I scoff.

"There was some dust on the floor; you were going to hit it and crash. I was saving you."

"Ohhhh. Well, thank you for saving me then." I brush my nose across his jaw. "Can I request a rematch even if I'm happy with the results?"

His strong arms tighten around me, dragging me a few more inches up his body so that we're lying face to face, chest to chest, hips to hips.

"Anytime."

It's only half of a word. The second half is lost as his lips find mine.

I exhale a whimper and melt against him as his kiss deepens. Kissing has never felt like this. Touching has never felt like this. I could kiss him for hours and days and years, and it would never be enough. As his lips play gently against mine, it's hard to remember that our first kiss was less than twelve hours ago. Everything about him feels so comfortable and natural. He feels like home.

This kiss is different than our desperate, clinging need in my cabin this morning. This is slow, gentle caresses of lips and tongues, the soothing weight of his palms against my back, and the scruff on his jaw under my fingertips. It tapers off slowly and effortlessly until I'm simply lying against him, our eyes locked and tender smiles tugging at the corners of our lips.

"Come on."

He leans up to brush his nose across mine, and the overwhelming magenta and gold haze of joy that surrounds us both brightens further still. *How is this really happening?* Maybe I finally cried myself to sleep last night, and this is a dream. Maybe I'll wake up, and I'll be alone in my cabin, the smell of cigarettes and bourbon and the memory of a stranger's touch still on my skin. I'm not sure I'm strong enough to survive losing these moments if I wake up and find this has been a dream.

Lying on top of Jayce on the floor is exciting and new and sensual. The two of us scrambling to our feet together is something less than elegant, however, and we break into laughter yet again as we awkwardly shift our limbs and cling to one another as we both attempt to stand while simultaneously helping the other. It's like a chaotic, no-holds-barred game of two-person Twister. While I don't know how old I am, I was certainly an adult when I arrived, so neither of us is in our twenties any longer, and springing up from the floor isn't what it used to be.

Hand in hand, we make our way to the blankets Jayce has laid out and settle back to the floor with small groans that leave us smiling into one another's eyes at the shared experience of being in our thirties. I stretch out on my side, head propped up in one hand, while Jayce relaxes cross-legged on the other side of the board.

I grin as I pop a piece of cheese into my mouth.

"That's your favorite, right?"

It's not like the small supermarket that sells cheap work boots and often expired Twinkies is the epitome of gourmet grocery shopping, so as there are a few types of cheese laid out, I'd just assumed he'd basically picked up one of everything that wasn't generic mozzarella or mild cheddar.

My hand freezes, hovering above the board as I reach for a grape.

"You remember that? You were so lost that day that you couldn't even pick out your own cheese, but you noticed what I chose for you?"

He beams with pride.

"I guess some part of me knew even then how special you are."

My hand moves to nervously slick my hair back, and I can feel my pale skin blushing.

"Jesus, Jayce. Warn a guy before you say things like that."

He bends forward, picking up the grape I'd been reaching for, and leans over to slip it into my mouth.

"This is your warning that I'm going to say as many things like that as possible for as long as you'll have me."

The shiver that runs through me is visible as I wrap my hand around his wrist, holding him briefly in place so that I can kiss his fingertips.

"I plan to have you for a very long time."

When I release his wrist, a quiet sigh escapes him as he settles back into a seat, and I can't help but smile in pleasure at the fact that he seems as enamored with me as I've been with him for so long.

It's romantic and comfortable and easy with Jayce as we pick at the food he's laid out and talk about nothing the way we usually do when we're together. The fact that neither of us can stop watching the other and the waves of love and lust that course through us and fill the room are new, but I'm thankful to find that these thrilling additions haven't affected the easy contentment we've found in one another's company over the past few months.

We sit and eat and laugh for hours before we're interrupted by the storm raging outside. The glass windows that make up the shop's façade rattle loudly enough that we can hear them from the mechanic's bay, and both our gazes shift to the front of the building even though the closed blinds prevent us from seeing into the waiting area.

I grin over at Jayce with as much lust-fueled playfulness as I can manage. "What do you say we head back to my cabin in case the storm ends up bad enough that we're snowed in somewhere for a while? We can use

it as an excuse to stay in bed together all day tomorrow.”
It’s not likely that we’ll get that much snow in September,
but I want Jayce to come home with me.

Jayce’s sharp intake of breath is loud enough that
it seems to echo around the bay. His lips part as if he’s
going to respond, but all he manages is a nod.

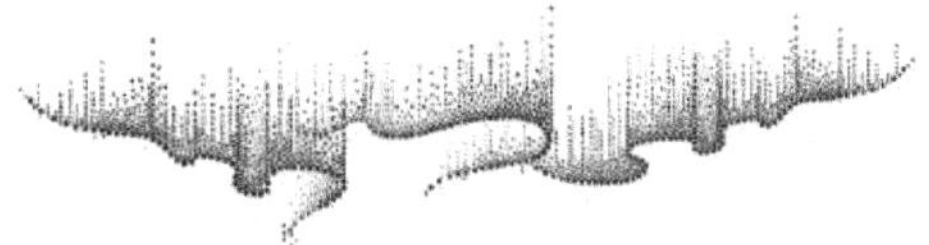

I’m nervous, standing in front of Jayce. There is so much
to feel in this moment. So much emotion flowing wild and
untamed - his and my own - combining and swirling
around us. Jayce has already offered me so much, even
though it’s only been one day. So much bright, explosive
love that I never thought I’d get the chance to experience.
I don’t want to feel it turn into fear. I don’t want it to slip
away.

I need to tell him before he sees.

“The way I feel...it’s not the only way I’m
different.”

His smile is tender and loving as he stands in
front of me. His pale-green eyes sparkle in the flickering
firelight, drawing me in and holding my gaze. They glow
blazing and bright and all-consuming in the best of ways,
and the love that wraps around me feels like a supernova
exploding inside my chest.

“I don’t care how different you are.”

His voice rolls down my spine, warm breath
passing over my neck as he steps closer, and his
fingertips find the tender skin of my belly under my

sweater. I'm trembling and struggling to remember to breathe as flames leap across my skin where he's touching me.

"Can I?" His fingers curl around the bottom of the fabric that separates us.

I can only nod.

He steps back, pulling the shirt over my head and dropping it to the floor.

I shift my fingertips to his waist. I want to know what he feels when he sees me.

He reaches out to trace the patterns that I know are dancing across my skin in ways they never have before. I've watched them in the mirror as I've thought about him. I've seen the way the black is nearly overtaken by the bright swirls of color when I remember what it's like to touch him and the way he smiles at me, colors that look like those I've only ever seen in the winter sky. The tender brush of his fingers leaves my skin tingling in their wake, and the sensation drifts across my skin, sinking its way into my bones and my heart and my soul.

"What is it?"

He's not filled with fear or confusion or anxiety over the fact that he's never seen something like this before, over the fact that it doesn't seem...human. His voice is filled with wonder and awe and reverence, and the love that burns so bright and gold between us radiates out from his skin until it encompasses me completely.

"I don't know. The hospital assumed it was an elaborate tattoo."

For years after I was found, the intricate patterning that covers the skin of my chest and stomach and back in a way that looks almost like smoke was pure black. The tendrils reach and twist, covering the majority of my skin while still leaving patternless, organic sections pale and untouched. The first time I saw it shift was the first time I experienced the emotion of another so strongly that I'd been unable to hold it at bay. I'd sat in the shower and cried as I attempted to wash away the grief I felt that wasn't my own, and when I'd stepped in front of the mirror, the black seemed to shift, darkening in some areas, blinking brightly in others as if tiny stars glowed behind my skin.

"It's the most beautiful thing I've ever seen. You're the most beautiful thing I've ever seen."

He's looking at me as if I matter, as if he can't get enough.

His words swirl and embrace me, and then his lips are on mine. They're dry and cracked and so gentle as they play against mine. His palm is pressed to my chest, and I know he can feel the rushing raggedness of my heartbeat as his tongue brushes the seam of my lips and asks for entry.

He is everywhere. His hand slides down my skin until it's resting on my belly. Fingers trace along my chest as lips move across my jaw, and his chin is pressing my head back, exposing my throat to the tip of his tongue. It lingers there, licking and tasting and trailing downward. His mouth pauses against my collarbone, and he's sucking, pulling the blood to the surface of my skin until it burns before moving lower, down the center of my chest, tracing along the edges where black markings meet white skin.

My fingers tangle in his hair as I arch into his touch. I'm clutching him against me as his lips burn across my skin, and then he's on his knees with my hips in his hands and his tongue dipping into my navel. I'm panting and dizzy and hard, so hard, as he drags the back of his knuckles across the denim covering my cock as it strains toward his touch. His lips lift from my skin, and his head tilts back, and he's staring up at me as his tongue flicks into my belly button once more. The breath punches out of my lungs as my body trembles, and I clutch at his hair as if it might anchor me to the world.

"Is this okay?"

"Please."

It's all I want. He is all I want.

His fingers fly over the buttons on my jeans, and then I'm naked in front of him, and his tongue finds its way back to my skin. I want to watch him. I want to watch this beautiful man kneeling in front of me, touching me and tasting me as if he'll never get enough, but my head falls back, and my fingers tangle in his hair as he sucks his way across my hip and down my thigh and into the bend where my leg meets my torso and there is nothing else. Nothing but Jayce.

I'm trembling when he finally stands and settles his lips tenderly against mine. I want more. More of his touch and his taste and more and more and more. My hands drag his shirt off, and I'm pawing at his belt as we stumble toward my bed. My knees hit the mattress, and I fall back, my legs spreading around him as if he belongs between them with his body pressed against mine.

My arms wrap around his ribs as I pull him closer. His cock grinds against mine, hot and solid as my hips thrust against his, needing to feel him, needing him to feel me. He's luminous and brilliant, and I don't know which feelings are mine and which are his because they're so strong and so identical and so blindingly bright.

His face is buried against my throat, and he's whispering as I arch and whimper and shudder against him. He's whispering curses and praise and my name, and I'm panting and gasping for air that smells like cinnamon and sweat. His jaw is rough against my own, his beard scratching and burning the tender flesh of my neck.

Then he's moving.

He's moving, and his body is sliding along mine. He's strong and muscled and so much bigger than me, and the fur on his chest and stomach glides across my skin, somehow rough and silken at the same time.

My head falls back, and my fingertips clutch at his shoulders, nails digging into his skin. His name falls from my lips again and again, and he's making love to me, and it feels like nothing I've ever known. My heel digs into the back of his thigh as our cocks slide together, slick and tight between our bellies. His panted breaths against my shoulder are hot and loud, and he's the only thing I can hear. He's the only thing that exists.

He shifts his weight onto one forearm so that he can clutch at my thigh, his fingers rough and strong and bruising as he pulls me closer while we rock together. My body curls around him, and he's clinging to me as if he's afraid I might disappear, and there is only this. Only him. Only the feel of his skin and the scratch of his beard and his cock thrusting slick and hot against mine until I'm on fire and shuddering and crying his name into the darkness.

His teeth catch on the side of my neck with a gasp, and he's trembling in my arms as heat spreads between our bellies.

I'm falling.

I'm falling over the edge of a cliff, but he's holding me tightly, and I'm safe, and I'm loved, and he is ecstasy. He is everything I didn't know I ever wanted.

Jayce

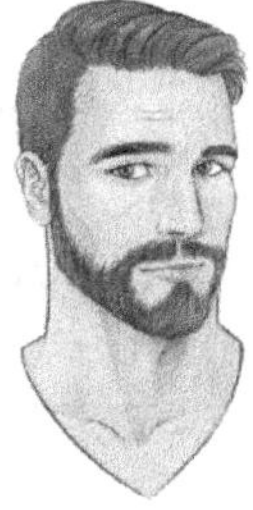

Namid is lying in my arms. We've shifted, and he's curled up against my side with his arm across my chest. My hand covers his tightly, and my head is turned so that my lips can rest in his hair, the scent of grapefruit shampoo and salt-covered skin and sex filling my senses. I didn't know it could feel like this. Nothing has ever felt like this. If I shift my gaze, I can see the dark patterns on his skin. They are calmer now, bright glistening points of starlight swirling through indigo and black. I don't know what it means, or what it is, or even who he is, but I don't care. Nothing matters except the way I feel in his arms. He is perfect, and he is mine.

I let my fingertips travel across the skin of his back, learning his curves and planes and harsh lines by touch. He's lean and muscular in a way that contrasts my bulk perfectly. The room has cooled around us, and his skin is so warm, and I'm so comfortable and so complete here in his arms. It feels as if we were meant to be like this, like we were made for one another.

"You know."

He shifts closer as I begin to speak.

"The last time I took the time to look at the sky, I mean to really look, before that night on your porch was when I was seventeen."

His hand tightens in mine, encouraging me to continue.

"It was only late April, but somehow, that night was warm enough to lie outside the way Jordyn and I did sometimes. There were so many stars, and even though it was late spring, the Aurora swirled in front of them and the glow lit up the world and held the darkness at bay. The sky wasn't black that night; it was indigo. It was the color of your eyes."

Namid shifts in my arms, moving to prop his head up in his hand, his elbow on the bed beside my chest. His eyes are soft and open and they hold the entirety of the universe as he watches me. He is my universe.

"Jordyn was out with his first serious girlfriend, and I was alone. I was happy for him, truly happy. He was so excited, and I wanted that for him. I wanted him to find love and happiness. He knew I was gay. So did my parents. I'd sat them all down and told them when I was fifteen. I knew I might lose them, a lot of people do, but they smiled and hugged me and told me they'd always love me. They told me later that they knew it would be harder for me here. Harder than it would be for Jordyn, harder for me to find someone, but I only half understood at the time. When I lie there that night, alone beneath the indigo sky, I knew that I'd always be alone."

Namid's eyes are still watching me; they're tracing the lines of my face, and the softest smile rests on his lips because he knows that I'm not alone now. He's found me.

"There are legends you know, about the Aurora. The Cree believe that it's the spirits of loved ones trying to communicate with those here on Earth. Some Labrador Inuit feel the same. They say it's the spirits lighting torches so that those who pass on can find their way home. They say that the whistling noises that sometimes accompany the Aurora are the voices of the spirits trying to communicate with the people of the earth."

Namid pulls his hand from under mine, and his fingertips trace along my jaw as I talk.

"That night, I asked the stars to bring me someone to love."

My eyes burn as he leans in and brushes his lips across mine, and when he finally pulls back, I lose my battle, and the tears slip down my temples.

His voice is a gentle whisper against my skin.

"Maybe that's why I have no memories. Maybe Ken was right. Maybe I fell the night I was found."

"Do you believe that?"

His brows furrow as he thinks for a moment before he responds.

"I don't know."

His lips brush my cheek, and he's smiling now.

"But I like it. I like the idea that I was meant to find you."

Chapter 14

The past six weeks have been surreal.

As far as anyone else is concerned, nothing has changed. Jayce is still who he's always been - one of the town's golden boys. A man who quietly lives his life, keeps to himself, and helps the community. I'm still who I've always been - a vaguely acceptable outcast who Jayce has recently taken pity on by employing me a couple of days a month. Jayce and I still meet at the shop every other Saturday for an hour or so while I work through his books, and every Saturday, we wander outside with our coffees when the weather is nice, but with winter starting to shorten the days and bring down the temperatures, we've spent more days inside than out.

In reality, the whole world has changed. Jayce and I are inseparable. On the days it's too stormy to walk through the park with our coffees, we no longer eat brunch at the shop. Instead, the one of us whose turn it is to buy picks up pastries and drives to the other's house. We make coffee at home and curl up on the sofa together, licking stray sugar from one another's lips.

I still have dinner with Ken a few nights a week, but now, Jayce joins us. He's fit with us from the moment he came to help us clear out the old cabinets, and these days, the three of us feel like a family. We cook together, laughing and talking about how our days went, sharing movies we love, and debating about the appropriateness of pineapple or mushrooms belonging on pizza. Jayce and Ken talk about football while I sit quietly and listen to their words and soak up the warmth of their emotions. I had no idea life could feel this way. Jayce still misses Jordyn, and Ken still misses his wife, Katherine. There are moments when the darkness of grief swims to the surface, and they have to fight to push it back, but it's mostly a soft, quiet thing that lives in the background of their souls. They are both lighter than I've ever known them to be.

Jayce and I spend most nights curled up in each other's arms, and on the rare occasion we sleep in our own separate houses, I miss him. I miss his smile and his eyes and his strong body pressed against mine. I know he misses me too. When he sees me for the first time after we've spent the night apart, I'm in his arms before I even realize he's closed the distance between us. His palms run the length of my spine while he grins and kisses me like he's just opened a gift on Christmas morning.

Every night we spend together surprises me. Each one is unique. Neither of us has ever had a real relationship before, and while neither of us is sexually inexperienced, we've only ever had quick fucks to dull the need. We don't want it to be like that when we're together. I don't think it ever could be, but we've been intentionally taking the time to experience every single thing together. We touch and taste and slide bare skin against bare skin, learning how to take the other apart and put them back together with fingers and tongues and words. Every time we're together, we learn something new. Some new secret spot on the other's body that's erogenous or ticklish. A slightly different, strangled moan as a head falls back. The sound of my name whispered in a rough, gravelly voice, choked off in a way I've never heard it before. Stars and supernovas explode around us each time we fall into pleasure-filled oblivion together. There is still so much more to learn. So many things to try. So much time to be together.

I've learned a lot about Jayce over the past six weeks outside of our beds as well. There are times when he laughs and jokes and rambles about nothing for hours, and I imagine it's how he was in his youth, before life brought him so much loss. He's witty and quick to tease me with dirty jokes and sexual innuendos and a smile so wide that it causes small wrinkles to appear beside his eyes. He's passionate and romantic, and anytime we're together, he's always brushing his fingers across mine or slipping his hand onto my back. There are times when he's quiet for long periods, but it's never awkward. It's filled with peace and gratitude, and we're both content to enjoy all of the small things life has to offer together.

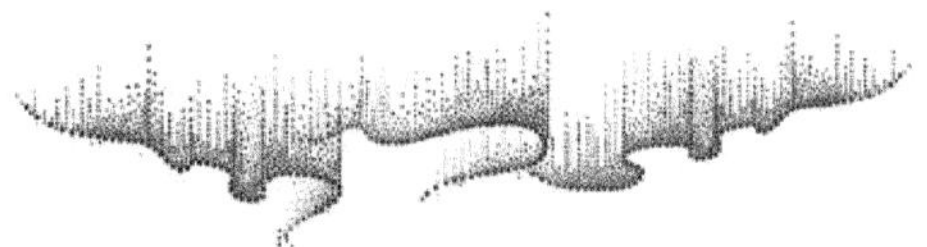

It's quiet as Jayce and I sit curled up on my small sofa, watching the flames dance in the fireplace. There is a storm raging outside my cabin, and we can hear the wind whispering even through the thick walls, but there's nowhere else I'd rather be.

Jayce is thinking right now, not about anything bad, and it's not like I can read his mind, but he feels contemplative. I don't ask. I know he'll talk when he's ready.

"You know that gallery in Seattle that sold a couple of my pieces a few years ago?"

"Mmhm." I'm engaged, of course, but I'm comfortable and lazy as I curl tighter into his side and mumble my response.

"They've been on me for a while now to get them some more pieces, but I haven't been ready to let any of my work go. I think I'd like to now though."

"I think that's wonderful if that's what you want."

"It is. I have to disassemble them and drive them down to Seattle. It's a long road trip and not nearly as fun in the truck as it is on the bikes. It's like forty hours of driving each way, but if you're open to it, I'd like you to come with me."

Shock rolls through me, and I shift back to search his gaze.

"Seriously?"

His fingertips trace my jawline as he smiles. I can feel that he's worried. Maybe he thinks I'll say no or that he's overstepped by asking.

"That seems like such a personal thing. You really want me with you?"

His laugh is warm and deep as it vibrates across my skin.

"It is really personal. That's exactly why I want you with me."

Oh. *Oh.*

I can't help the rush of pleasure and desire and warmth that rushes through me. The way he loves me and accepts me and wants me by his side, the way he's let me into his life and his soul will never cease to amaze me.

"I'd be honored."

Our lips meet tenderly in an unhurried kiss as we curl tighter together. His body is perfect, a striking combination of softness and strength, and being in his arms feels like home.

"The weather is supposed to be good next week, no big storms. I'd like to go before winter really hits and I have to wait for spring. Would that work for you?" he mumbles into my hair.

"I'll go anywhere with you. Anytime you ask."

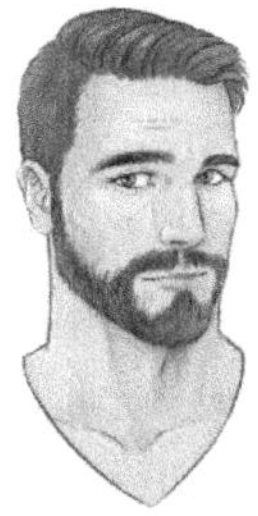

I didn't know life could be this way. Namid and I spend nearly all of our free time together. We spend nights in one another's homes, where we cook and eat and laugh and fall naked into bed to explore and touch and tease. We still have coffee and pastries together every Saturday. We have dinner with Ken and talk about football, and it feels comfortable and familiar. It feels like I've found a family.

We've spent all day in my studio together, painstakingly disassembling four midsize sculptures, wrapping and labeling each piece, and Tetris-ing them into the bed of my truck. They're not really meant to be taken apart, and I had to cut a few of the original arc-welded seams in order to make it work. If I ever do this again, I'm going to make the gallery pay for some shipping containers and a long-haul truck. This time, I don't mind. Even though I'm emotionally ready to let go of some of the pieces that feel like grief to me, this trip is more about spending some time with Namid away from the constraints of our small town.

Namid has treated each piece like delicate, important things made of glass. There's no way for anyone to accidentally bend or break them without the aid of power tools or welding equipment, but watching the way he cares for them because I'm the one who made them has been heartwarming.

We're exhausted by the time we shower and crawl into bed, but the excitement about starting this new adventure tomorrow is still thrumming through our veins. Namid seems in no more hurry than I am to fall asleep as he climbs into bed, where I lie on my back, crawling up to straddle my hips. His skin is still hot from the shower, and small drops of water fall from his hair to land on my chest and cheeks as he leans forward, kissing me and rolling his hips down against my belly.

I watch him move, naked and brilliant, with his jet-black hair and indigo eyes and galaxies swirling across his skin. He is magic and passion and possibility. He is the very embodiment of the universe. He is everything.

Namid once told me that the night sky doesn't always look black to him. He said the lights from so many stars help the sky hold on to the slightest bit of blue, almost like they're protecting it until morning. It's the color of my dreams and of Namid's eyes. He may wear the stars on his skin, but his eyes are the indigo they rest upon. That blue is a color that now fills my world.

He's kissing his way down my chest and belly, his tongue flicking out across my skin as he moves, pausing from time to time to suck blood to the surface of my skin until it prickles and burns and my hands tighten in his hair and on his shoulders. I'm hard and leaking against my stomach as he sucks his way along the underside of my shaft nearly as relentlessly as he sucked bruises into my skin on his journey down my body, and I can't help the way my hips buck and my back arches up toward him, needing even more of his hands and his breath and his mouth.

He moves lower still, suckling along my inner thigh as he presses my legs open further, his fingertips exploring places he's never before ventured. He brushes them delicately down my other thigh, moving from my knee toward my body, pausing where my leg meets my torso, his fingers tapping lightly for a moment before tracing one single fingertip across the inner curve of my ass cheek.

"Don't stop." My whisper rushes out with a gasping exhale.

"I was wondering if..." His voice rumbles against my skin when he speaks.

"Yes. God, yes. Please. I've wanted this for so long."

I've dreamed of this, of his long, lithe body kneeling over me, in front of me, behind me. Of letting go as he turns me inside out, as his body slides into the heat of my own.

His lips tremble as he kisses my inner thigh once more, a single fingertip stroking across my opening with slow, strong circles. I throw my head back and moan his name as his teeth drag along sensitive skin that's rarely been touched.

"Please. God. Fuck. Namid. More." I'm rambling now, almost incoherently, as his fingertip presses harder.

He pulls away, and the absence of his warmth is staggering. It takes me a moment to realize he's leaning up and over the side of the bed to retrieve something from my nightstand. He settles back between my knees with a bottle of lube, quickly popping the top and slicking his fingers.

I find my gaze locked onto his chest and belly as he kneels between my legs, lost in the brilliant swirls and starlight that dance across the inky expanse that's etched into his skin. It moves like a part of his soul is on display, and it responds to me like his body does, like his heart does.

When I finally tear my gaze away, indigo eyes are smiling at me.

"Everything okay?" he asks as he leans forward and flicks his tongue along the underside of my shaft.

My body twitches so hard it must have looked like a small seizure.

"Everything is perfect."

His slick fingertips press against me, and my hands are searching, clutching at the sheets, at anything I can reach. My legs tremble so hard they're nearly vibrating as I spread them further, offering him access in a way I've never offered it to anyone before. He presses forward, a single slick finger sliding deep into me with one smooth move. I fight to keep my eyes open and my head from falling back so that I can watch the way his shoulders flex and his black hair falls across his forehead as he leans forward, watching his finger slip in and out of my body.

This isn't my first time. I've been touched like this before, but it's never felt like this. It's never felt like I need less and more at the same time. Like this singular point of contact is enough to make me explode while still leaving me begging for him to keep going. He slips another finger inside of me, twisting, spreading, opening me. *Fuck.* I'm whimpering and groaning and grinding down against his hand.

His fingers curl toward my belly, making me jolt and cry out his name as the stream continuously leaking from my cock rolls toward my hip. He strokes in and out, fingers curling and pressing and stretching me wide. He adds a third, and I've forgotten how to breathe. Gasping inhales and sharp shuddering exhales and the sound of his slick fingers fill the room, and I'm on fire. Lightning sizzles through my belly. I don't think I've ever been this hard, and I can feel my cock pulse with each racing heartbeat.

I lean up, my hand reaching down to join his.

I'm holding his wrist so tightly I'm afraid I'm going to hurt him as I pant and focus on my breath. He tries to pull away, and I force my eyes open only to find his close, so close. He's leaning over me; his eyes are wide, and something bordering concern is etched into the lines of his forehead. He tries to pull his hand away once more. He thinks he's hurting me.

"No. It's not..." I shake my head.

"I'm too close. I don't want this to be over yet."

His fingers relax inside my body, and a smile as bright as the sun spreads across his face as he leans in to brush his lips across mine. They're so warm and so soft, and I never want them to leave my skin. I want him touching me always, kissing me always.

My eyes fall closed, and I breathe. I breathe in his scent, the sharp citrus of his shampoo, and the pine and earth that always seem to cling to him from all the time he spends in the woods, even when it's far too cold for a rational person to be outside. My body slowly calms, and my fingers loosen their grip on his wrist.

When he moves again, it's with his body still curled up over mine, both of our arms reaching down between my legs. His fingers move slowly now. They're not pulling out and pushing in; he keeps them buried deep, his fingertips gently exploring and circling. It's like he's memorizing every slick curve and ridge inside of me. It's hard to breathe, and I'm clutching at his wrist and squirming and trembling, and I've never known something like this, something so powerful and intimate and all-encompassing.

I can't catch my breath, and I'm panting and clinging to him. It's so perfect, and he's so close, and a part of me wants to come like this, with his fingertips gently pulling me undone, but I want more. I tighten my hand around his wrist again, and he lets me guide his hand away.

He lifts his head from my shoulder, his eyes never leaving mine as I lie back. I'm still trembling as he shifts to kneel once more, his hands pressing against my thighs, spreading my legs further. Slick fingertips trail along my skin, up to my knees, and I might shatter into pieces before he's even inside of me. He runs his hand along his length, his body shivering at his own touch.

Then he's touching me once more, long fingers clutching my hips as indigo eyes search my soul and then pressure, gentle and slow. A sharp sting as I stretch around him. Then there is nothing else. The heat of him inside me, the grip of his fingers on my skin, his lips on the inside of my knee.

The slick skin he's been stroking is so sensitive that my back arches, and I cry out as he settles his body into mine. He's inside of me, hot and hard, and I've never felt so full as he inches forward. I can feel everything, every movement, every pulse of his cock inside my ass and twitch of his fingers against my hips. I'm writhing against him, desperate for more. I'm coming undone.

Namid's eyes are wide, the deep blue barely visible around his black, blown-out pupils, and he's looking at me like I'm everything, like I'm his entire world. He pulls back, nearly slipping from me before thrusting back in, slow and deep. I'm trembling so hard I might shatter, and I barely hold on for two strokes before I lean up and pull him down to me, the weight of his body pushing my legs up to my chest.

Our foreheads press together and we share breaths as he thrusts, long and slow.

I clutch at him, needing him closer, deeper. Needing him to become a part of me, to merge his body with mine in a way that can never be undone. My calves tighten against his biceps, leveraging myself as my hips lose control, thrusting, grinding, straining up to meet his movements. We're desperate, rocking together, lost in need and heat and ecstasy.

His lips tremble as they cover mine, his breath coming in harsh bursts, and I know he feels what I feel. This is different, so different than it's ever been. There is only him, only us. The pressure is building deep inside of me, so hot and all-consuming, and I can't stop it. I don't want to even try. Namid's eyes lock onto mine. His shoulders are tense, and his hands curl into the sheets beside my head, and then he's falling over the edge, screaming my name as his forehead drops to my shoulder and his body shudders against me. His thrusts are hard and slick and hot. I've never let anyone come inside of me before. I've never felt the rush of heat and the way his cock barely seems to touch me for a moment as his release floods into me, separating our skin for the briefest of moments until his thrusts force it deeper. I cling to him, whimpering his name as my body tenses and shudders as I follow him over the edge.

Chapter 15

Namid

I brought my suitcase with me yesterday morning when I came to help Jayce disassemble and pack his sculptures, and even though he'd semi-convinced me that it would be a good plan to get on the road by nine, when I woke with him curled up naked and warm against me and sleepily whined that I was still tired after last night's activities, it was enough to convince him that we should sleep in a bit longer. By the time we rolled out of bed, showered, and got the cooler and suitcases in the back seat, it was close to eleven.

It turns out that no matter how enjoyable your company is, driving for ten hours straight is *brutal*, and by the time we pull into the motel parking lot somewhere in Canada, I'm a firm believer in two things. First, truck drivers need far more credit. Second, this is probably what it feels like to do drugs.

Despite having limited my junk food intake to only three small packs of chips and one set of Reese's in addition to the healthy sandwiches and juice that we'd packed for lunch, I'm somehow both starving and nauseous. I also feel like I'm climbing out of my skin and ready to challenge random strangers to race me around the parking lot, yet also like I'm as exhausted as I would be after running a marathon.

The three-day drive down and three-day drive back up just might have killed me if we hadn't decided to spend a week in Seattle. Jayce usually takes two weeks off to make the trip on his bike every year, and I've never been on a vacation. There was no way either of us wanted to simply drop his work off at the gallery and head back.

We check into the small, strip-style motel and shower before settling in to eat another set of sandwiches for dinner. We're still in the middle of nowhere, and aside from the gas station–McDonald's combo at the freeway exit and a taco stand trailer that looks like a fifty-fifty shot at getting murdered or food poisoning, the motel is the only thing around. I'm grateful, as even the emotions coming from the couple in the room next to us are grating on my nerves after today's drive.

Even though there have only been a handful of nights together where we haven't spent at least a little time exploring one another before drifting off, tonight, I just need to curl up in Jayce's arms. Somehow, he seems to know even before I say anything, and after he strips and climbs under the sheets, he lifts the covers and gestures for me to crawl in against his side, immediately pulling me into his arms and tucking me in like a little spoon against his chest.

"I tried to pick places that are out of the way. Are you going to be okay here tonight?"

My fingers tighten around his forearm as I turn my head to kiss his bicep.

"The people next door are fighting, but they're far enough away that I'll be able to block them out with a bit of work, and then I'll sleep just fine. In truth, I'm much better at managing other people's feelings when you're around. Yours tend to overpower them for the most part."

A chuckle vibrates through his chest and across my back.

"Do you need me to, like...think sexy things or something?"

I can't help but laugh and snuggle in tighter in response. "Somehow, I don't really think that would help me fall asleep."

"Well, I'm willing to take one for the team if you need me to."

"Very generous of you, but I'm sure I'll be asleep in just a few minutes." I brush my lips across his arm once more and close my eyes as he hugs me tightly.

The next two days are nearly identical. We take turns driving, munch down sandwiches and snacks, stop at gas stations to pee and reload our coffees in order to ensure we'll stay awake and need to pee again in a couple of hours, and spend the nights curled up in cheap motels. By the time we hit the freeway signs that announce Seattle's exits are coming up in about fifty miles, I'm definitely ready to spend some time away from the truck, even if it is in a crowded city.

I've never been to a city larger than Anchorage. I've seen plenty of cities online and in movies, of course, but somehow, nothing prepared me for just how unique Seattle seems to be. As the freeway swoops high and circles around, I can see skyscrapers and tall luxury condo complexes crowded together in a sea of shimmering glass and harsh cement that extends for miles. I'd expected that. What I hadn't expected was just how much nature seems to have found a way to harmonize with the harsh, man-made structures and materials. One entire side of the downtown metropolis is bordered by the Puget Sound. Docks and piers covered with restaurants and small shops notch up against tall glass office buildings. Sailboats and large shipping vessels loaded high with steel containers float across the gentle waves to tie up at the water's edge. The city itself is filled with green. There are parks with trees and rooftop gardens, bright flower patches, and vines climbing down balconies and concrete walls. Freeway overpasses are covered with wild blackberries, and the road's shoulders are filled with Scotchbroom and ivy and laurel. The road itself, though eight lanes wide, seems to have been carved straight through a forest, and pines and redwoods tower over us on the side of the road that doesn't face directly into the city center.

"Hey." Jayce's hand squeezes mine, pulling me from my revelry.

"You okay?"

"Of course, why?"

He looks at me for longer than he probably should, considering he's the one driving at the moment.

"I said your name twice."

Embarrassed laughter escapes before I can stop it. "Sorry. I've just never seen anything like this before."

The lines around his eyes soften, and he squeezes my hand once more.

"It's beautiful, isn't it?"

"It really is. I'm surprised how much I like the look of it."

Concern fills his gaze once again. "Are you going to be okay here? I mean, this is a huge city. Is it going to be too much for you?"

I can feel my brows furrow even though I try to keep my expression neutral. "I think I'll be okay. I mean, it's not like I can go to a ball game or anything super public like that, but as long as we just try to do things that aren't overly crowded, maybe the beach or something, I think I'll be able to handle it just fine. I've always been able to manage a few nights a year at the bar."

He nearly growls, "Looking for strange men."

My laughter bursts out loudly, echoing in the truck's small cab. "Not usually. Besides, you used to do the same thing. Hell, there were probably times when we'd hit on the same dude. It's not like there were a lot of options to choose from."

Jayce just glares and huffs out a jealous snort, and I can't help but laugh at the visible effort it takes for him to pull himself together and change the subject.

"Is that what you want to do while we're here? Beaches? We can do anything you want, so if there are other things on your list…"

"I guess I haven't really given it a lot of thought since it's hard for me to be around a lot of people and all. I want to spend a few days at the beach. I know it's probably going to stay cold and rainy, but I've never really been to a beach, and it's definitely going to be a lot warmer than it is at home most of the time. Maybe we can find someplace to go hiking too? I never realized that this city is just like…plopped down in between the ocean and the forest. Maybe there are small little towns not too far away we can drive to see? And…okay, this one might not work out all that well, but I think I'd really like to try to visit a museum."

Jayce nods as I ramble, his smile lighting up my universe.

"Done. I will make all of that happen."

I hesitate for a moment. "Do you want to know what I want to do more than anything?"

"Of course."

"I want to hold your hand." I feel my cheeks flush at the admission. "It's different here. It's a big city, and one that's LGBTQ+ friendly. I want to walk down the street and through parks and along beaches with your hand in mine so that people know that I'm yours."

He exhales sharply, and for a moment, I wonder if I've said something wrong. He doesn't feel upset with me. He just feels...in love.

"Jesus, Namid. What was it you told me once? Warn a guy before you say things like that."

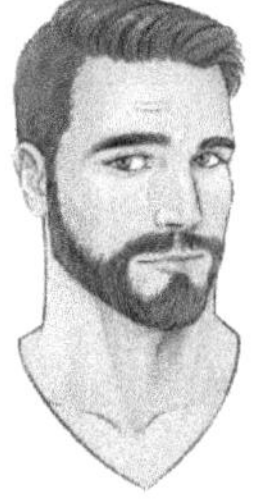

I know that this is going to be hard for Namid, maybe harder than he realizes, so I've tried my best to make arrangements that might help. It's late afternoon by the time we finally finish driving, and I can tell that the past few days have taken a toll. Namid has never traveled like this before.

He raises an eyebrow in my direction as we come to a stop in the half-empty underground parking lot of a fancy downtown condo complex.

"I know that a hotel would probably be hard on you, so I did some research and found this short-term rental for the week instead. It's a top floor, corner apartment, so the only people who might be close enough for you to feel are the older couple who lives across the hall and the single, twenty-something university student directly underneath our place. I checked with the landlord."

Namid surges across the seat to throw his arms around me and crush his lips to mine.

"Thank you." His voice trembles quietly.

"Anything for you, sweetheart."

His lips curl into a smile against mine as he nips at me before pulling away.

It will take all day tomorrow to unload and reassemble the sculptures at the gallery, so I'm just going to have to hope that they're safe enough in the bed of the truck overnight. We did have to punch in a code to get into the garage, so hopefully, none of the building's residents think that hundreds of pounds of steel wrapped in canvas is worth taking.

Although there were a handful of pictures online, I'm still surprised by the spacious beauty of the apartment. It has one large bedroom with a fluffy king bed and a master bathroom with a separate shower and tub - both of which look like they can easily hold two large men - and I'm very much looking forward to getting Namid naked and into each of them at least once on this trip. The living space is an open floor plan kitchen, dining area, and living room complete with cushy sofas, reading chairs next to fully stocked bookshelves, and a gourmet kitchen. The highlight, though, is the window seating. One entire wall of the apartment is composed of floor-to-ceiling picture windows, and running their length is a cushioned leather bench that even extends a few feet in the other direction in the one corner that has windows in the shape of an L.

"Jayce, this place is incredible!"

"Yeah? How is it for you? I mean, can you feel too many people, or are you going to be okay here?"

"It's perfect. The neighbors are home; I can feel all three of them, but barely. With the distance and having you here with me, I hardly even notice them."

"Thank God." I laughingly groan in relief. "I was so worried that this trip would be a bad experience for you because we couldn't stay far enough away from people."

"I don't think it's going to be an issue at all. I don't know how you managed to find this place, but it's better than anything I expected."

I slip my arms around Namid's waist, pulling him close, his lithe body instantly molding to my own larger form. I've only gotten to hold him like this for seven weeks, but he's so perfect for me. Everything about him is so perfect. He already feels like he's meant to be mine, and I want to hold him for the rest of my life.

"It took a long…long time and so…so much effort to find the perfect place," I mumble against his lips. "I definitely think you probably owe me some kind of thank you for all of my hard work."

The laugh that rolls through his chest is deep and smooth, and I tighten my arms around him instinctively. I need to feel that sound again. I need it to vibrate along my skin and settle into my bones until it becomes a part of my soul.

"I suppose that can be arranged." His voice is dripping with innuendo.

"Do you think there is a Hallmark store nearby so that I can buy you a card?"

"Baby, I'm insulted." I growl and nip at his bottom lip. "This place is definitely worth at least a couple of roses."

His lips are already crushed against mine as his whisper crawls over my skin. "A dozen at least."

We only manage to pull ourselves apart once our lips are red and our breath is fast from the thrill of pressing against one another. We unload the food from the coolers and hang our clothes in the closet before deciding that we should take advantage of being in the city and order delivery for supper. We settle on a Thai restaurant; it's something Namid has only tried making for himself a handful of times, and I've only had it once on a road trip. This week together seems like the perfect time for us to explore new things.

We're both tired from the long few days of traveling, and tomorrow is going to be one more exhausting day unloading and reassembling everything at the gallery before we get to relax into vacation mode. Our sleep schedules were so different at the start of our relationship that we've had to work to find a compromise that works for both of us, but tonight, we're both ready to crawl into bed long before our normal one a.m. bedtime. It's barely eleven when we strip, shower together, and slide into one another's arms. Although, in fairness, by the time we drift off, clinging to one another, sticky and sweaty and sated, it's probably close enough to one a.m. to count.

It's the fastest week of my life. After spending our first day in Seattle getting everything set up at the gallery, we have six days before we head home. We start our mornings in the apartment Jayce has rented with coffee and pastries from a different bakery each day. I'm half convinced that I could manage to live in the city if it meant I had access to dozens of bakeries all the time. We spend two days wandering along rocky shorelines, exploring old lighthouses and dark-sand beaches. The weather cooperates with us, and even though it's only in the fifties, the sky is blue and the air is crisp and heavy and filled with the tang of salt and the sharpness of pine.

We wander quietly together, lost in the sound of birdsong and the thrum of the waves. Our fingers linger on backs and arms and intertwine tightly together as we walk, the sand scuffing against our feet for hours and miles. We study the sky and the surf and the ground, contemplating the shape of clouds and playfully arguing over who is able to find the best rock or shell. Only when the light is fading and we've managed to come to an agreement do we slip the day's single treasure into a pocket to take with us. The priceless artifacts will live on our mantles when we return home.

We spend two more days exploring small towns and woodland trails. These days begin with a ferry trip across the Puget Sound to the peninsula. When we're waved onto the ship and directed to park, packed in like sardines with a hundred other cars, I panic at the swirling pile of emotions that seems inescapable with this many people in such a close space. Jayce takes my hand, and I focus on his smile and the tiny lines of concern that frame his eyes. As the huge boat starts to move, most people abandon their cars for the passenger decks, and we're left largely on our own, sitting in Jayce's truck with the rumble of the engines vibrating through us as waves crash against the thick sheet metal sides of the ship just below the passenger side window.

We drive along clean black stretches of road, bracketed by mile-high pines so thick that when I watch the forest as it speeds past, I can't see any further than a few feet into their depths. The sun shines brightly, breaking through their shadows and casting almost blinding rays of light in front of us as we curve and sway, the dense forest breaking from time to time to offer views of large pastures filled with horses and cows and sheep, old red barns, and farmhouses with pickups and camping trailers parked in gravel driveways.

We pull off whenever signs announce an upcoming nature trail and wander slowly, listening to the breeze swirl through the trees and the crunch of soil under our feet. We battle to find the best pinecone to join our small collection. When we pass small seaside towns, we stop to find tiny family-owned bakeries and small out-of-the-way bars with patio dining areas that are largely empty on the chilly November days. The cold, cozy tables are the perfect places for us to pull our chairs close and cuddle together for warmth while we eat something small for the fourth, fifth, or sixth time that day without more people around than I can handle.

One of our days is spent at a fine art museum. I almost change my mind when we pull into the crowded parking lot. I can't imagine there's any way I'll be able to manage the emotions of all the people inside. Jayce slips his hand onto my low back as we purchase our tickets and whispers into my ear that we can leave any time, but we should try before giving up. He's right.

The first room we enter holds a handful of people, all standing close to paintings, staring as if they're looking through windows that can transport them to other times and places. Their emotions rush over me, covering me and dragging me down. They're overpowering. So overpowering that I have to fight the instinct to turn and run. Jayce's hand tightens on my back, his fingers dig into my skin, and I breathe. I step closer, leaning into his shoulder and letting the scent of cinnamon from his morning chai and the oil that lingers even after a week away from the shop wash over me as I work to push the emotions away. It takes a few moments to find my way out, but once I do, I notice something I've never experienced before. The emotions are easy to push away if I try. As immense and overwhelming as they seem at first, they're not floating free in the ether like emotions usually are - they're distant and focused. They're being projected onto the artworks that are causing them to surface. As we step into the next room, it's the same - a handful of strangers with huge emotions - but I'm okay, and they don't need to affect me. It's so easy to push them aside like thin, sparkling party streamers hung from the ceiling, to watch them exist instead of letting them sink under my skin. By the time we move into the third room, the emotions of the audience have become a part of the art for me. When we step up to a new work, the joy or grief or peace that those staring at it feel are as much a part of the paintings as the colors and textures of the brush strokes. We stay until the museum closes. For nearly seven hours we wander, lost in a sea of color and light and emotion that leaves me breathless and filled with wonder.

Each night, we return home to wander the quiet streets as night gently settles over our apartment's small residential neighborhood while the glow of streetlamps, whose rays don't quite reach the ground through the mist, cast a peach glow over the world. We choose a new restaurant each night, taking our food home and eating on the window benches with cardboard and Styrofoam containers spread between us. We make love in the shower and linger in one another's arms in the tub. We kiss and touch and hold and lose ourselves under the sheets of the large bed while the golden city lights shine through the large windows and caress our skin.

I can feel what Jayce feels. I can always feel what my lovers feel, of course - pleasure or pain or lust, but not like this. Nothing has ever been like this. Nothing has ever been like Jayce. I can feel everything as I touch him, as he touches me. I can feel the pleasure coursing through him as we take one another apart, falling into the abyss in one another's arms. I want this forever. I want him forever.

Chapter 16

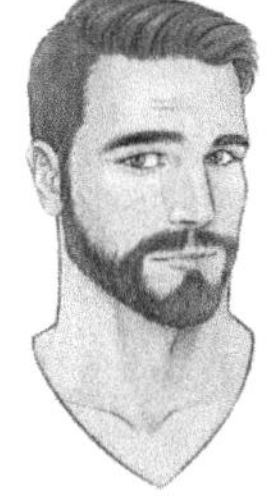

My breath catches in my lungs as I step out of the
bathroom to the vision of Namid pulling a deep-blue V-
neck cashmere sweater over his head. The patterns on
his chest and belly swirl brightly; they always do these
days. He's the most beautiful man I've ever seen, and my
chest aches at the fact I get to call him mine. He smiles
and ghosts his lips across my cheek as he walks past me
and into the bathroom I've just vacated to fix his hair. He
still keeps the sides shaved tight, but the raven-black
tresses on top are longer than they were when we first
met. He usually lets them fall wildly free, and it takes him
a few moments to actively convince them to behave when
he wants them to.

We spent the day lazily wandering around the
neighborhood and lounging in the window seats in one
another's arms as we read books from the condo's large
collection. When I told him I'd made plans for this

evening, we'd both felt like some downtime beforehand would be nice. When he'd asked what we were going to do and I told him it was a surprise, he'd simply grinned and said okay. The way he trusts without reservation that I'll consider his needs, the way he trusts me to care for him, always astonishes me.

I pull on the black jeans that I still think are too tight. I've never owned skinny jeans before, but Namid looks so delicious in them that I ordered a pair online to surprise him when he'd agreed to come on this trip with me. I know he won't take long with his hair, so I hurry as I button the cream and white plaid that Ken told me looked both modern and fancy yet still somehow like me. I'm still working the top button when he steps back into the room.

"Jesus, Jayce." His face lights up as I spin in a slow circle, warmed by the way he's looking at me with enough love and lust that I'm afraid we may not end up leaving the apartment.

"You like?"

He crosses the room as I spin, and his fingers reach out to trail down my chest.

"You look unbelievable." He nearly growls as he raises an eyebrow. "Are you sure we can't just stay here tonight?"

I can't help the laugh that explodes out of me at the fact I'd just been thinking he might say that very thing.

"I'm very, very sure. I put a lot of work into tonight."

"Still a secret?" He cocks his head to the side, his hair staying largely in place as he does.

"Yep." I pop the P for emphasis.

"Let's do it then." While he offers his hand, palm up, an indication that he's ready for us to head out, his leering smile and suggestive tone are clearly meant to hold two meanings.

It's a twenty-minute drive to the Space Needle parking lot, and Namid's clearly growing concerned as we head into the city center and park at one of the busiest tourist attractions in town. I know he trusts me, but I'm sure this doesn't make any sense to him yet.

Our hands link as soon as we're at one another's sides, and I lead him toward the entrance.

"Jayce." He stops us, confusion written across his face.

"I'm taking you to dinner. I've never gotten to take you on a romantic restaurant date the way most folks can."

"Jayce. All of our dates are romantic to me. Every breakfast and coffee we've ever had, our dinners at home together, the first date you ever set up for me at the shop. Hell, even when we walked around the park together when we first met. Our dates were romantic for me before you even realized they were dates."

"I know, beautiful. They are for me too." I lean in to taste his lips tenderly. "But let me do this."

"Jayce, I really want to, but you know restaurants are hard for me."

I kiss him again and again. Small, light pecks that travel from his lips along his cheekbone and forehead.

"You really need to trust me."

His exasperated snort is almost hysterical. I know that he trusts me, and I know that he knows that I know.

I grin at his fake glare and tighten my hand in his as I drag him to the entrance.

A single security guard stands in the empty lobby beside the elevator.

"Good evening, sirs." He nods quickly as he presses the elevator button.

"Good evening," we reply at the same time, my voice chipper and struggling to contain my excitement, Namid's a bit warier.

His voice is laced with suspicion as we ride to the Sky Lounge on the top floor. "Why do I feel like there are only...five people in this entire building?"

For the life of me, I can't rein in my smile. It's probably wide enough that it's borderline creepy at this point.

"Jayce...What did you do?"

I'm saved by the ding as the elevator opens, and an elegant grey-haired man greets us with a kind smile and leads us to a table. We're the only ones here.

The Sky Lounge is one of the most popular and high-end restaurants in the city. It's located at the top of the Space Needle and takes up the entire floor just below the observation deck. It's walled entirely by windows, and they serve five-course, Michelin-star gourmet meals and have an extensive wine collection, in addition to keeping one of the city's hottest bartenders on staff. It can take more than a year to get reservations.

Namid is both trying to glare at me and repress his blinding smile as we settle in at the table and the grey-haired gentleman walks away.

"What did you do?" he repeats, almost laughing through hissed teeth.

I reach across the table, and he lays his palm against mine without hesitation.

"Jordyn saved our whole lives. He never used any of it. He never got the chance. He never found anyone worth spending it on. I never thought I would either. While I'm not some millionaire who can buy out the city's hottest restaurant with two weeks' notice very often, this matters to me. Giving you this matters to me."

The tears that threaten to fall from the corners of his eyes make the indigo sparkle like lapis in the golden sunset light that streams in through the windows surrounding us.

He shakes his head with a long, deliberate, laughing exhale as he squeezes my hand.

"I shall only allow such a ridiculous gesture once a year at most."

"Done."

His eyes are my world as his gaze holds mine across the table, his fingers strong and warm in my hand. I could stare into them until the world stopped spinning, and I'd never even notice that anything around us had changed.

The sound of a throat clearing shakes me from my revelry.

"Champagne, sirs?" a smiling server with wild teal hair and eyebrow piercings asks in an amused tone. His gaze is soft as he watches us, clearly approving of whatever it is he can see flowing between us.

Dinner is long and leisurely, and we laugh and talk and make exaggerated, nearly sexual moans as we move through course after course and finish the bottle of champagne. There are only five people on staff tonight, and Namid tells me that every one of them is radiating joy and happiness. Maybe they're simply happy to have such a relaxed evening with only one table to cook for and serve, but I like to think it's because they can see what Namid and I have together. I like to think that they can see how in love we are and that they find joy in that. I've spent my whole life hiding who I am, so afraid that I'd never find love. So afraid that no one would accept me for who I am, but Namid accepts all of me. These people here tonight, Max and the other two gallery owners, everyone we've encountered at bakeries and bars on this trip have accepted us together without question. I know that's not really how the world is. I know there are many people who won't like seeing us together, but this week has been a gift, a glimpse of the future we can have together. I never want to let it go, and I know that I'm going to hold onto Namid for the rest of my life.

We barely step foot inside the door before I reach for Jayce's shirt, my fingers battling with the buttons in my haste.

"Need you." I moan against his throat. "Need you inside of me."

His hands join mine as we step further into the apartment together, clothes falling as fast and furious as summer rain along the way. I can't help the hungry whimpering that escapes my throat as I suck my way across his collarbones and down his chest. He walks backward as I guide him around furniture with my hands on his hips, fingers gripping so tightly I'm afraid they'll leave bruises. It doesn't matter; nothing matters but the scent of his skin and the sound of his moans and the way his fingers curl tightly in my hair.

I walk us back until we're in the corner of the room, the one where the window seat forms an L against the glass.

"Here. I want you to take me here," I mumble against his chest before sucking his nipple into my mouth hard enough to draw blood to the surface.

He nearly screams as his hands press against the back of my head, urging me to continue. I take the nub with my teeth, rolling it between them as I increase the pressure until he's panting, harsh, ragged breaths infused with moans and whimpers.

"Fuck."

"Yes."

"God."

He's rambling, and I can feel the slickness already leaking from him against my hip as I step closer and pull my mouth away from the abused, pink skin. It's darker than the other, nearly red with the bruise I've sucked into it.

He looks stunned as I grin at him and trail one fingertip along the underside of his cock.

"Kneel for me while I get the lube." His voice is broken and rough and desperate, and he's already stepping toward the bedroom before I can respond.

I kneel on the long side of the bench, my head facing the corner with my knees and forearms on the cushions. He's back in seconds, settling on the bench behind me, and I can feel the need and lust dripping from him.

His fingertips are tender as they trace long strokes along my spine and follow the edges of the patterns that stretch across my back. The scruff on his chin is rough against my hip and the curves of my ass as his tongue wanders across my skin. He's slow and gentle and deliberate with his touches as one cool, slick finger presses softly inside of me. His lips and tongue never leave my back as he teases, coaxing out whimpers that leave me trembling and wanting more as he draws out my pleasure.

A single finger twists and slides and curls until I'm moaning and straining back, searching for more. It's never felt like this. I've never felt like this. Never needed more and more and more while at the same time, his gentle touch captivates me so completely that I don't want it to ever change.

I welcome the pressure with a shudder as a second finger effortlessly joins the first, and I lose the battle to hold myself up, my chest sinking to the cushion as he twists and spreads inside of me.

"Please."

"I need..."

"God..."

I've lost the ability to speak; only whimpered words and quiet curses fall from my lips.

His fingers slip from me, his voice so deep and harsh I barely recognize it, the waves of desire thick and heavy as they envelop us.

"Kneel up for me."

His arm wraps tightly around my waist, my arm resting along his, fingers laced together tightly enough that our knuckles whiten with the strain. His other hand clutches my hip. I want him in a way I've never wanted another. I've never wanted someone in a way that makes my heart race and my breathing stop. I need more. More of his touch, of his taste, of him.

I turn my head over my shoulder, reaching my free arm back to sink my fingers into his short hair, holding him to me. Our cheeks press together, our panted breaths mingling and fogging up the glass beside us.

His hips shift behind me as he holds me close, and then he's inside of me, a deep pressure working its way up my spine as he eases forward until his hips press against mine. We're both gasping and trembling and clinging desperately to one another. There is nothing else. There is only the touch of his skin and the way he's wrapped around me and the fire deep in my belly that's growing as he begins to rock, pleasure radiating outward from where we're connected until every nerve in my body is vibrating.

His forehead is resting on my shoulder, hot breaths skittering across my skin as his fingers clutch at me, holding me still as he pulls back, his body nearly slipping from mine before thrusting forward with one deep, smooth stroke. Each of his movements drives me higher, closer to him, further from the rest of the world.

I pry my fingers away from his to run my hand along my stomach, ignoring my leaking cock to press my palm hard against my lower belly. I can feel the pressure of him moving inside me against my hand. He shudders in pleasure, and his teeth scrape across my shoulder as I press my fingers harder, pinning him tighter inside of me, and I'm lost in the sensations of his length within me, the warmth and strength of his body behind mine, his fingers clutching my skin, and the way he's moaning against the back of my neck.

I tilt my hips slightly, crying out when sparks of pleasure almost too intense to bear shoot through my pelvis and belly, and I'm shuddering almost violently, spasming and tightening around him as I fall into the darkness.

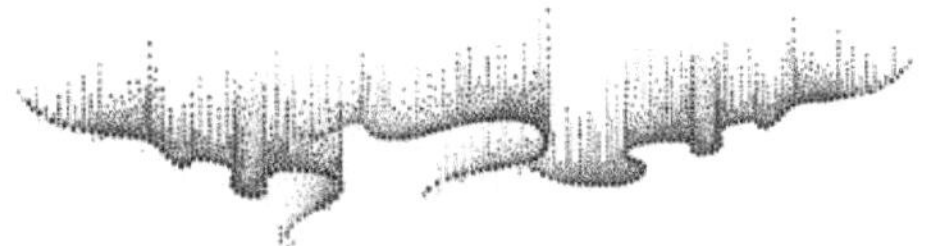

Silken sheets rustle around us as I curl tighter against Jayce's side. His fingers are trailing along my spine, raising goosebumps in their wake. We'd showered together, taking our time with lazy kisses and lingering fingers as we cleaned one another before slipping into bed and curling up tightly. I'm surrounded by warmth and cinnamon, and there is nowhere on earth that I'd rather be.

"Do you know what I thought my life would be like?" Jayce's deep voice is nearly a whisper, and there is a muted pain flowing through him as he starts talking.

"I thought that I would hit a gay club once a year when Jordyn and I took our road trips down here in the summers like we always did. I thought I would be the best man at his wedding. I thought I would be a good uncle..." He chuckles for a moment, but the pain and grief are still there. "Okay, I didn't know if I would be a *good* uncle, but I'd definitely be a fun one."

I wait while he pauses to gather his thoughts, my fingers curling tighter into his auburn chest hair.

"I thought that one day, if I was brave enough one day, that just maybe before I got old enough for it to be really pathetic, I would save up enough money and go on a gay cruise. I thought that maybe if I was really, really lucky, I might meet someone the first night who I clicked with, and then for a few stolen nights, I'd get to find out what it was like to have the same person in my bed more than once."

I shift, lifting my head to rest my chin on the back of my hand against Jayce's chest so that I can stare up into his pale-green eyes. His fingertips rise from where they were resting next to mine on his chest to tuck a stray hair that's lying across my forehead back behind my ear.

"I never once in my wildest dreams thought I would find someone to love who actually loved me back. I want to be yours. Only yours. Always. Everywhere. I want the world to know that we belong together, and I don't care what anyone back home thinks about it. I want to love you every single day of my life without hiding and without reservation."

His emotions swirl around us, mixing with mine, so genuine and happy and full of love, but I can't help the sliver of worry that still lives in the back of my mind after having spent the last decade as an outcast.

"Jayce. I don't think people will make it easy for you. It could affect your business, your friendships…being with me could affect everything you have."

"I'd have you. If you think that for even one minute that I'm ever going to regret you or treat you like you're anything less than the most important thing in my world, you're mistaken."

His eyes are glossy, and his voice cracks as he continues.

"Twice in my life, I've known what it's like to lose someone I love, to know what it's like to lose time I thought I had, to leave words left unsaid. If you'll have me, I've never been more sure of anything in my life."

I slide my body up along his to capture his mouth in a kiss as deep and passionate and loving as anything I've ever offered, anything I've ever known. I want that too. I want a life with him, a full life. I want to live and love together for the rest of our days.

I hover close enough that we share breath as I search his pale eyes with a smile.

"I love you. I never dreamed I'd ever find someone either. I want that. I want a life with you. A life with a small house and a dog and you in my bed every night. I want what we've had this week. If you're truly okay with the town knowing, then so am I."

Jayce's fingers trace along my cheekbone before wandering down my jaw.

"Together then?"

"Together."

Chapter 17

Namid

The three-day trip home is nearly as excruciating as the drive to Seattle was. I'm not meant to sit in a small, confined space for days on end, and I can't decide if knowing what to expect after suffering through the drive down has made the experience better or worse. Jayce and I feel...different...on the way home. Something shifted between us the night before we left, and there is something warm and weightless enveloping us and holding us effortlessly together even outside the cab of his truck. When we stop at gas stations and check into our motels at night, his fingers clasp mine tightly, and our shoulders bump together as we walk. Neither of us cares who sees. Neither of us even thinks about it. We aren't Jayce and Namid any longer. We're *US*.

When we leave the final motel on day three, it's just before dawn, and while I should be excited to watch the sunrise as I've only been awake to see a handful of those in my life, I'm too tired to care. Jayce has two cups of coffee waiting for me by the time I stumble to the truck, but I still don't feel remotely human until well after we stop for lunch. If anyone ever decides to torture me for information, this will be the way they do it. I am not built to survive waking with the dawn, but the early start means that we'll be home in time to have dinner with Ken before settling in for the night.

A lot of folks might find my relationship with Ken a bit odd. After all, not many grown men have dinner with their parents several nights a week. It works for us though. He's not only the closest thing to a father I've ever known, he's also my friend. He's been kind to me from the moment he found me, and for a long time, we've been the only person the other has had. Jayce has never felt like he thinks our relationship is odd; if anything, he's always felt slightly envious. Not in a mean-spirited way, of course. It's just that by the time I met Jayce, he'd already lost all of his family. Ken and I are his family now. We all feel that way, and it warms my soul to know that not only have Jayce and I found one another, he's found a new family with Ken as well. Jayce and I have been so caught up in one another while we've been away that we've only texted Ken a handful of times. But I've missed him, and even though having a family dinner together could easily wait another day, I'm excited for us to spend the evening together like we always do.

The weather has cooperated throughout our journey home, and no storms stand in our way as we drive for hours along the nearly empty, swerving, black asphalt that cuts through the forests for miles and miles. It's late afternoon when the gravel driveway in front of my small cabin finally crunches under the weight of Jayce's truck, but this late in the year, it's already dark. We dump our bags just inside the front door and stumble to the bathroom in a daze. Neither of us is feeling particularly sexual after three days on the road, but after nearly an hour together in my tiny shower, during which we cling and touch and hold one another, we're feeling more like ourselves.

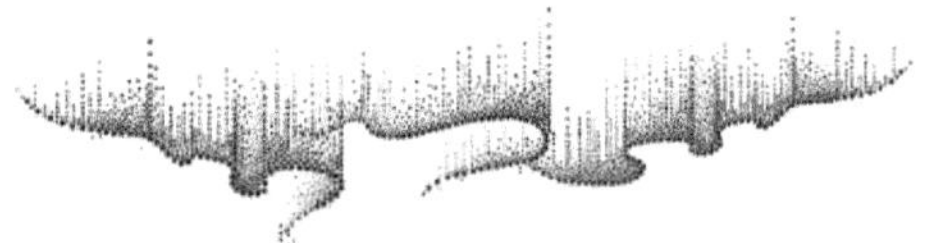

The moment I pull open the front door to Ken's house, we're greeted by the scent of roasting meat and vegetables. It's the same meal he's cooked every Sunday since I came to live with him. It smells like home. Ken rises from his armchair the instant we step inside, moving quickly to pull me into a tight hug. When he lets go of me, he pulls Jayce in and squishes him without a hint of uncertainty or hesitation. Jayce is his family now, too, and I can't help the way my heart melts at the happiness and sense of belonging that floats up from each of us, swirling together to fill the room with soft greens and golds and silvers.

We quickly fall into our normal dinner routine, chatting idly and moving in well-synchronized unison as we fill our plates in the kitchen and settle in around Ken's old, scuffed oak table. Dinner lasts for hours as we regale Ken with stories about our trip, and conversation ebbs and flows easily between the three of us. Somehow, it feels like it's always been the three of us. Jayce fits here - he fits with me. We laugh together as we tell him about the day we nearly got stuck on a sandbar when we didn't notice the tide coming in during one of our beach trips, and when I describe the date Jayce arranged at the Sky Bar, Ken's soul is filled with love and support and longing. The longing takes me by surprise. It's not something I've ever felt from Ken before, and I find myself wondering if the years he's spent without Katherine have been lonelier than I realized.

Ken is amazed as I describe the way I was able to spend the day at a museum. When he unwraps the small painting of a sailboat pulling into the harbor we've brought him from the gallery where Jayce's sculptures now reside, he breaks into tears of joy and gratitude, not over the gift, but rather over the way three men who found themselves alone in the world have managed to form a new, loving family.

"You know, Kat and I went to Seattle once," Ken offers, changing the subject with one last quiet sniff as he carefully settles the painting onto the coffee table in front of the couch.

I'm taken aback when he mentions Katherine. It's not that he hasn't talked about her over the years, but rarely has he shared specific memories. I wonder if it's been too hard for him. Maybe her memories have been precious things that he's hidden away for himself the way I once thought I'd end up holding onto my moments with Jayce before my wildest dreams came true.

"Ethan was only about twelve, so it was a long time ago." He laughs as he gets lost in the memory, but even years after her passing, loss still stains the edges of his happiness.

"It was a good trip though?" Jayce asks.

"It was wonderful. Even though it was a couple of decades ago, I imagine the city wasn't that much different than it is now. In fact, the first time I saw it from the freeway, I remember thinking almost exactly the same thing Namid described. It really is magical the way the entire city seems to almost co-exist with nature in a way."

"Maybe we could all go back sometime? I mean, Jayce usually goes every summer...maybe next year we could all go together...as a family." I know my voice is quiet and tentative as I ask, but I don't want to push Ken or make Jayce feel like I'm trying to somehow replace his memories of his trips with Jordyn.

Loss and love flood the room as Jayce reaches over to take my hand.

"I'd really like that." His voice cracks as he forces out the words, but he means it.

I'm so lost in his gentle, jade eyes and the tender, hopeful smile that tugs at his lips that I'm almost startled when Ken's hand comes to rest on top of our intertwined fingers.

"I would too."

A long, heavy moment passes as we each take comfort in the life we've built together before Ken pulls his hand away and snorts out a laugh.

"I definitely think we should fly. It sounds like Namid may not survive another road trip, and I'm too old for roadside motel beds."

My eyes roll automatically. "You're not old, Ken."

"Well, I'm not young, that's for sure."

"Sixty-seven is not old."

Jayce snickers. "I don't know, Ken. I mean, if you were old, wouldn't you be retired?"

"Who's going to take over here if I retire now? This one?" He gestures to me with a mocking frown, clearly trying to fight the smile that threatens to burst free. "You think he'd be any good at facilitating funerals with that smitten kitten smile on his face he's always wearing these days?"

I nearly choke to death as water makes its way up my nose and tries to drown me when I snort out a laugh while taking a drink. Any witty retorts from either myself or Jayce are lost as I try to cough and laugh simultaneously, which only leads to more snorting. The three of us collapse into laughter for long enough that our sides ache by the time we manage to catch our breath.

While I've dreamed of it nearly every day since Ken found me, not once in my life have I truly believed I would manage to find this sort of happiness.

Chapter 18

Jayce and I don't go out of our way to announce our relationship; there is no one we want to tell. It turns out that, unsurprisingly, two weeks after we return, everyone knows anyway. Early on a Sunday afternoon, Jayce is dusting a kiss across my cheek, and his hand is resting on my arm as we finish our conversation when a customer walks in to drop off their keys. The rush of shock and disgust that floods the reception area is nearly strong enough to knock me over. While the man doesn't say anything to either of us, by the time we head to the grocery store to collect our afternoon pastries, I can feel a change in nearly everyone we encounter.

There are nights during the weeks that follow when Jayce comes home upset or frustrated. On a few occasions, I've pushed him to talk about it, hoping that the knowledge he's not in this alone might help. I think it does in a way, but he's still hurt and surprised by how quickly the people he's known all his life have changed the way they treat him. I don't think anyone has been actively aggressive or insulting. If they have, he hasn't told me. All he'll say is that business is a bit slower than it normally is, and a few folks have been a bit more abrupt with him than usual. I know there's more to it than that, but I don't press him. I know all too well how it feels to be treated differently, and I wish I wasn't the reason people have become less accepting of him. I wish I could take away his pain, but I know that's not really how life works. All I can do is love him and remind him that he's not alone. I'll be by his side for as long as he'll have me, and I'll do everything I can to make sure he knows just how loved he is.

For me, things are a bit more...intense. I try not to let Jayce know how bad it's gotten. People who were already wary of me before now go out of their way to avoid being in my presence for longer than absolutely necessary, and people who have always felt mildly curious are now almost openly inquisitive. There is also a handful of folks whose fear or hatred seems to overwhelm them when I pass by on the street or in the shops. It reminds me of the way the town felt when I first arrived. While I've never been sincerely accepted by many, at least most of the emotion directed my way had become more subdued over the years. I hadn't realized how subtle it had grown until it shifted after the town found out about me and Jayce. It's anything but subtle these days, and while it's not exactly a wonderful way to live, I try not to let it bother me. I'm not ashamed of who I am, of who we are together. I have Jayce by my side, and having him is enough. He'll always be enough.

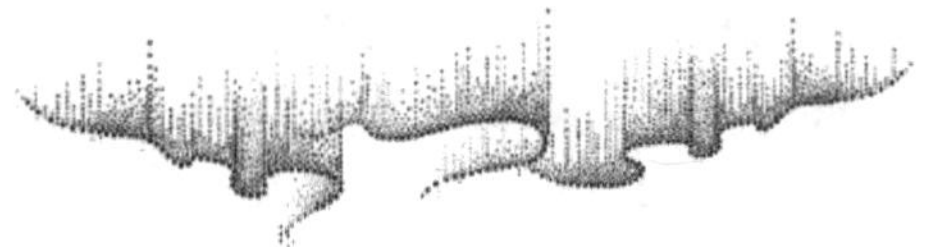

"I'm sorry, hun. I ran into a bit of trouble, and I have another half hour before I finish up here." Jayce's lips brush my cheek briefly as I lean over the engine he's working on.

I've just finished sorting the shop's accounts for the week, even though it's a Thursday night. At this point, as long as there aren't a lot of people coming to pick up or drop off, there's no reason for me not to be at the shop whenever I have the time, and I've taken to spending at least a few hours a week here just to keep Jayce company.

"It's a nice night. Why don't I head over and get the few things we need for dinner? That should take about forty-five if I walk."

"You sure you don't want to take the truck? It's freezing outside!" We came in together a couple of hours ago for Jayce to finish up the alternator job he's still working on.

"Nope. It's a clear night, and it's not really that cold. Besides, it's only four blocks. Pretty sure with all the...exercise...I get these days I can manage to walk a few blocks with a bag or two of groceries." I shoot him a leering glance as I pat his shoulder and turn to head out.

"I'll be finished by the time you're back," he promises as I shoot him a wink while I walk backward through the glass door into the reception area.

It really is a beautiful winter evening. The sky is clear, and the snow piles left by the plow glow with an almost pale jade-green light as the colors from the Aurora and nearly full moon bounce across their surfaces. It reminds me of Jayce's eyes. The quick walk to the grocery store is calm and refreshing, and I savor the way the cold air burns my lungs and stings the tips of my ears. It's a shame that the peace that falls over me during the walk is tainted the moment I step through the shop's sliding doors and feel the way the other shoppers shift from passive, distracted emotions to intense and almost painful ones when they notice my presence. I keep my head down as I grab the few items on our list as quickly as possible, and don't bother looking up when I pass anyone in the aisles. I know all too well that none of them are happy I'm here without having to see their smirks and glares and frowns.

The gentle amusement that approaches me as I slip apples into a bag is unexpected enough that I glance up, surprised to find Shelly bagging lemons nearby with an almost playful grin on her face.

"Guess I won't be seeing you at the bar anymore, huh?"

I can't help the way my lips twitch into something close to a smile. "You know I'm not exactly social as it is. I'm there, what, three times a year max? You'll probably still see me a couple of times a year; I'll just only be after a good drink when I come in."

Her face softens, and something that feels almost wistful drifts from her.

"I'm happy for you guys. Truly. If you ever need anything at all, you let me know, okay?"

I'm stunned enough that it takes me a few breaths to come up with any response at all, and when I finally do, I find myself struggling to keep my voice from cracking. I guess I haven't realized just how isolating it suddenly feels to have everyone hate me again.

"Ya. We will."

Her smile softens even more as she nods once and turns.

"Shelly."

She glances back without hesitation, and I press my hand to my chest.

"Thank you."

Joy. She's happy. She's genuinely happy for me, for *us*.

"Anytime, Namid."

I'm still distracted by my interaction with Shelly as I grab the last few items and check out. I still feel the way those around me stare and wonder and secretly wish I'd just go away, but I'm able to keep their emotions from affecting me. I think I may actually have found a friend.

While it's uncomfortable, I'm getting used to feeling unease and suspicion and hatred from folks in town again. It's a low thrum that never completely disappears unless I'm physically too far away to feel the angry red and black emotions directed my way. Fighting to keep them at bay has become automatic for me anytime I'm in public. Maybe that's why I don't notice until it's too late. Until they're already on top of me.

I'm only a few steps away from the edge of the parking lot, two bags of groceries in one hand as I head back to the shop. I'm lost in my own head, trying to decide what Jayce and I should have for dinner and replaying my unexpected encounter with Shelly when I hear my name.

The man I've never seen before is close, far too close. He's spitting my name like it's a curse as he steps closer still. He's filled with rage and hatred and disgust. I've never felt anything like it before, and it turns my stomach as my knees threaten to buckle. I don't know how he managed to get so close to me feeling like this. How did I not notice?

I tear my gaze from his snarl as a second man, one I've seen in town on a handful of occasions but never actually met, steps out of an old pickup a few feet away. It's not in a parking space. It's stopped at an awkward angle, only half in the parking lot in front of me. The rear tires are resting on the sidewalk, and it's clear they've stopped there deliberately to block my path. The second man feels exactly like the first, an endless wall of anger and loathing.

I turn back the way I came. If I can make it back to the store, maybe I'll be okay. If I can even make it to one of the streetlamps that cast light on small sections of the nearly empty parking lot, maybe someone will see. Maybe someone will help. I've never been in a fight before, and I know that I won't be able to stop whatever these two men have planned for me unless I can get away before anything physical starts.

A hand curls into the back of my shirt before I can take a second step.

"Knew you were trouble the minute you showed up." The low voice drips so thickly with animosity that I can barely make out the words as I struggle to think rather than succumb to panic and crumple to the ground.

"Knew you were just biding your time. I always thought that you were trying to take advantage of Ken somehow, but I never thought that you'd manage to get your hooks into someone like Jayce."

A hand clamps onto my shoulder.

Another grabs my wrist, twisting my arm and pressing me down to my knees on the asphalt. The hand on my wrist twists until a loud snap fills the nearly soundless night.

I can feel everything. Every nerve in my body is on fire, but it's burning in the distance. I'm far away. Detached. I'm no longer made up of the cells that are caught in the flames. I'm merely an observer.

The pavement is clawing its way across my skin where the back of my shredded shirt no longer exists to protect it. The pain in my ribs and arm is sharp and throbbing, and I imagine if I were still connected to my body enough to move, I might feel the shift of broken bones under my skin. The rage and hatred that swirl through the air around me no longer sink into my soul, and the grunts and curses and the scrape of leather on blacktop and the sound of skin connecting with skin start to fade.

The stars are so beautiful overhead. Their light shimmers so brilliant and bright across the universe that they seem to hold back the darkness, and the sky appears deep blue rather than black. Jayce says that blue is the color of my eyes...

Jayce

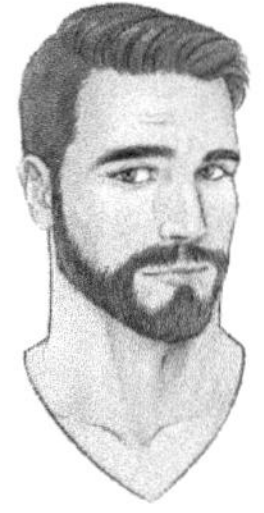

I can't stop the small smile that takes up residence on my face as Namid brushes his lips across mine. I can't stop the way I stare at him as he shrugs on his coat to head out to pick up groceries for dinner. I don't even want to try. These days, I often find myself doing things I've never done before. I find myself watching the way Namid moves, so elegant and fluid no matter what we're doing. I find that the small smile that never seems to leave my face isn't something I can control, not that I'd want to. I find myself excited at the end of each day to go home and spend time with my family before falling asleep in Namid's arms. I'm still adjusting to the fact that I get to love Namid and that he loves me in return. In truth, I hope I never get too used to the feeling. I don't want it to ever become expected or mundane. The way we love one another isn't something I ever thought I'd get to experience, and I hope it always feels this precious.

We haven't talked about the future much, not about the specifics anyway. I know that Namid is my future, and he's made it clear that I'm his as well. Since

returning from our trip, there hasn't been a night when
either of us has insinuated they want to be alone for the
evening. I can't imagine living apart from Namid, even for
a night. I know he loves his small cabin, and I'm not
overly attached to my house; maybe he'll let me live with
him. It would be tight, but we'd make do. Maybe we'll
keep moving between my house and his. I want to be
with him; it doesn't matter where we are. He is my home.

I shake my head with a small laugh, pulling my
attention back to the car in front of me. Namid will roll
his eyes and tease me if I'm not finished by the time he's
back, so I need to focus on what I'm doing. It's so easy to
get lost in my thoughts these days. I suppose it's always
been that way, really, but now I find myself enjoying the
moments my mind drifts in on itself instead of forcing my
attention instantly back to the present the way I've had to
in the past when my mind held nothing but pain. When
my thoughts drift now, they're always about Namid.

Black.

The patterns that stretch across Namid's skin have
swirled with color and sparkled with starlight,
captivating me from the moment I first saw them.

They're black now.

Only black.

I can't tear my eyes from his skin. I can't look
away from the wide swaths of lifeless black and the angry
red scuffs left by asphalt and knuckles. I'll never be able

to forget the greens and purples and blues that mar the normally pale and pristine stretches of skin. I can't look away from the hard white cast that encases his wrist and the tops of his long, elegant fingers or the bandages that obscure one of his cheeks and sections of his chest.

I hadn't thought much of it when I'd heard the police siren rush past the shop yesterday evening. I'd been too absorbed in trying to finish changing a finicky serpentine belt before Namid was ready for us to head home to consider what trouble someone in town might be causing. Even a town this small has a few teens and unruly adults who take things too far once in a while. When the ambulance passed by moments later, I found myself wondering who in the world could be causing such a disturbance that they'd needed an ambulance at six at night. When the second and third police cars had rushed past, I'd paused my work and stepped outside to glance around. They weren't at the bar. They were parked four blocks away, barricading the entrance to the grocery store parking lot. The grocery store where Namid was picking up the ingredients for supper.

I ran.

I'd arrived before they had a chance to call me, before they'd gotten him strapped onto the gurney or lifted him into the ambulance. I'd arrived to find the man I love lying on asphalt that is pale and greyed with age, save for the glistening strips of this year's tar over new cracks and the streaks of blood that slowly spread from his all-too-still body. A young EMT, one I'd met a handful of times, knelt over Namid, his knees spread, hands cupping Namid's temples to prevent any neck movement.

I didn't remember the EMT's name, but he'd always been kind to me when he brought the ambulance in for oil changes and tire rotations. He'd been kind to Namid as well. He didn't hold my gaze for long when he saw me arrive.

When I'd followed Namid to the ambulance without a word, the EMT had held out his hand to help me step into the back of the vehicle as soon as he'd settled in at Namid's side. I was grateful for that.

Namid was still unconscious when we arrived at the hospital, and it was only moments before he was wheeled down a hallway and out of sight as a nurse I'd never met held my wrists and told me I couldn't follow. I'd have to wait. Ken arrived to find me standing in front of a heavy, closed door, staring down a bleak white hallway through the small, wire mesh-embedded window. He'd led me to the small cluster of chairs next to an old oak coffee table that held sticky magazines and a box of tissues, and we waited.

Namid had woken up in a panic just before they'd started a CT scan to check for head trauma. They'd sedated him after that. Ken and I were grateful for that, too. We had to beg them to keep him sedated, telling them that he suffered from anxiety and panic attacks so severe that he'd surely wake in the same state he had the first time if they didn't listen to us. It was close enough to the truth.

They told us he'd been lucky. The men had broken several of his ribs and one of his wrists. They'd used their fists and knees and boots. He was cut and scraped and bruised and bloody, but there was no internal bleeding, no head injury, nothing that would take him from us. We stayed in the hospital until the following evening while they gave him IV fluids, anti-inflammatories, and antibiotics. Then we'd signed him out against medical advice and brought him home. They could do no more for him than we could, and when he woke, he needed to feel safe.

They told us this morning that they'd caught the two men quickly. They told us that Shelly had been in the checkout line two people behind Namid and that she'd entered the parking lot only a few minutes after he had. They told us she'd saved his life. While there had been a handful of people around when Namid had walked across the parking lot, none of them had intervened when the two men blocked his way. None of them had spoken when his bags had fallen to the ground. None of them had helped when he'd cried out. Shelly had. She'd run toward them, yelling and threatening. They hadn't expected her, and they'd run, leaving Namid bleeding on the pavement as Shelly tried to wake him and called 911.

The silence in my small bedroom is overwhelming after the endless chatter of nurses, continuous beeping of equipment, and muffled shuffling of feet through hallways that have filled the past thirty-six hours.

"Here, son." Ken is at my side, holding out a mug that smells like soup. "You have to eat something. You won't be any good to him when he wakes up if you don't at least try to take care of yourself, too."

I haven't let go of Namid's hand in hours, not since I laid him gently in my bed. He'd still been lightly sedated when we'd left the hospital, and we'd had to fight with everything we had to remove him before he woke. That was three hours ago. Three hours and twenty-two minutes. He should wake up soon. He will wake up soon.

"Thanks," I mumble as I shift so that I'm only clinging to Namid with one hand, reaching for the mug with the other.

Ken settles into the second chair we've placed beside my bed, and I manage to tear my eyes from Namid to look at him. He looks as tired as I feel. For the first time since we've been spending time together, Ken looks old.

"Did I do this, Ken? Is this my fault?" I can barely hear my own whisper.

"How in the hell would this be your fault?" He sounds genuinely confused.

"I told him I didn't want to hide. I kissed him at the shop. I told him we'd make this work."

Ken shifts forward to rest his elbows on his knees with a sigh. "Namid would have asked you the same thing eventually, Jayce. He wouldn't want to hide forever either."

When I open my mouth to respond, Ken cuts me off.

"I know he's a quiet man, and I know he's been happy with me since he arrived, but the way he loves you...it's the type of love not many people get to experience. He wouldn't want to keep that secret for the rest of his life."

"I could have lost him, Ken."

"I know, but you didn't."

"But I…"

"You didn't," Ken cuts me off again. "You and I know what it's like to lose people we love, but you can't let fear control you. The two of you deserve to live the life you want. Together."

I stare into the mug of quickly cooling soup for a long time before managing to find words that hopefully match what I'm feeling.

"When I lost Jordyn, I lost half of my soul."

Clearing my throat does little to clear the harsh, gravelly tone from my voice.

"I thought I'd spend the rest of my life feeling like half of a person. I thought I'd move through the world, managing to eat and sleep and work, but that was all. I was alone. I had no family and no one to love. There was no one left who loved me. I didn't expect to find love again. I didn't really ever expect to live again. For as long as I can remember, my soul has never felt whole on its own, and when I lost Jordyn, the emptiness that was left simply became a part of me. It became who I was."

A smile pulls at my lips, as it always does when I think about Namid.

"Namid snuck in, slowly and quietly, and somehow…the emptiness faded away. While Namid's love is completely different from Jordyn's, he's become the other half of my soul. I can't lose him."

Ken reaches over to pat my shoulder briefly. "You won't."

Chapter 19

Namid

Fear.

My entire body hurts, and I want to retreat back into the darkness. Worse than the pain is the fear. The room is filled with it. It's so uncontrolled and intense that it takes me a moment to push it aside far enough to force my eyes open and attempt to figure out what's going on.

Jayce. It's Jayce's fear, Ken's too.

When I finally manage to blink away the blurriness that clouds my vision, my gaze lands on Jayce. He looks tired and ragged as he sits in a dining chair beside the bed. He's leaning forward with his elbows resting on his knees. One of my hands is clasped between both of his, and his thumbs are slowly tracing across my skin. I focus on the sensation, the warmth of his touch, the roughness of his callused palms. It helps push the fear back a bit further.

I tighten my hand in his, gripping his fingers.

Jayce's head snaps up, his eyes panicked and searching. He's on his feet in an instant, leaning over me and cradling my jaw in his hands as he peppers soft kisses across my forehead and cheeks, and the relief that floods the room engulfs me.

"You're okay. Jesus, Namid, I thought I lost you. You're okay, love. It's all okay now."

I tilt my head back so that I can brush my lips across his. They're wet and salty, and they tremble against my skin. As I shift against the pillows to reach a hand up to his face, sharp waves of pain shoot up my arm and across my chest. *What in the actual fuck?* I suck in a ragged breath as my gaze shifts down. My arm is in a cast, bandages cover half of my chest, and bruises litter my skin.

"Fuck." A half-groaned, half-sighed curse is all I can manage as I suddenly remember how I ended up like this and why the room is filled with fear.

Jayce moves at my side, and his brilliant green eyes fill my world as his fingers gently trail across my cheek once more.

"I know, baby. I know. But it's okay. It's your wrist and a couple of ribs, but that's all. You're going to be just fine."

His voice cracks as he speaks, and he feels frightened and desperate. He's so worried about me. He loves me so much, and he's so worried. I never thought I'd know what it was like to have someone care about me like this.

"I love you."

It's all I can think to say to try and calm him, to reassure him. Even if I could find more words, it's all I really want to say. Nothing else matters.

He chokes out a strangled sob as his lips twitch into a small smile, and a rush of blue and gold and magenta love and relief and peace rush around us, forcing away the anger and fear that have radiated from him since I woke up.

"I love you too, beautiful."

His lips catch mine in a slow, tender kiss that says we'll get through this together, that we'll always be together. His kiss lingers, soft skin playing against soft skin, until Ken starts to feel uncomfortable enough being in the same room that I can't stifle a chuckle as I pull away from Jayce.

"Sorry, Ken."

He stutters out a response. "It's okay. You can keep going if you're not finished."

I snort out a laugh. "You're already more uncomfortable than I've ever felt."

"Stupid feeling everything," he mumbles under his breath, even though he knows we're both able to hear him.

Ken reaches out to rest a hand on my shin as Jayce settles back into his chair with my hand between his once again.

"As long as you're happy, I'll learn to live with watching you play kissy face." He exhales a deep, shuddering breath. "We were scared, kid."

"I know. I was too." My admission quickly squashes the moment of humor, and even though the room is still filled with love and relief and gratitude, there's concern as well, from all of us.

"I still can't believe something like that happened here." Ken's voice, normally smooth and professional after the years he's spent speaking quietly with those who've lost loved ones, is harsh and rough. "I know it's a small conservative town, and I know a lot of folks have always been wary of the way you showed up here, Namid, but I grew up here, and I've always believed that in their hearts, these were good people. I really thought that even though it might take time for people to accept the two of you being together, eventually they'd see that you were happy and let you live your lives in peace."

Jayce sighs as sadness and hurt envelop him. "I wish I could say the same thing, but I'm not all that surprised. I'm stunned that anyone resorted to actual violence, but I never expected to be accepted, not really. I figured a handful of people might learn to be okay with us, but I've known since I was a kid that I'm different enough that most people in a town like this would never treat me the same if they knew."

My hand is still nestled between Jayce's, and I squeeze his fingers tightly. "We have each other now. That's enough, right?" I glance over at Ken. "All of us."

Ken squeezes my shin as Jayce brings our hands to his lips and kisses my knuckles.

"Ya, beautiful. It is."

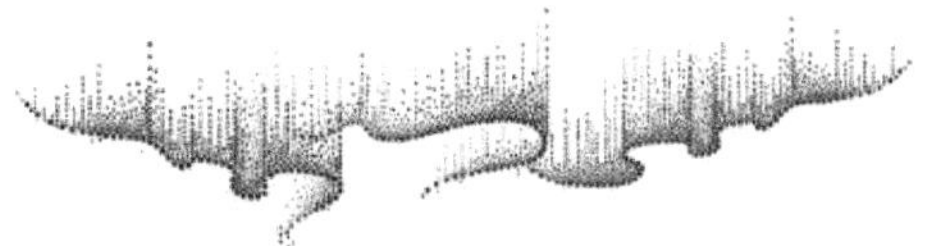

The next few weeks feel like moments out of time, and everything blends together in a haze. It's almost as if we've stepped outside of our reality and are simply existing as we wait for some sense of normalcy to return. Jayce puts up a sign saying that the shop is closed for an indefinite period of time, and he stays home to help care for me. I don't actually need all that much help after the first few days, but I like having him around. While neither of us wants to dwell on what happened any more than necessary; we both feel the need to be close to one another most of the time. My ribs hurt every time I move, but it doesn't take long for me to learn to accomplish basic tasks without twisting my torso too much, and like Ken, I've lucked out in the sense that it's my non-dominant wrist that's broken. While I'm perfectly content to have the man I love washing me with lingering, sensual touches while whispered words of adoration fall across my skin every time I shower, I'm grateful that I don't have to experience the embarrassment of needing him to help with other...daily activities.

Jayce is cautious when he touches me, which is something my ribs appreciate, but there are times it feels like more than that. There are moments when it feels like hesitation and fear force him to hold back. When we curl up together at night, he clings to me as if he's afraid I'll be gone when he wakes up. But when our kisses become desperate and our hands stray across bare skin, he seems to temper the fire that I know burns through his veins in the same way it courses through mine. I want him to let go. I want him to touch and taste and overwhelm my senses until there is nothing but him. When we talk, he tells me that he's fine, that he's simply waiting for me to recover, but something has shifted between us, and it feels like a part of his soul has slipped back into darkness.

While Ken declines Jayce's offer to stay in the guest room, he comes by for a few hours every night, and we have dinner as a family. We laugh and joke and try to keep the mood loving and light, but there is a shadow that hovers around the edge of our existence. Everything is the same, but at the same time, everything has changed. The calm, comfortable bubble that we'd woven around us at home and at Jayce's shop no longer feels safe. There is a dim, grey film that seems to cover the world no matter how hard we try to scrub it away.

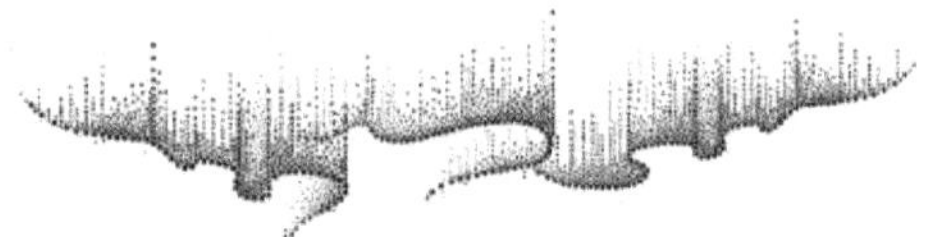

"I don't want to reopen the shop." Jayce's voice is calm and quiet, but his words echo loudly around his small kitchen as our little family sits together at the dinner table.

I'm too stunned to speak, but after a long, silent moment, Ken recovers. "What would you do if you didn't have the shop?"

"I'm not entirely sure, but even though it was only two people who attacked Namid, that was three weeks ago, and Shelly is the only person who's called or come by to see how we're doing. I don't want to do work for anyone who can so easily ignore something like that happening in their own town."

"You just want to give it all up? Everything you and Jordyn worked for?" I can't believe it's something we're even talking about.

"I've been thinking a lot, and it's not just that I don't want to reopen the shop - I don't want to stay in this town. I want a life with you, a real life. I want what we had in Seattle." Jayce's eyes flash with a ferocity I've never seen before.

He glances over at Ken as he continues. "You too, Ken. I think we should move, all of us, as a family."

He reaches across the table and curls his trembling fingers around my hand. "We've all lost too much here. We don't need to lose anything else."

He leans closer, raising our hands and pressing a kiss to my palm. "I almost lost you, Namid. They almost took you from me. I won't let them. I won't let anything happen to you again. We could move to Seattle. We could have a new start, a new life. We could build a life together."

"What about everything else: your house, Ken's business? We can't just...leave." I'm struggling to process everything that's happened, everything that he's saying, but deep down, I'm excited by the idea.

"Yes, we can. Those things don't matter. All that matters is that we're safe and happy. All that matters is us. You're my whole life, Namid."

He feels so eager, so hopeful, and a shiver runs through me as his warm breath ghosts across my skin and his emotions wrap me in their embrace.

Can I say yes? Can I really let them give up their lives here?

Ken's voice is hesitantly thoughtful when he finally speaks, breaking our long silence, and I can feel it as his emotions shift. He's still concerned for me, still scared and upset over what happened, but excitement and hope are slowly starting to build in his soul as well.

"I think that's a really good idea. I'm tired of loss, tired of death. I watch the two of you together, and I realize that I miss Kat. I mean, I always miss her, but I realize that it's not just *her* that I miss. I miss having a partner. She was the great love of my life, and I don't know that I'll be lucky enough to find that type of love again, the type you two have for each other, but Seattle is a big city. Who knows, there might be someone out there for an old man like me."

My gaze darts back and forth between them. They're waiting for me to say yes. They want me to say yes.

I take a deep breath as my lips twitch into a smile. "Okay. Let's build a new life."

Epilogue

My life is different from anything I've ever imagined.

The past two years have been a whirlwind. Less than a month after I was attacked, Jayce, Ken, and I started to make plans to move away from our small town. Jayce reached out to Max at the gallery, and she connected us with a realtor. It had taken three months for me to fully recover, for Ken to find a buyer for the business, and for us to find the perfect home. When we saw the listing for six acres of land on the peninsula, half cleared for structures with a yard and a small pasture and half still covered with dense forest, we knew instantly. The main home is a three-bedroom, ranch-style house that we've furnished and repainted together. There are also two large shops, a shed, a chicken coup, and a small two-bedroom cabin scattered across the cleared acreage. Ken always paid me a salary, and he never charged me rent on the cabin, so with my small savings account and the sale of Ken's and Jayce's homes, the three of us had been able to buy the property outright without touching the money Jordyn had put away.

Our land is surrounded by a national forest, and there is a small, secluded strip of beach with fine grey sand and smooth dark rocks less than a mile away. Jayce and I walk there often, spending our time hand in hand, arguing over who can find the most interesting shell or rock or stick. Our home smells like the salt that rides across the ocean breeze and fir trees and grass and damp earth. The singing of birds and the chattering of squirrels and the shifting of pine boughs in the wind are the constant quiet background soundtrack as we go about our days.

We can't see the Aurora from here, but the stars are bright and brilliant on crisp, clear nights. Jayce and I built a small deck in the middle of the property, and on warm nights, we curl up together under piles of blankets and sleep under the stars. I don't often miss the swirling teal and gold and magenta skies that I've always known; with Jayce at my side, they ripple across my skin endlessly.

There are several small towns in a thirty-mile radius - seaside enclaves with tiny main street shops and bakeries that tourists flock to during the summer months. We've gotten to know the owners of small bookshops and bakeries and bars by name, and we walk along sidewalks and piers and park trails with interlaced fingers without a second thought. People smile at us as we pass by.

This place looks and smells and feels different from the only place I've ever known, but this is home.

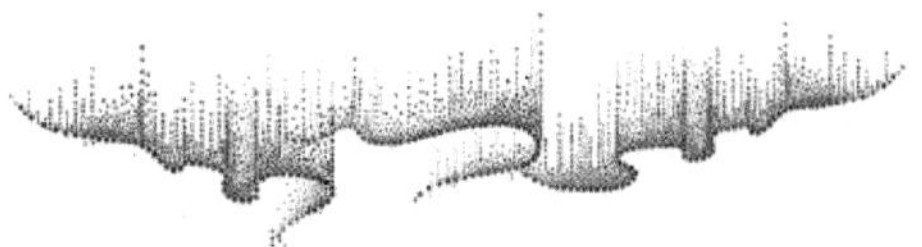

Apparently, it's so common for artists to be reclusive or eccentric that the gallery's three owners, Max, Emily, and Troy, didn't bat an eye when we told them we wouldn't be attending the opening of Jayce's first solo exhibition.

Max, however, was insistent that we do something to mark the occasion, and after a relatively long debate, we landed on having the owners and their families over to our place for a mid-summer barbecue. I've met each of them and their partners a handful of times, and they've all been kind and understanding of the fact that I seem quite antisocial. They've always respected my need for space while still actively trying to make me feel included, and I've never felt any frustration or anger toward me or Jayce from any of them.

By having an outdoor barbecue at our home, we figured I'd be able to keep my distance or seek refuge inside our house for a while if I needed to. I haven't needed to. I've been outside for nearly two hours laughing and enjoying the company of nine people, and not once has one of their emotions strayed to something negative enough that I've had to step back. Emily's five-year-old is a tad challenging. I've never spent time around children, and his rapidly shifting emotions have come as a surprise, but it's not something I can't handle. Having Jayce nearby always helps. His emotions sink into my soul in such a way that they become my whole world. I still feel the emotions of those around us, but the overwhelming love that envelops me when he's by my side helps temper them.

The people who currently occupy our large grassy yard have spent the sunny afternoon enjoying good food and good company in celebration of Jayce's work.

Fifteen sculptures currently stand tall in the downtown gallery. The building's other two floors have been temporarily closed, and Jayce's work is the only thing on display. Each of them towers at least ten feet, with the largest nearing seventeen. Jayce has thrown himself into his art, and our new life has inspired him. I've taken some part-time, remote accounting work for a few of the small shops in nearby towns, but I spend much of my time laughing at Jayce's side or quietly reading in the corner of the old barn studio while he works.

Sky of Souls has already garnered critical acclaim, and the exhibition's opening night sold out in under a week. The gallery doesn't expect even the largest of pieces to remain unsold for more than a few days.

I don't know if the burgundy room in Ken's old funeral home had actually absorbed the intense emotions I always seemed to feel there. I still don't know if that's really possible. What I do know is that the steel that comprises Jayce's work has done just that.

Each of the sculptures triggers the same emotional reaction from everyone who sees them.

They are passion and need and gratitude and love.

They are *US*.

They are Jayce and me, public and proud and unashamed. Standing strong and tall for the world to see.

Jayce startles me from my revelry as he slips a strong arm around my waist.

"Do you think he knows?" The flood of emotion that runs through him contains traces of the grief he wore when we first met, but the emotion is small and soft and tempered by more love and happiness than it should be possible for one person to feel.

I don't have to ask what he means, and I can't help the grateful sigh that slips from my lips as I lay my head onto his shoulder. "He knows."

His lips brush my hair. "I think he'd be happy for us, with what we've done with the money, with the life we've built."

"I think so too, my love."

As we laugh and shift to the left to dodge the beanbag that has escaped Ken's grasp on yet another of his horrific throws toward the cornhole board, Jayce's grief fades. Those lost to us, Jordyn, Katherine, Jayce's parents, they're always here, but we choose to honor them with laughter and memories and stories about the way they were loved. While grief will always be a part of our lives, it's become a part we're thankful for as, in some inexplicable way, it brought us to one another.

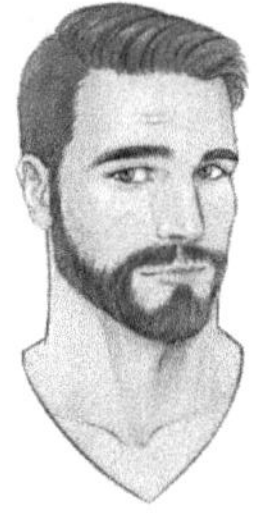

One soul that speaks to another can come in any shape or size or form. They can be a sibling, a friend, a lover, even a pet. When you find a soul that fits yours, it doesn't matter who they are or even what they are.

They can show up when you least expect it, even when you've given up hope.

They share our love and our pain. They carry our secrets and protect our dreams. They become such an integral part of ourselves that we aren't complete without them.

My brother was my first soulmate. My first friend, my first confidant, my first partner in crime, my first love.

I have a different kind of love now. The kind I never dreamed I'd ever get the chance to experience.

If you find a soul that speaks to yours, hold it close. Cherish it. Notice all of the little moments that normally get overlooked in the day-to-day experience of living. Embrace all of the earth-shattering events and grand gestures.

Offer that soul your whole heart, and you might just be lucky enough to receive theirs in return.

To be continued...

The wave of grief that threatens to overwhelm me is more intense than anything I've felt from Jayce in more than a year, and it's hard to believe that he actually made it through Jordyn's loss, feeling like this every day.

As his grief slowly fades, I can't help the way my eyes are drawn to the tan stretch of skin that peeks out under Jayce's shirt as he finishes lifting the storage unit's roll-up garage door. I'll never get enough of him.

"Are you really sure you want to do this?"

He chuckles and shoots me a glare as he shakes his head. His grief has shifted to a dull grey ache, and he's filled with love and amusement. "Have I ever told you it's annoying when you read me like that?"

I grin. "Nope. Not once. I'm not even sure what you're talking about, to be honest."

Jayce has tried to tell me on many...many...occasions that the way I'm able to instantly tell what he's feeling is annoying at times. He doesn't mean it. I can feel that too. As strange as it seems, his teasing is actually his way of telling me that he loves it.

I kiss his cheek and draw my fingers across his low back as I step into the dark unit and grope around for the light switch, only to instantly regret finding it as the aggressive halogens flicker to life.

His sigh is deep and sincere as he leans against my side. "I don't think we should keep much, but there are a few boxes that are important: photos, things like that."

When Jayce had finally terminated the lease on Jordyn's apartment after he passed, he'd been unable to let go of nearly anything; instead, he'd packed it all up as quickly as possible and put it in storage. Three years later, he finally feels settled enough in our new life to let it go. He loves Jordyn, and he misses him deeply. He always will, but he keeps him close with memories and mementos, not a storage room filled with couches and T-shirts.

It's nearly dark by the time we've sorted through all but a few stray boxes. Many things, like boxes of old socks, were quickly put into the donation pile, but there is a handful filled with personal mementos like old photographs and diplomas that we've set aside as we've worked, and we're now sorting through them one item at a time. It's been a strange and enlightening experience working next to him all day and feeling the way his grief for Jordyn is so deeply tied to love and joy and happiness. His emotions are fluid and dynamic. Each time he's pulled out an item that's triggered a specific memory, the strong wave of darkness that has rushed over him has been followed by something beautiful, sometimes even laughter. It's made me realize that maybe grief serves a purpose after all. Maybe, in its own way, it helps us to remember the good things.

"What it the world..."

Jayce's eyes flick up to the yellowed paper in my hands. We're sitting cross-legged on the floor facing one another, the last two boxes in front of us as we rifle through the precious items to weed out nonsense like old power bills that somehow got mixed in during the chaos of the original move into storage.

"Do you have any idea who this is from?" I hold the letter out in his direction.

His brows furrow as he swipes the paper from my fingers, his eyes darting quickly across the faded blue pen strokes scratched into its surface.

Confusion and surprise envelop him.

"No...I..."

His eyes shift quickly as he reads it again, flips it over - looking for more - and then reads it a third time.

"I always thought he told me about everyone he dated, but I don't remember anyone with the initials E.J., and I definitely don't remember him ever telling me that he'd truly fallen in love, or that someone had fallen in love with him."

My fingers carefully take the aged paper back.

"Do you think they ever spoke after this?" The unrequited love that drips from the page is heartbreaking. "It sounds like whoever it is, Jordyn broke their heart."

"I...I don't know."

"I think we should keep it." I fold the letter carefully and slip it back into the stained envelope. "Jordyn wouldn't have kept it all this time if it didn't matter to him a great deal."

"You're right. Ya, let's keep it in with the photos and things for now."

I can't help the groan that escapes as I stand to slip the letter into the only remaining unopened box we've decided to take home.

"Anything else?"

Jayce's deep sigh whispers through the cool metal room, echoing back with loss and longing and resignation.

"I think that's it."

His hand rests on the small of my back for a moment as I tape the box shut before he bends down to haul it up onto one shoulder, his fingers lacing tightly through mine as we make our way toward the truck, taking only the memories that matter home with us.

My dearest Jordyn,

There has been no moment during the years we have known one another in which I believed our time together would end the way it has. You have been my anchor when I've found myself drifting out to sea, my light whenever I have known darkness, and my laughter when life has threatened to overwhelm me. I don't say such things in an attempt to sway your heart or change your mind. I say them so that you'll know what you have meant to me and so that you may always remember your worth.

I understand that the battles we would have had to face together seem insurmountable, and while I would confront any obstacle for you without hesitation, I do not fault you for choosing an easier path.

It is my fondest wish that whoever you give your heart to in the future should love you the way I have. Unconditionally and without reservation.

Should you ever decide that I might be enough, I'll be waiting.

Always your love,

E.J.

9 7 9 8 2 1 8 4 6 3 6 9 4